THE COLOUR
OF MERMAIDS

CATHERINE CURZON &
ELEANOR HARKSTEAD

The Colour of Mermaids
ISBN # 978-1-83943-876-9
©Copyright Catherine Curzon & Eleanor Harksetad 2020
Cover Art by Erin Dameron-Hill ©Copyright March 2020
Interior text design by Claire Siemaszkiewicz
Totally Bound Publishing

Published in 2020 by Totally Bound Publishing, United Kingdom.

THE COLOUR
OF MERMAIDS

Dedication

CC — But is it art?
EH — For G, who *does* know one end of a
paintbrush from the other.

Chapter One

Of course Eva wasn't going to turn down her invitation to the private viewing at the Hawley Gallery. Daniel Scott, *enfant terrible* of the international art world, was exhibiting in Brighton of all places.

She arrived fifteen minutes early, but the gallery was almost full. It seemed as if everyone who was anyone on the Brighton art scene had turned up for vast amounts of free drink and air-kissing. Eva waved to people she knew, and finally spotted her friend Lyndsey on the other side of the room in front of one of Daniel Scott's canvases. Somehow, a glass of Prosecco had appeared in her hand by the time she had squeezed through the crowd to reach Lyndsey.

"Hello, gorgeous!" Lyndsey put her hand on Eva's arm and leaned in to dart her lips to her cheek. As she did, she dropped her voice and whispered, "Not many laughs on these walls tonight!"

"Hello, darling!" Eva kissed Lyndsey back, her friend's summery floral scent enveloping them both like a cloud. "No, his work's not a laugh a minute, is it?

But it's so exciting that the exhibition's *here*. And thanks so much for sorting me out with an invite."

"I don't actually understand what it *is*. I don't think I like it." Lyndsey peered up at the canvas before her. From it, *something* vaguely human glowered down, a twisted, misshapen silhouette of a human face in a mist of fog. She cocked her head to one side then the other and shrugged. Then she smiled and murmured, "It needs a kitten or two, then we'll talk."

Eva laughed. "Like the ones on tea trays that grannies used to have? You do crack me up! I love his paintings… I'm always drawing *things* in my illustrations. It must be so freeing to paint emotion."

"I haven't met him yet, but Rupert says he's *super* intense." Lyndsey took a glass of Prosecco from the tray of a passing waiter. "He wouldn't let us so much as hang a single work until he'd been through the space a dozen times. We've had some tricky artistic types through, but *nothing* like this. Rupert'd let him paint the place neon green if he wanted, though, for the exposure we're getting."

"I can't say I'm surprised that he's intense. I mean, to produce art like this." Eva recalled the photos she'd seen of him in newspapers and magazines, dark eyes like coals that seemed to burn through the paper. "Then again, I bet he's been really spoiled over the years. Don't you think? Mr Rockstar Artist!"

"I just want another lovely sculptress to come and give us all biccies like that one from Cornwall." Lyndsey pouted. "She was so nice, like the perfect mum! I mean, nobody came to see her work but…that meant biccies for the office!"

"Sorry about that, Lynds… I was busy." Eva hadn't been, of course, but at the time she hadn't wanted to go out and her own studio had been her sanctuary. "She sounds lovely, though. No biscuits from Mr Scott, I take it?"

"No, nothing from Mr Scott other than shirty emails from his people about the quality of the light and the spacing between the works." She took a sip from her glass. "You know none of them are for sale, and we've had offers on every single one?" Lyndsey dropped her voice again and confided, "I can't tell you how much because Rupert won't tell me. He just says think of an insane number and then add at least one zero. Mr Man-in-Black apparently *might* let some go once the exhibition closes. Personally, I can't think who'd want one! Would you want these things above your bed?"

"Possibly not!" Eva looked up again at the canvas. She had trouble turning away from it. She'd seen his paintings reproduced in books and everywhere else, but actually seeing his artwork up close—close enough to see each individual brush mark—made the emotion it represented all the more intense. "But imagine it in the lounge, it'd be quite the conversation piece at parties!"

"The problem is, to buy this you'd have to sell your house, so you'd have no lounge to hang it in!"

"That's true!" Eva laughed. "Thing is, don't you think he should, I dunno, up his game a little? Develop his style a bit? It is exciting seeing all these works up close, but it's as if he's painting to a tried-and-tested formula. The Daniel Scott Method!"

"Are you accusing our *enfant terrible* of painting by numbers?" Lyndsey affected mock outrage. "Tell me more, Ms da Vinci!"

Eva gestured towards the painting while she sipped a mouthful of Prosecco. "Well, I do paint myself, as you know, and I try to...do different things. I mean, imagine if he broke from type and did a landscape.

Although I suppose if you get to be as famous as him you're trapped in one style, because everyone expects to see a Daniel Scott, and this is what they want."

"Oh, don't stop there," a male voice said from behind the two women. "I'm enjoying learning from a master."

Eva didn't recognise the voice, although it seemed familiar. Some annoying hanger-on, no doubt, who thought they were an expert. But when she turned, her eyebrow already raised in scornful retort, she was facing Daniel Scott himself.

His coal-black eyes held Eva fixed to the spot. "I...erm... My God, Mr Scott. If I'd known you were stood right behind me, I really wouldn't have said all that. Sorry. Erm..." She swallowed, then held out her hand to him, an awkward grin on her lips. "Eva Catesby. I am actually an artist, before you ask! Not just an opinionated bystander."

"Eva Catesby." He took her hand very briefly and narrowed his eyes as though trying to recall her name. "Did I see you exhibited at the Met last season? Or was it the Tate Modern? You'll have to remind me, I seem to have forgotten."

Because, of course, he has to be an egomaniac.

Eva rolled her eyes. "How unfortunate that you can't remember. By the way, you also appear to have forgotten your sunglasses. We *are* indoors." She indicated his Ray-Bans, which were perched on his dark hair.

"Eva!" Lyndsey whispered urgently, no doubt seeing her job as PA to Rupert Hawley flashing before her eyes.

"That's why they're not on my face," he replied, deadpan. "As you correctly say, everybody wants to see Daniel Scott and they'd be disappointed if I didn't have my sunglasses. I've always been a people pleaser."

"Is that so?" Eva arched her eyebrow again. He was dressed entirely in black. His suit, his shirt. Was it an act, and at home he tooled about in flip-flops and Bermuda shorts? "Of course, some people are much harder to please than others. And I'm one of those people, I'm afraid. What can I say? I'm sure you're not all that fussed by the views of a provincial artist you've never heard of."

"Mr Scott." Rupert Hawley was suddenly beside them, as if conjured from nowhere. He was almost bowing, Eva realised, his hand extending to shake Daniel's. "I was hoping to announce you, you managed to evade me!"

"I was meeting the locals," Daniel told him. He subtly turned from Eva, angling his body away from her a little. "Tough crowd."

Rupert glanced to the two women for just a moment, but word of the artist's presence seemed to have spread and an interested crowd was gathering. Everyone was eager to meet the star in their midst and none of them, Eva knew, would tell him that he needed to try something just a *little* different next time he put brush to canvas.

"That's Brighton for you." Rupert managed to force a smile to accompany his words. He moved to put his hand on Daniel's back as though to steer him away, but it hovered there before falling. *He can't touch the icon, can he?* All he could do was wring his hands and say, "Let me introduce you to some people. Excuse us, ladies."

"Ms Catesby," Daniel addressed Eva, the hint of a smile chilling on his lips, "thank you for the notes. I'll keep them in mind."

"Oh my God," Lyndsey groaned as they departed in a crowd of excited chatter. "Oh my God, oh my God. Why did you do have to do that? You didn't have to do that!"

"Do what?" Eva sipped her drink as she watched Daniel walk away. *Cocky sod.* Although, she had to admit it, a very good-looking sod, which was probably part of the problem. A man who had lucked out thanks to the universe granting him both a handsome face and talent. "I was merely expressing an opinion. That's the point of a private viewing, isn't it? I mean, I know everyone *really* just comes out for the free booze and schmoozing, but there are paintings on the walls, and we're allowed to comment on them. It's not my fault he was eavesdropping. His work is great, but I just think... Bloody hell, if he pushed himself, it could be amazing."

"It's *Daniel Scott*," Lyndsey reminded her. "His last exhibition was at the Pompidou and when he came back to England he didn't go to the Tate or the National, he came to our humble little gallery. You were really rude to him, Eva, that wasn't on. It costs nothing to be nice, you know."

"I did apologise, but then he came out with all that egotistical bollocks, and I saw red." Eva adopted a snooty tone. "*I've exhibited at the Met, I've exhibited at the Tate Modern, I'm a great big poser with my sunglasses on my head, I dress in black because I want everyone to think I'm a badass, I still sleep with my teddy.*"

"It was rude," Lyndsey told her again. "And you were saying you loved his work, why didn't you tell him that?"

"Because that's all he ever hears!" Eva watched his progress through the room, handshaking with some of the most annoying people in Brighton. Everyone was smiling and fawning over the man. "Look, when I do outreach with those kids, I don't just say *well done* to everything they paint. I'll say, *well done*. And next time, what if you do *this* a bit differently. There's nothing wrong with pushing people. As long as it's a gentle shove."

"He's going to complain about you." As Lyndsey spoke, Daniel glanced over his shoulder at them for a moment. Eva flashed him a sarcastic grin and momentarily raised her glass. He raised his own in turn, the red wine catching the light before he turned away again. "And Rupert will blame me for inviting you and I'll lose my job. You know how moody Rupe can be. You'll have to go out for drinks with him again and save my job!"

"Oh God, Rupe and his lacklustre snog." Eva wrinkled her nose and giggled like a gossipy schoolgirl. "There's someone I won't be going on a date with again. Ewww!"

"Bless his socks, give him another chance." Lyndsey laughed. "You know, in three years of working with him, he's never had a girlfriend for more than a couple of months. You looked so cute together, and he still likes you!"

"He's a nice bloke, but really…" Eva shook her head. "He's not for me."

Whereas Daniel Scott…

What a thing to think. But he *had* been a bit flirty with her, although he was probably like that with everyone. Eva watched as Daniel lowered his head to speak to a woman who fashioned genitalia in colourful pottery. She was giggling at him. *Giggling.* Eva looked back up at the painting again. Something in it which she hadn't seen before, which she wouldn't have been able to describe even had she attempted it, made her come out in goosebumps.

"Do you want to see the rest of them?" Lyndsey touched her arm. "And maybe accidentally bump into Mr Scott and grovel at his feet? Tell him he's amazing and how sorry you are? *Pweese?*"

"I'd love to see the rest of them, but speaking to him depends on how likely he is to keep talking to that woman about her pottery pudenda." Eva snorted with laughter. "Am I mean? It's just...my foundation art course was bulging with them, and *she* somehow makes a living from crockery cocks!"

"She's probably not being rude to him." Lyndsey slipped her arm though Eva's. "Come on, talk me through these scenes of horror, it's not a world I often inhabit!"

"After that show last year of the comedy seagull photos, I'm not surprised you find them a bit" — Eva glanced at her friend's benign face, then up at a canvas of swollen, dark paint, which seemed to throb before her eyes — "unfathomable. You could see that one, for example, as...a bruise. An emotional bruise. We all have them. I suppose that's what frustrates me. He's putting all this emotion on canvas, and it could be dark and disturbing, but I feel almost as if he's cranking them out to order. Do you see?"

"I liked the seagulls," Lyndsey smiled nostalgically. Then she glanced over her shoulder, satisfied that Daniel was at a safe distance, still surrounded by acolytes. "But when I look at this... It's like there's something wrong with him. What's going on in his head?"

"Who knows? Does *he*?" Eva tipped her head to one side, to see the painting from another angle. "But don't you think that's the point of art, really? I look at this and it makes me think of...well...splitting up with Miles. An emotional bruise, which faded. And

14

everyone else looking at it thinks of something painful that happened to them. And maybe — *maybe* — he does it on purpose, but in his production line way, stirring those feelings up, forcing people to *look* at that pain inside them. Or maybe horrible things *are* going on in that handsome head, and he spills it out in paint." Eva sighed. "Maybe it's a cross of the two."

"Oh God, he's looking at us," Lyndsey whispered, quickly turning her attention to the painting. Years in gallery administration had left her with the talent for looking both interested and appreciative even when she wasn't, a skill that Eva knew her friend was justifiably rather proud of. A skill that had saved her career on more than one occasion. "You've *really* upset him, Eva, so you'd better hope what's in his head *isn't* as horrible as his pictures."

Eva met his glance as she combed her fingers through her long hair with a careless swish. He was doing a very good job of not looking upset at all, despite what Lyndsey seemed to think.

"He's smiling, Lyndsey. He doesn't look upset to me."

"I'm not going to look at him. He might put me in a painting if I do!"

Eva nudged her, laughing. "Don't be silly, you'd *love* it if he did that!"

"Only if I could have bunnies," Lyndsey told her cheerily. "But if he painted bunnies, he'd probably paint them with...I don't know, horns or something. Horny bunnies, can you imagine?"

"Horny bunnies?" Eva laughed loudly and hid her mouth behind her hand. "Is this a new *ladies' toy* that's just hit the market?"

"I wouldn't know." Her friend laughed. "Go on, show me another Daniel Scott masterpiece, before he asks us what we're talking about. I'm a teeny bit terrified of him!"

They went on to the next painting, but all the while Eva was aware of someone's gaze following her. She glanced over her shoulder, only to see Daniel again, assured and confident as he toured the room, watching her. Had she got under his skin?

Good. Because he's got under mine.

"This one... It looks like a scream, doesn't it? Not that you can see a mouth, as such, but it *feels* like a scream. There's tension in it. You can almost hear, can't you?" Eva gestured towards it, her silver bangles jangling on her wrist.

"I wouldn't want it in my loo! It'd scare my little Pears Soap children witless. They'd run out of their frames."

"At least you don't have a crocheted crinoline lady on your toilet roll, or she'd faint!" Eva laughed. "But this sort of art, it's not meant to be background noise. It's not meant to be lift muzak. It's supposed to challenge you. And it does..."

Lyndsey nodded, her lips pursed as she considered the canvas. Then she admitted, "I think I sort of fancy him, though. Isn't that awful?"

"He's a handsome sod, there's no getting around it. He knows it too... But are you sure you find it attractive, all that intensely intense business?" With a return of her schoolgirlish mischief, Eva giggled. "I do hope he wears black underpants, though. Or perhaps none at all! If you found out he wore ones with cartoon characters on, it'd be pretty disappointing, wouldn't it?"

"Or horrid grey y-fronts." Lyndsey gestured to a waiter and took two more glasses, handing one to Eva. "Or silky lady's knickers! He's too intense for me. I like someone a bit more…you know. A boy who'll wine and dine me, not one with things like that in his head!"

Eva took the glass. He was watching again, she knew, and the thought of it made her burn inside. He was playing with her, though—of course he was. The man could have anyone he wanted. And, if rumour was to be believed, he regularly did. But it was exciting to think that Daniel Scott, of all people, was flirting with her. As she sipped her drink, she caught his glance again, so she ran the tip of her tongue across her lip. "Oh, I don't know, I think he'd be rather fun."

He lifted his hand and brushed it through his dark hair, catching his sunglasses in his fingers as he did so. Still holding her gaze, he slipped them into his jacket and raised one eyebrow, as though to ask, *happy now?*

"I bet he's really dirty." Lyndsey giggled. "In the bedroom, I mean."

Eva raised her hand casually to her hair but shielded her face from Lyndsey as she gave Daniel a wink in response that her friend couldn't see.

Then she turned her back on him. "Dirty as in covered in paint?" She laughed. "Oh, but I know what you mean. I bet a man like him would be incredibly naughty!"

"You fancy him!" She took a sip of Prosecco then whispered through giggles, "Eva and scary artist sitting in a tree, k-i-s-s-i-n-g!"

Eva blushed as red as her satin dress. "Well? And so what if I do? Tons of other people do as well. He's hardly going to be interested in me, is he? Especially not after my terrible review of his paintings!"

Lyndsey glanced at her watch and pouted. "I have to leave you alone and round up the punters. Rupes wants to do a little talk and pay homage to the great man in our midst. Promise me that you won't insult anybody while I'm gone?"

Eva patted Lyndsey's arm. "Worry not, I'm on my best behaviour."

"I was going to say enjoy the artworks, but" — Lyndsey gave a theatrical shudder — "maybe not!"

The she trotted away on her ballet flats, quietly ushering the patrons towards the centre of the gallery space. Lyndsey Davis was perfectly suited to this sort of schmoozing, petite and smiling and neatly turned out in her rose-patterned sundress, a red cardigan over her shoulders. She gave her boss and his guest a wide berth, concentrating instead on the great and the good who had been invited to this monumental occasion in the history of the gallery. Of course she would leave the guest of honour to Rupert's care, because nobody loved the limelight like Rupert Hawley.

Eva stood in the crowd of dinner-jacketed men and women in their evening gowns, of artists so dedicated to the cause that they had turned up in ripped jeans and raggedy knitwear, of reporters tapping notes on their phones. But she didn't pay any attention to them. Her entire focus was absorbed by Daniel Scott. *The handsome sod.*

She fanned herself with the exhibition programme that she hadn't got round to looking at and waited.

Rupert moved to stand beneath the largest painting, a canvas drenched in reds of every imaginable hue, thickly coated with streaks of paint, the textures leaping from the surface as though it were an alien landscape.

Blood by numbers.

Daniel stood ten feet or so to the side, his arms folded across his chest, his face unreadable because, for reasons best known to him, he was wearing the Wayfarers that had been nestled in his hair.

Indoors. Because of course, he was Daniel Scott, who had made art the new rock 'n' roll. Allegedly.

He wouldn't be giving a speech — Eva knew enough about him to know that. She also knew enough about Rupert to know that he would have more than enough to say to make up for Daniel's avoidance of the limelight. He was just that sort of man.

"Ladies and gentlemen." Rupert clapped his hands and glanced back at Daniel, as though seeking some approval. He didn't receive it, Eva noted, as Daniel merely waited, arms folded, his mouth set in a tight, serious line.

"Ladies and gentleman," Rupert began again, not at all deterred. "Please join me in welcoming Daniel Scott not only back to the UK, but to Brighton and the Hawley Gallery."

He turned to Daniel again and applauded, joined by the enthusiastic audience. Every eye in the place fell on the bad boy of English art and he rewarded them with the briefest, most cursory tip of the head that Eva had ever seen.

'Was it the Met or the Tate Modern?'

But the applause just went on. And Eva didn't join in.

It was too warm in the gallery, too many overdressed people packed in together. Too much free booze. And far, far too much sycophantic twaddle. Eva made for the French windows at the back of the room and headed out onto the terrace. A cool breeze came in from the sea and fluttered the pages of her programme open on a moody photo of Daniel. A gushing blurb, doubtless penned by Rupert, filled the opposite page. Eva read it under her breath.

"Autodidact... Self-taught genius... No formal training. Raised in care. Visceral...controversial... Cocking a snoot at the Art Establishment...the Met...Tate Modern...Pompidou. BBC 4 documentary...household name."

It told her nothing new about the man. These were merely the same facts that were always trotted off about him with the ease of myth. The man who had upset the art establishment apple cart, then been taken for a lap of honour in it.

Eva took her time leafing through the programme. The photos really didn't do justice to Daniel's paintings. They had to be seen in person, to stand under them and take in their size. But if only... *If only he'd push himself.*

Inside, she could hear the steady drone of Rupert's speech, the occasional burst of polite laughter or applause, but out here, all was calm. The sun was setting over the ocean, reflecting red on the surface as the heat of the day bowed to a sultry night. Eva took a deep breath of fresh air, her only companion a distant yacht sailing a peaceful horizon.

There was another rustle of applause from inside, this one going on longer, signalling the end of the speech. Tribute had been paid to the man who wore sunglasses indoors and was, she imagined, being adored by his public even now. Standing beneath his paintings and silently preening, the quintessential man in black.

She vaguely heard the sound of a cigarette lighter igniting close by but didn't pay her fellow escapee any attention. She wasn't in the mood for sharing platitudes about how marvellous it was to welcome Daniel Scott to Brighton. Besides, Lyndsey would be back with more Prosecco soon enough — all she had to do was wait.

"I've wracked my brains," she heard a man say. "Was it the Moscow Modern?"

Daniel Scott himself.

Eva slipped the programme into her handbag. "Yes. And MOMA in Glasgow." She raised her eyebrow at him. "And my most famous work, the border of dancing cakes on every page of a bestselling cookbook."

"That was *you?*" Daniel took a long drag on his cigarette. His eyes were still hidden behind the lenses of his Wayfarers, but she sensed his gaze was on her. "You must be due a retrospective?"

"Put it in your diary, you won't want to miss it, it's next month at the South Bank Centre." *You infuriating, good-looking bastard.* "You're not annoying me, you know. You *are* outside now, so I won't complain about the sunglasses. Although once the sun's set, they should really come off again."

"Call it the *Daniel Scott Method*," he suggested, repeating Eva's own words back to her. "Should I include a sunset in my landscape? *The Haywain, with Sunset and Dancing Cakes.*"

"Don't you even want to try?" Eva's gaze drifted down from the sunglasses, which only showed her reflection, to the triangle of exposed skin peeping out from his unbuttoned shirt. The man radiated sex, and standing out here on the terrace with him—and only him—Eva was deeply aware of her attraction to him, of every reaction in her body at his closeness. She was at risk of making a fool of herself, she knew, but...she wanted him.

"Do you think I should?" He held out the cigarette to her. "It's a genuine question."

Eva took the cigarette and placed the filter, damp from his mouth, between her lips. She coughed on the first puff, then took another, inhaling deeply. She breathed out slowly, the smoke carried away on the strengthening breeze, and passed him the cigarette back.

"Yes, I think you should." Eva pushed back her loose hair, her bangles clicking. "You are an exceptional artist and you know it, but I just feel that you could go that little bit further. Don't you like a challenge?"

Daniel didn't answer. Instead he put the cigarette between his lips and allowed himself the time to take a leisurely draw. When he removed it, he still didn't speak for a long moment. Finally he broke his silence to tell her, "The first twenty years of my life were one long challenge."

"Yes...so it says in the programme." Eva wasn't unsympathetic towards what must have been a difficult childhood, and one so different from her own middle-class Home Counties upbringing. But she had heard Daniel's myth so often that it had become a cliché. "But your work goes for thousands now, *millions*. You can do whatever you bloody well like."

"What I do — *everything* I do," he replied, holding out the cigarette again, "Is instinct. I don't plan, I don't think about tomorrow. Maybe I'll wake up one day and give you your landscape, maybe I'll work through the night and paint *you*. My instincts tell me what's right and I don't argue with them."

Eva took the cigarette from him. The filter was still tinged red with her lipstick, and this time when she puffed, she shaped a perfect smoke ring. "What if you told your instincts to give you a shove? Or doesn't it work like that?"

"How does it work for you?" His voice was a little lower and she felt his gaze on her again. "What do Ms Catesby's instincts tell her?"

"Do you mean in my studio…or do you mean right now?" She held his gaze for as long as she could, then stared off at the horizon. "Do you suppose my instincts aren't worth a damn because I'm not an art world bad boy?"

"I'm asking you as one artist to another," he clarified. "I don't care if you're a bad boy or a dancing cupcake."

Eva chuckled at that. "You must have seen me in my costume! That lot in there, half of them won't speak to me because I'm *commercial*. It's not *proper art*, according to them. But it still comes from in here." She placed her hand on her chest, her heart's determined beat thudding beneath her palm. "Instinct, perhaps. Even if it's a dancing cake."

"Nobody has any right to tell an artist what constitutes *art*," Daniel decided, in the way that only someone who charged millions for a work could. "And they'll all want to talk to you now, because here you are with Daniel Scott. Exchanging philosophies of *proper art*."

Eva dropped her hand from her chest and held it against Daniel's, his heart under there somewhere beneath layers of clothes. "Is this where your instincts live, Daniel? Like mine?"

"You found me out." He smiled. "What do your instincts tell you right now?"

"They're telling me to run away from the bad boy," Eva whispered. "But I don't want to."

"Tell me what you want."

Desire rose inside her with such strength that Eva could barely speak. "I want you. I want— Oh, fuck it, I'm making an idiot of myself, but…" She tipped her face up towards him, trying to seek out his lips with her own. Yes, she *was* an idiot, even more of a fawning fan than the people she had earlier mocked. An art groupie, was that it? If he pushed her away and someone saw, everyone would find out, the commercial artist rejected by the man who created *proper* art.

"Can I get anybody anyth..." Lyndsey's words trailed away as she realised that she had interrupted a moment. She just about managed to stifle her awkward giggle as Eva and Daniel looked her way. "Excuse me, I didn't—"

"Is there anywhere private we can go?" Daniel asked.

Eva smoothed down her hair. "To discuss something."

Lyndsey bit her coral-pink lip and Eva could see the worry in her eyes, even at this distance. She glanced back into the gallery then quickly took her identity laminate from around her neck, holding down her wooden necklace to keep the two from tangling as she did so.

"Buzz through the fire door at the end of the terrace." Her voice was hushed, but Eva saw something else in her friend's eyes, the excitement of a secret shared. "Up the steps and buzz through the first door into Rupert's office. Just... Leave it as you found it?"

Daniel took the laminate from her and pressed his other hand to the small of Eva's back. He didn't thank Lyndsey, just wordlessly urged Eva to move.

What the hell am I doing?

But she couldn't stop. She didn't want to. When they reached the fire door, she whispered, "Are your instincts telling you to fuck me?"

"They're telling me that you want me to." He pressed the laminate to a small box beside the door. It gave a low beep and she heard the sound of the lock springing back a moment before Daniel pulled the door open and followed her inside. A flight of steps stood before them and the door slammed behind them.

"Then they're right." They went up the steps, and Eva saw the office door with Rupert's nameplate on it. The man who had taken her on one date and hadn't got any further than a kiss. *Sorry, Rupert.* "And do you want to fuck *me*?"

At the office door he caught Eva's wrist in a gentle grip and turned her to face him. He was still wearing the sunglasses, of course, because — Why? Because he was as infuriating as he was attractive.

"You know I want you."

Eva stroked her other hand down his cheek, then gave him a soft peck on the chin as she caressed lower, over his torso and down to his groin. She breathed out in surprise as she touched his erection through his clothes. "Oh, I most certainly do."

Daniel touched Lyndsey's card to the reader and the click sounded again. Then he reached past Eva, his arm lightly brushing her hip, and turned the door handle behind her, finally letting them into the sanctuary of Rupert's carefully ordered office.

"On the desk?" Eva popped open the top button on his trousers and drew down his zip with care. "Kiss me, you delicious bastard."

He slipped his arms around Eva, one hand sliding down to rest possessively on her bottom as he kissed her. This wasn't the awkward collision she and Rupert had quickly written out of their brief, aborted dating history, but a gesture born entirely of his beloved instinct, full of the heat and passion that had lately gone missing from Daniel Scott's artwork. There was nothing *by numbers* about it.

Eva responded with desire burning in her kiss as she dragged one hand through his hair and slid the other into his trousers. She closed her hand around his erection, unhindered by underwear, as the *enfant terrible* wore none. Her touch drew a gasp of pleasure from his lips and into their kiss, before he lifted his hand and the edge of Rupert's desk pressed against Eva's thighs.

"Tell me how hard you like it," he demanded breathlessly, catching the edge of her earlobe lightly between his teeth.

"Do you think you *can* do it as hard as I need it?" Eva grinned, stroking his long, girthy erection. "You're bloody big… I'm going to enjoy this."

Daniel's lips met Eva's again, his tongue moving with hers as he urged her dress higher. The office air was cool on her naked skin, his fingers sure as they revealed her body, and all the time he was kissing her with that same intensity, that same heat.

She broke away from his lips to whisper, "There's a condom in my handbag." Was he going to think she'd planned this, that she'd left for the exhibition intending to seduce him? *Let him, if that's what he wants to think.*

"So you're a fan then?" He tightened his hands on her hips and lifted her up onto the desk.

Eva laughed. "You really are the most arrogant man I've ever met! But you also have the biggest cock… Are the two things connected?"

"Definitely." Daniel reached into his jacket and took out a folded leather wallet. He opened it with a practiced flick of his wrist and retrieved a wrapped condom. With the wallet safely returned to his pocket, he tore open the wrapper with his teeth then told her, "If you ask very nicely, I might even sign your programme before we leave."

"And if I don't ask nicely?" Eva arched an eyebrow. "Will you put me over your knee?"

"I probably should, just for your opinion of my work." He held out the wrapped condom in a wordless invitation.

Eva took the condom out and threw the wrapper over her shoulder. She slid the condom onto him, her hand trembling just a little as she did so, then she linked both hands behind his neck and locked her legs around his middle.

The sunglasses weren't coming off, Eva realised that now. Just to goad her, of course. To stoke her ire. An urgent fuck between two people who had done nothing since their first meeting but spar and flirt with each other.

Why not?

He deepened the kiss, stroking his tongue against hers as he caught his arms around her waist and pulled her closer, finally joining their bodies with one determined thrust of his hips. There was no preamble, no pretence of affection, just the primal desire to share this most intimate of connections.

Eva moaned into their kiss as he thrust, possessing her in the most visceral way he could. She rocked her hips against him, urging him as deep inside her as he could go, answering a need within her that had been left unsatisfied for too long. Pleasure rolled through her, and she was hungry for him, ravenous and greedy for every inch of him and every thrust. Even if she couldn't see his eyes behind those bloody sunglasses.

Daniel's fingers were in her hair, tangling, twining, bringing her mouth back to his. Every thrust drew a gasp from him, every second stoked the fire between them and Eva tightened her limbs around him until they were as close together as they could be. Downstairs they would be wondering where their star was, but it was a secret they'd never share. It belonged to Eva Catesby.

Eva's pleasure built steadily from a tremble in her limbs, growing until she shuddered with its intensity and something inside her burst and flowed out through her body. She moaned Daniel's name as her pleasure grew again. The urgency of his kisses and the deep, hard strokes of his cock told her that his own orgasm couldn't be far off, and the promise of it sent a shiver through her. In reply, Daniel's embrace tightened just a little, his hand creeping round to caress her bottom as he pulled Eva's body against him.

Eva grasped his buttocks, feeling all the power in him, which at that moment was for the pleasure of them both. "Harder...*harder*..." she sighed, lost in a place of passion and sensation, no thought in her head besides this man. Their kisses grew more fervent and, as she turned her head away to gasp, she knocked his sunglasses flying.

"Shit!" Daniel spat the word out and she looked into his eyes, seeing a flash of annoyance and desire in the depths. Then he twisted his fingers in Eva's hair and kissed her again, obeying her command as his hips moved harder than ever.

They were so close that his eyelashes brushed against her face. Such a small thing, but—

"Oh, Daniel." Whatever else Eva would've said was lost in a long, drawn-out moan as she climaxed again, her body shuddering and her veins alight with vivid desire. It was if a thread joined them and it pulled taut at that moment, pushing Daniel to his own climax even as she found her release. He bucked against her, a cry of exertion torn from his lips as his orgasm claimed him.

Eva held him tightly, her mouth pressed against his neck as tremors still ran through her body. "Sorry about your sunglasses," she whispered.

Daniel tilted his chin up and she felt the pulse in his throat. It was racing.

"You were determined to get me out of them," he eventually murmured, but she couldn't tell if there was any humour in the words.

"It wasn't intentional, even if you don't believe me." Eva laughed. She touched away his hair from his face. "I suppose I can't have the star of the show all to myself for the whole evening…"

"And you'll be in demand now." He put one finger beneath Eva's chin and raised it so he could kiss her lips. "Your public awaits."

Then Daniel gently disentangled himself from Eva's embrace and took a couple of steps back. He turned away and she knew exactly what he was doing, because she already knew that he wasn't the sort of man to appear dishevelled in *anyone's* company.

Eva hopped down from the desk and let her dress fall back down to her ankles once more. She reached for her handbag. What she was about to do might well make her look needy to a man like *the celebrated Daniel Scott*, but she couldn't just walk away. She held out her business card to him. "Now you're a Brighton resident…if you ever need some company, or illustrations of dancing cakes, give me a ring."

Daniel Scott, the guest of honour in Rupert Hawley's gallery, threw his used condom into his host's wastepaper basket as though it was his God-given right to do so. When he turned back to Eva his clothes were tidied once more, and those dark eyes were sparkling.

He took the card and slipped it into his pocket without even glancing at it. Then he picked up his sunglasses and put them on, hiding his gaze from Eva.

"Do you want me to sign that programme now?"

Daniel wasn't going to ring her, Eva knew that. This was a one-off and nothing more, and she was sure he'd laugh about her later, the gall of a nonentity like Eva Catesby thinking he'd want more than five minutes over a desk with her. But she was certain he had enjoyed it.

"Go on, sign it, then." *What a memento.* Her handbag was already open and she pulled out the programme and passed it to him along with a pen from Rupert's desk tidy. He took the pen and put the programme down on the desk where, moments earlier, they had fucked each other.

For a second Daniel appeared to be waiting for those much-vaunted *instincts,* then he set to work. He was drawing something, Eva realised, and she craned closer to watch.

It was a scribble of a cupcake with a rather jolly smile and its eyes hidden behind a pair of sunglasses. Its spindly legs and arms were raised in a dance and beneath it he had written, *"Today cupcakes, tomorrow landscapes?"* Beneath that Daniel scrawled his signature, before he picked up the programme and held it out to her.

"Maybe!" Eva laughed as she took the programme from him and put it back in her bag. "Well...it's been fun. Thank you. I should really..." Eva pointed to the door.

"I'm sure I'll see you down there." Only then did he smile, the expression just a little arrogant. No, *very* arrogant. She knew why when he added, "Always a pleasure to meet a critic."

Eva grinned as she opened the door. "Is that how you deal with all your reviewers?"

"Only the ones with attitude," was his reply. "But I *never* sign autographs afterwards."

Eva didn't look back and headed downstairs to the gallery. The overheated room was loud with conversation, and while Daniel's paintings were the source of fascination to some, most of the crowd were quaffing Prosecco, the exhibition preview a social occasion rather than one to consider art. Eva tried to take in Daniel's work, but rather than his art, she was aware of *him*, and every fibre in her body still thrummed. She could still feel him inside her.

"We appear to have misplaced our star attraction." Rupert was at Eva's shoulder, his voice merry. "Tell me that you've seen him, my nerves will thank you!"

Eva sucked in her cheeks as she tried to think what to say. The very man whose desk had been despoiled and he hadn't a clue. "He…was out on the terrace about ten minutes ago. Smoking a fag. Being intense. You know how it is."

"I shall leave him to his own devices, I'm sure he'll return when he's ready to mingle," Rupert decided. He slipped one hand into the pocket of his elegantly cut trousers, something in his studied manner a little *too* casual.

Eva felt the need to make conversation, to assuage herself of her twinge of guilt. "Well done, by the way, on getting this gig. Really puts you on the map, doesn't it!"

"I wish I could claim the credit, but the inspiration came from Lyndsey," he told her, the admission one Eva would never have expected. "She was the one who seemed to think we might be able to convince our bad boy to exhibit once word went round that he'd bought the house. I never in a million years thought he'd say yes!"

"How on earth did you guys do it? He's so full of himself! The man who keeps his sunglasses on" — Eva paused, seeing again in the dark lenses the reflection of her face softened by need and desire — "indoors then vanishes from his own private viewing. Although I suppose he has a reputation to live up to."

"Believe me, it was far from easy. The pottery chicken and charity eiderdown brigade are much easier to deal with." He took a sip from his glass. "But they don't bring in the national press, do they? For that we need — Oh thank God, he's back!"

Rupert glanced across the room and she saw again Daniel Scott, standing beneath that red canvas once more. One hand was in his pocket, in the other he held a glass of ruby-red wine and on his face was the barest hint of a smile, but even though she couldn't see his eyes, Eva knew they wouldn't be smiling. The floor around him was empty, and beyond that exclusion zone, a gaggle of press photographers snapped the publicity shots that would be on tomorrow's arts pages, both paper and electronic.

"Far be it from Daniel Scott to miss a photocall." Most of the Brighton art crowd were making a show of not watching, as if they saw photocalls like that all the time and found them thoroughly tedious. But Eva wanted to watch. She wanted to see *him*, the man whose desire had met hers for a few delicious minutes. Who would think that her business card was in his pocket?

If he hadn't already thrown it away.

Eva grabbed a Prosecco from a passing tray. And if he had chucked it in the bin and he never contacted her, so what? They'd had their fun.

"What do you think of the work?" Rupert asked. Across the room Daniel shifted his pose just a little, tilting his head, turning his foot, and Eva had the sudden, strange feeling that his hidden gaze was on her. "Isn't it marvellous? He's a visionary, of course, our generation's Bacon. One could study these works for a lifetime and never tire of listening to what they have to say, don't you find?"

"Maybe..." Eva sipped her drink. "But don't you feel as if he's always saying the same thing? I mean, everyone who looks at the paintings will take something away from them that's slightly different, I realise that...but I'm sure you'll hear from Lyndsey, there was a little incident earlier when Daniel overheard me say that I think he needs to push himself."

Rupert's eyes grew wide. "What? I need to know what happened, Eva, this is damage control time."

Eva laughed and patted Rupert's shoulder. "No need to panic, Rupe! He and I...got our heads together and sorted out our differences. It's not as if I don't admire his work, I *do*, but I don't think he's making the most of his talent. It's something people like him need to hear when they're surrounded by yes-men and arse-kissers."

"And how go things for you?" Rupert smiled. "Is *painting for chavs* still rolling on, or are they all in a borstal by now?"

"It's called art outreach, Rupert..." Eva rolled her eyes at him. "I did wonder about bringing them here to see Daniel's work. He grew up in care, as we all know. He might not be an ideal role model in some respects, but maybe seeing his art in your gallery might inspire them."

"Some little bastard scratched the Jag last week when I was at dinner," he grimaced. "So if you bring them here, you need to keep them in line. The new Bloomsbury set?"

"The Burberry set," Lyndsey helpfully supplied as she joined them, then she and Rupert exploded in a gale of laughter.

Eva guzzled her Prosecco. Her date with Rupert had included a lengthy monologue from him on his disdain for *pointless middle-class do-gooders*, like Eva and her art outreach. Quite how he'd thought that was the way to impress a woman, she didn't know. Maybe he'd expected her to melt as soon as she'd got into his Jag and declare that he was perfectly right about everything. She thought of him at his desk tomorrow, leaning against the very spot where she and Daniel had fucked, and it made her smile.

"Think of Mr Scott, though," Lyndsey told them. "Isn't he the role model for your kids, Eva? He had a terrible childhood, yet look at him now. Such a shame that he wouldn't be interested in talking to them — imagine how amazing it'd be if he did!"

"Not interested?" Dispirited, Eva tugged at her earlobe, only then realising that her earring had fallen out. Because now, of course, everything would go wrong. "Did you ask him about the local community art projects and all that? Did he say no?"

The gallery owner and his PA shook their heads as one. Rupert told her, "I don't think we need to ask, he won't do it. We weren't even sure he'd show up tonight!"

Eva swallowed. The intense joy she had felt while in his arms was ebbing away. She'd behaved like a fool, the willing toy of an entirely unprincipled man. "That's a shame. He's in a position to really do some good. At least, *I* think so. But maybe he can't *do* nice. It wouldn't go with that *enfant terrible* image, would it?"

"Don't offend him again," Rupert warned, as though she were a naughty child. "Lynnie, we must circulate. Ciao, Eva!"

"I might go home, actu—" But she wasn't sure that they had heard her. Across the room Daniel's photographers had scattered and he was nowhere to be seen. Perhaps even now he was in the office with another woman, another notch for the bedpost. Eva ran her fingers through her hair and they caught on a tangle, which she started to tease out. She was a grown woman, and she wasn't going to let some little voice in her head make her feel ashamed for enjoying herself. She just hoped it didn't become public knowledge amongst the Brighton art crowd.

"Do you ever drink red, or is it only knock-off champagne that suits the girls of Brighton?" Daniel emerged from a small gaggle of guffaws to her right. He held two glasses of red wine, one of which he held out towards Eva.

"Thank you." Eva took the glass with a grin. Despite her reservations, her body was reacting again to his presence, desiring his touch once more. Could he tell? "I'm an equal opportunities drinker. As long as it's got bubbles in it, I'll drink it, even if it's not champagne. But I suppose I'll have to rough it with red wine."

"No bubbles in this, I'm afraid." He sniffed, brushing his thumb briefly across the tip of his nose. "You've seen all the works now, I assume?'

She recognised that gesture. He was a bad boy, after all, and what self-respecting bad boy wouldn't snort the occasional line? That explained the raging ego, at least. "I've seen them all, but I've only looked properly at a few. Gutsy work, but you know what I'm going to say, and I'd say the same to the art outreach kids. Don't be afraid to push yourself. Try to do things differently."

"So try a dancing biscuit rather than a dancing cake?" He nodded thoughtfully, then brought his sunglasses up into his hair. She knew then that she was right about the line—she could see it reflected in his dark eyes. "Is that what you do? Outreach?"

"Believe it or not, my day job is as an illustrator. The outreach is something I do because..." How exactly did she phrase this without sounding patronising? "I was a lucky child, growing up. And there's lots of kids who aren't. So I do outreach in my spare time, just to, I don't know, create a bit of balance in the universe."

"Does it help? You, not them." He slipped his hand into his pocket and leaned his shoulder against the wall. "Does it assuage your middle-class guilt?"

Eva rolled her eyes. "Should I just do nothing, then? Sit in my nice house drawing anthropomorphic rabbits and not care a straw for anyone else? I just want to help where I can, that's all."

"And what help is it? I'm not arguing, I'm intrigued."

"It gives kids confidence, an outlet, a different perspective. A different way of seeing things." Eva drank her wine, and wondered if it was the alcohol talking now or not. "And someone who'll listen to them, when they feel as if the world really isn't that bothered whether they exist or not."

"Sometimes the world *isn't*. The world would rather they *didn't*," he replied. "Promise me that you'll never tell them that."

"I promise." She smiled at him over the rim of her glass. "Actually... I was saying to Rupert earlier, it'd be nice to bring them here to your exhibition. Could we arrange something? I know you're really busy, but maybe…just give it a thought. It would be wonderful to bring them here, and if you talked to them about your work—"

"I don't think that's my scene, but you should bring them to the show." He gave a soft chuckle. "I'd like to get an opinion that isn't rehearsed, sycophantic and meaningless. Present company excepted."

Eva ran her fingertip down his lapel, her gaze fixed on his. Could she really not convince him to meet her kids? "See? I don't hate your art. Far from it, it's brilliant, but I think you could be *more* brilliant still."

Daniels flicked his sunglasses down over his eyes and sniffed again. "Where can I see your work? Besides cookbooks?"

"Here and there," Eva said. "The Met…the Tate Modern…"

"Snap. Small world." He glanced around. "Small town. Maybe we'll bump into each other."

"Hope so!" Eva nodded. "If you still have my card, get in touch."

"Do you think I've thrown it away?"

Eva glanced at the pocket she'd seen him put her card in. "I really wouldn't like to assume one way or the other."

"But if you had to? If your life depended on the guess." He took another drink. "Did I keep your card or throw it away?"

Eva tipped her head to one side. "I reckon you've kept it. But you'll forget it's there. Then you'll take your suit to the dry cleaner's and find it in your pocket, and you'll remember what we did. Every last little detail will come back to you." She finished her drink. The question was, if he did remember her, would he want to see her again?

"But you won't forget," he told her with more than a trace of arrogance. "And when you're in bed tonight you'll be replaying it in your head. And you'll be as wet then as you are now."

How dare he assume – Eva tightened the grip on her glass. "Count yourself lucky that this glass is empty or I would've flung red wine in your face."

"What a cliché you would've been." He held out his own glass to her, still half-filled with red wine. "But if you insist on melodrama, be my guest."

"No thanks." Not for the first time that evening, Eva questioned what she was doing. If his arrogance annoyed her so much, why was she still courting his company? But she knew the answer. He was handsome, yes, there was that, but she liked it when he infuriated her. Too much. "I've monopolised enough of your time this evening, and all the art world of Brighton want to speak to you."

"Bring your kids." He glanced back at Rupert, who raised his glass. 'And ask them, *how can this be improved?* We're ready for our next *enfant terrible*, don't you think?"

Eva smiled at him—a genuine, warm smile, because she was fairly sure that she had just been allowed a peep through the crack in Daniel Scott's conceited armour. "Yes, we are. We really are."

"Goodnight, Ms Catesby." He leaned closer and kissed her cheek like a friend might. "Think of me tonight."

Eva's kiss in return was the most impeccably platonic she had ever bestowed. "Oh, I will. But only because you'll be thinking of me."

"Count on it." Then he turned and finally gave his attention to Rupert and his hangers-on.

Chapter Two

She did think of him that night, of course, but with a wry smile. And she was still thinking about him when she got up the next morning, and kept an eye out as photographs of the private viewing went online.

Handsome sod, posing in his sunglasses.

One local news site had several photos showing Daniel with local artists, and there was even a picture of her and Daniel mid-flow, standing beneath one of his paintings.

"Oh no!" Eva scrolled quickly past the image, not wanting to spend another second looking at her red cheeks or the sparkle in her eyes. But after seeing some photos of Daniel with Rupert, Eva scrolled back up again to the picture of her with the *enfant terrible* and downloaded it to her computer. She flicked through the programme, smiling at what he had written, and sat it on her desk.

He didn't contact her though. Just as she had expected. He might be recovering from a hangover or a comedown, but equally, he might have already moved onto someone else.

And I don't care.

Although, as she worked on her illustration, she kept her phone beside her, and she checked her emails at half-hour intervals. Just in case her agent wanted to speak to her. Or even if Daniel Scott should happen to —

But he didn't.

* * * *

Two days after the private viewing, and Daniel still hadn't contacted her. That was it now. She stopped hovering over her phone and her emails, and put the programme away in a drawer.

By the third day, Daniel Scott was a pleasant memory. She thought of his grip on her waist as he took her, the heat in his lips as they kissed, the urgency of their coupling, the smoulder in his eyes. Eva would never forget any of that, but it seemed that he had.

She stood on the tiny balcony at the back of her studio, overlooking her modest garden as the shadows lengthened. Her phone buzzed in her pocket.

It wouldn't be *him*, not now.

But who else would have sent her a message that read, *Are the cakes still dancing?*

She stared at the screen, laughing, but she desire uncoiled in her once again. She tapped out her reply.

It's bees this week.

Eva put the phone back in her pocket, wondering if he would reply. Surely he was expecting her to say something else. A gushing *omg how are you?? Xx,* perhaps, but it wasn't her style. Her bees might have put paid to their budding whatever-it-was.

She held her glass of lemonade to her blushing cheek. The ice in her drink didn't seem able to cool it. Maybe she should send him another text. Nothing about bees this time, though.

Just as she took out her phone, it buzzed with a message.

I want you.

Nothing else, just those three words. Eva clutched the balcony rail, trembling as a wave of need swept through her. She shouldn't, she really shouldn't, but—

I want you too. Where are you?

In his new house overlooking the sea, or had he jetted back to New York? The thought that he might not even be in the same country as her anymore left Eva feeling desolate. She shouldn't have let him get under her skin, but he had.

His reply was faster than before.

Where would you like me to be?

The answer to that was easy, at least.

Between my legs, she replied.

And waited.

The phone rang, but whoever the caller was, they had chosen to remain anonymous. She knew who it was, though. Eva let it ring for as long as she could bear before she swiped the screen to answer.

In her most deliberately breathy voice, Eva said, "The Palace of Dancing Cakes, Eva speaking, how can I help you?"

"Tell me how wet you are," Daniel said, his voice husky with desire.

Eva's hand shook. She couldn't stay outside here, where her neighbours would overhear. Or see.

Heading back into the studio, closing the window behind her and drawing the curtain, Eva replied, "Wet enough for your enormous cock. Is it hard yet?"

"Hang up the phone," he told her. "I'm calling you back."

"If you must…" Eva ended the call. Curious now as to why he needed to ring off and call back, she dropped down onto a beanbag. Her own breathing was the only sound in the room as she waited, quick, shallow breaths as her heart raced. A couple of minutes passed before it rang again, this time with a video call from that same withheld number.

Should I?

Eva swiped the screen before her hesitancy could stop her.

And there he was, Daniel Scott, beneath a cloudless sky of the brightest blue she could imagine. From what Eva could see, he appeared to be on a lounger of some sort, his sunglasses on, a glass of wine in his hand and, of course, he was wearing black. This wasn't the smart shirt in which she had last seen him, though, but a T-shirt that was covered with a hundred paint spatters that conjured the canvases she had seen in Rupert's gallery. This wasn't the clinical, careful exhibition space—this was the raw creator.

Eva was self-conscious of the view he'd have of her. A corner of her studio with an old chintz curtain behind her. No makeup, and her figure-skimming satin dress replaced by a white Babushka blouse. She ran her hand through her hair. "So your instincts have been busy, then?"

"Always." He raised the glass of red wine. "Tell me about these bees."

"They're flying through a clump of plants. It's to raise awareness about bee-friendly gardening. See, exciting, isn't it? But important. I like bees." Was she really talking shop with *him*? Eva chuckled. "Do you have some sort of massive balcony there, Daniel? Because I want to see some bee-friendly pot plants out there. And I don't mean *that* kind of pot either."

"I don't grow my own," he informed her, then reached out. The camera moved, sweeping over the vast terrace with an array of colourful plants in pots, which she certainly hadn't been expecting.

Neither had she been expecting—well, perhaps she had a bit—the infinity pool with its pacific blue water. As Daniel continued to pan around his domain, the house came into view. A vast, white art deco structure with huge floor-to-ceiling windows, the sort of place where a knowing Belgian detective might find a murder victim.

"What a gorgeous house you have!" Eva knew she hadn't sounded sarcastic or seductive, and she also knew that she was at risk of making his head expand to ever more massive proportions by flattering his home. But it *was* lovely.

"I was thinking about you." The camera settled on Daniel again, a longer shot this time. His legs, clad in paint-spattered black trousers, were stretched out before him, crossed at the ankle. His feet were bare and even there, Eva saw, some paint had landed.

"And became so distracted that you dropped paint all over yourself?" Eva laughed. But she was all too aware of her unslaked desire behind everything she said, and she whispered, "I want to wash your feet."

"That's more polite than I was intending to be," he replied, but had she imagined the pause before he answered? The sound that suggested the slightest catch of his breath?

"Were you going to be rude, Daniel Scott, *art world bad boy*?" Eva ran her tongue over her lips. "Is there something you wanted to show me? Not just your house and your garden, I assume, or your paint-covered toes. What was it?"

"I thought, since you were so keen on *private views*, that you might like another." Daniel took a sip from his glass then reached to place it down beside the camera. He didn't relax back onto the lounger, though, and instead peeled the T-shirt up and over his head, casting it aside.

Eva held the phone more tightly. *Had he really just –? He had. She recalled the sensation of him thrusting between her legs, and the thought of having that toned, bare chest against her if they ever had a repeat performance left her struggling for words. She slid her hand up under her skirt and let her fingertips rest against the soft skin of her inner thighs. "That's really not a bad view, as views go."

"It's only half the exhibition," he deadpanned. "Do you want to see more?"

"You're sitting outside!" Eva laughed, a dirty chuckle. She wasn't shocked at all, merely amused that every preconception she'd had of him was true. "Go on then. If your neighbours won't complain."

"I don't have any neighbours, but I'd hate to shock you, Ms Catesby."

"Even though I might draw dancing cakes for a living, I'm not easy to shock, Mr Scott." Eva danced her fingers farther up her thigh. "That might surprise you, I know, but you'd have to get up very early in the morning to shock *me*."

Daniel stood and she saw that the trousers were actually some sort of ludicrously decadent lounging affair, the sort of wide-legged silky number that only someone with far more money than they knew what to do with would wear to paint in. He cocked his head to one side and unfastened the tie with one hand before, as though it were an everyday occurrence, he slid them down.

Eva brought her hand up to the top of her thigh and touched herself. She was wet, just as he'd known she would be, and she stared at the body that he had revealed to her, the cock she had caressed and that had thrust inside her, but that in their eagerness, she had barely stopped to see. He looked like a lewd satyr, and Eva stroked herself faster, sliding her fingers inside as she remembered how it had felt to be fucked by the man who presented herself on the screen for her now.

"Tell me what you're doing," Daniel instructed as he resumed his place on the lounger, his ankles crossed again and his cock standing out from his groin. He reached down and took his erection in his hand, lazily stroking. "I want to know how you feel."

Eva lay back on the beanbag and spread her legs wider. "Can't you guess, Daniel?" She gasped as her frustrated desire for him began to melt into pleasure. "I wish you had your hand under my skirt right now."

"I don't want to guess." She saw the tip of his tongue flick over his lip. "I need to see you. I need to touch you." Eva pulled up the hem of her skirt, still holding the phone. He must've seen the length of her legs before she stopped, her skirt now around her middle and her phone resting on her thigh. The angle could have given him no doubt as to what she was doing. "Touch me, then. Do it. I want you."

"Next time we're together —" His hand jerked a little faster, a moan slipping from his parted lips. "Before I fuck you, let me taste you?"

"I'll insist on it, never you worry about that." Her hips rose of their own accord, as if chasing her hand. "Over Rupert's desk again, is that where you'll lick me and fuck me?"

"That *prick*," he spat with a venom that surprised her. "Every time we see him, we'll know that his office is *ours*."

"Rupert wants to fuck me. Did you know?" Eva's climax was getting closer, the memories of that intense evening flooding back and urging closer to her orgasm.

"He never took his eyes off you," Daniel told her breathlessly, his back arching as he fought against his own approaching orgasm. "Will you let him have you?"

She shook her head. "No, never. He kissed me and I felt nothing. I burned up when you kissed me, and it was nothing like that. Every bit of me."

"And you've been thinking about me?"

"Yes..." Eva didn't really want to admit it. She didn't want him to think that she'd waited and waited for him to contact her. "...to begin with."

"Then you forgot me?"

"Didn't you forget me?"

"Not for a second."

There was something in his voice that pushed Eva over the edge, and her climax soared. Her body jolted, sending her phone flying from its perch on her thigh onto the floor. As bliss shook through her, her only thought was *he hadn't forgotten me*. She clumsily reached for her phone again and propped it up so she could see him.

"I didn't forget you either," she admitted in a whisper. He lifted his sunglasses to look at her, his other hand jerking hard and fast. Then Daniel Scott, the *enfant terrible*, the man with paint on his toes, closed his eyes as his orgasm swept through his body.

He looked ridiculously hot as he came, all the muscles in that toned body working together, moving under the surface of his skin. If only she could see it in the flesh, if only she could kiss his perfect stomach and take him in her mouth.

"We need to meet. *Now*, Daniel."

"Where?"

"I'll come over to yours." She didn't know why she hoped he wouldn't think that sounded desperate. They both craved each other — *desperate* barely came into it. "I can't drive, not after that, but I'll get a cab. Text me your address."

"I'll send a cab for you," Daniel told her. "Where are you?"

"Kemptown. Hang on… I'll send you my address." As she brought up her text messages and typed, she realised that he was now getting a hugely unflattering view of her nostrils. Once she'd typed out her address, she lifted the phone to a more flattering angle. "There. Got it? How long have I got to get ready, or do you want me as I am?"

"Come just as you are. How long do you need?" He smiled and added, "And how do you want me?"

"Give me fifteen minutes." Eva heaved herself up from the beanbag and left her studio, turning off the light behind her. She went through to her bedroom, which was at the front of the house, and stood in front of her large bed so that he could see it behind her. So that it would imprint itself on his mind and he could think of them romping there. "You? Hmmm... I think your bad boy black suit and shirt, don't you?"

"Consider it done," Daniel told her. "I'll see you very soon?"

"Definitely." Eva blew him a kiss and waved at the screen. He rewarded her with a wink, then put the sunglasses back on.

"The champagne'll be on ice." And with that, the call ended.

Chapter Three

The cab arrived exactly fifteen minutes later. Eva had flung an antique cloak around her shoulders and thrown some bits and bobs into a bag. A swift slick of mascara and lipstick, a squirt of perfume, and she was prepared.

The cab's engine was loud in the courtyard outside her mews house. A curtain twitched, because an area couldn't claim to have a *village vibe* without at least one nosey neighbour.

After five minutes in the cab, Eva leaned between the front seats to speak to the driver.

"Are there diversions in town? Only, I'm not sure this is the right way."

"This is the address I was given," the driver told her. "We're nearly there."

"But—"

But this was the Brighton promenade, a row of Georgian town houses, not secluded art deco palaces by the sea.

"This is you," the driver announced, brakes squeaking as they pulled up outside a hotel. "The fare's taken care of."

He glanced into his rear-view mirror and she saw a glimmer of humour in his eyes. "All I know is, *this is you*. Have a good afternoon."

"Are you absolutely certain? There hasn't been a mix-up at the cab office?" Eva glanced at her phone. It was infuriatingly silent, with no calls or texts from Daniel.

He pressed a few buttons on the mobile phone that sat in a cradle on his dashboard and peered at the screen.

"You're Ms Catesby?"

Eva nodded. "Yes."

"Booked and paid for, pick up, drop off at The Mallard." He peered through the windscreen at the white double-fronted building. "Do you want me to drive you back to the pick-up point?"

A hotel. How very Daniel Scott—and what a saucy trick to play. "No, it's fine… I thought I was going to a different hotel, that's why I was confused. Thanks."

Eva climbed out of the taxi. As it merged with the traffic, she realised why the driver had been smiling.

He must think I'm an escort!

In a way, she was, summoned by desire.

A couple emerged from the hotel, dressed as though they had just stepped out of a roadside diner in the heartland of 1950s America. The young man held the door open for Eva, waiting for her to enter.

Eva thanked him and went in. The hotel was lavish and clearly expensive, and a hush fell over Eva as soon as she entered. But there was something else, too, a definite frisson in the air, the unavoidable impression that wildness went on behind its respectable façade.

Otherwise, why else would Daniel have chosen the place?

"Good afternoon!" The *too* polished woman behind the desk greeted her with a grin as bright as her red hair. "Can I help you?"

"Hi, I'm looking for—" Eva stopped herself before she said his name. Surely he wouldn't have booked in under *Daniel Scott*? "A friend. I'm sure you know what I mean."

The woman's smile confirmed everything that Eva had suspected about this place. She turned away from the computer screen and instead opened a large paper diary, then tapped her manicured nail against the page.

"Mr Carswell's guest." She closed the diary with a thud of finality. "Let me show you up."

Carswell? The name seemed familiar, but Eva couldn't place it. It was probably a pompous gallery owner or a fatuous curator who had dared to cross the *enfant terrible*. And he was here, somewhere in this building, and the thought of it seared her with desire.

"Can I take your bag?" The receptionist emerged from behind the desk, her gait assured despite the sky-scraping heels on her patent shoes. She held out her hand expectantly, the smile never wavering.

It was clearly not an overnight bag, but Eva suspected that the receptionist would have been surprised if it had been. Then the bag was taken from her and the woman led Eva from the foyer and into a corridor, its walls decorated with rococo swirls in silver and turquoise that continued up the sweeping staircase they climbed, past rooms on which large numbers had been painted in gold. It was undeniably chic and undeniably decadent.

It was very Daniel Scott—or Mr Carswell, as he was today.

They climbed a second flight, and though the stairs continued on upwards, the women did not. There was only one room on this floor, its cold number identifying it as 7. Here the receptionist turned to hand back the bag. She didn't knock on the white door but instead broke that immaculate smile to say, "Enjoy your stay."

She didn't look back as she descended the stairs.

Eva's heart thudded in anticipation. The video call earlier had only stoked her lusts, not slaked them, and as soon as the receptionist had disappeared around the angle of the stairs, Eva knocked.

She didn't know whether Daniel would make her wait and she didn't have time to wonder, because the door opened less than a minute later.

And of course he was wearing sunglasses.

Eva threw her arms around him, her lips already on his before the door had shut behind her. She dropped her bag to the ground and ran both hands through his hair. "A hotel, you utter sod." She laughed.

He silenced her laughter with a kiss, his answering embrace pushing Eva back against the door as it closed. The kiss went on as his body pressed to hers, his clothed erection already hard against her. Daniel didn't speak until he broke the kiss so they could breathe and he murmured, "That's why you want me."

"There's another reason, too." Eva slid her hands down to rest on his buttocks. "This fabulous body you flashed at me earlier."

"It's all yours," he breathed. Then he pressed a kiss to her throat and whispered, "Champagne?"

"No Prosecco for Daniel Scott! I mean—Mr Carswell." Eva gently ran her hand down his chest. A bed this time, not a desk. Not five minutes stolen from an evening. *Oh, the fun we could have.* "Yes, please, to champers."

"The mysterious Mr Carswell." He took her hand and drew her into the airy room. It was stunning, as stunning as her companion, though only one of them was all in black. The bed was vast, piled with bright pillows and covered in crisp white linen that seemed to glow in the light of the three windows that reached from floor to ceiling, overlooking the promenade and ocean far below. In front of those windows was a large bath, perhaps promising even more possibilities later, whilst a sofa and chairs in bright turquoise surrounded a coffee table on which there was a champagne bucket and two glasses.

Only as they crossed to the table did Eva realise that Daniel, resplendent in his black suit and sunglasses, was still barefoot. Paint still spattered his exposed skin and she recalled again the sight of him naked, relaxing on the lounger, just for her.

Eva unfastened the clasp on her cape and let it fall to the ground, revealing her blouse and what lay beneath the gauzy fabric. She felt the heat in Daniel's gaze as it swept over her, lingering for just a moment at her breasts before he turned to retrieve the bottle of champagne from its cocoon of ice.

"I've been thinking about you," Daniel admitted.

Eva perched on the edge of the bed and kicked off her shoes. She rubbed her bare toes against his ankle. "And what were you thinking? *That bloody woman telling me to up my game!*"

"I was thinking of how it felt when you wrapped your legs around me." Daniel tore off the gold foil and threw it onto the table. "And how much I wanted to fuck you again. And how much thinking about that was getting in the way of my work."

Eva's gaze shifted away from Daniel. How on Earth had that happened? A world-renowned artist distracted by a one-night stand with *her*? Surely the world was full of women willing to be bedded by Daniel Scott.

"Should I apologise because you find me irresistible?" It sounded like one of his lines, but Eva was in a cheeky mood and she wanted to see how he would react.

"I'm getting you out of my system," he replied, but she saw a quirk of humour touch the corner of his mouth. Then he took the cork in his fist and popped it from the neck of the bottle. "Once and for all."

Eva lay back against the pile of pillows as if she was posing for a painting as an odalisque, her arm arched behind her head because she knew it would make her breasts pert beneath the thin blouse. "And I *fully* intend to work you out of mine."

"You'll have to work hard," he told her with a hint of mischief. Then he filled the two glasses and approached the bed so that Eva could see herself reflected back in the lenses of his sunglasses.

"Oh, very hard. I imagine I'll work up quite a sweat."

"That's why we have the bath." Daniel held out a glass of champagne. "And nobody to disturb us."

Eva closed her hand around the glass and kept her eyes on the lenses of his sunglasses as she drank. Then she held up her champagne. "This is good stuff. You have *excellent* taste, Mr Carswell."

"Which is precisely why *you're* here," he replied smoothly. Then he sank to the bed to sit beside Eva and bent lower to kiss her. She tasted the champagne on his lips and caught the scent of his cologne in the air, every sense wonderfully alive.

Eva tangled her fingers in his hair, capturing him. "My very own bad boy for the evening. Aren't I a lucky girl? Do you intend to be bad, Daniel? Very, very bad, I hope."

"For my loudest critic?" He kissed her again. "*Very* bad indeed."

Eva's breath hitched. The memory of him inside her came back to her so strongly that her hips involuntarily shifted towards him. "I want you. I'm ready for you. Touch me."

He reached out and set his glass down on the bedside table. His fingers were on her skirt, teasing it higher as his leg slipped between hers. Eva knew that he would take his time, because this was their dance, and the more he knew that she wanted him, the more he would tease her.

Eva sighed deeply, trying to master her impatience for his touch. She tugged the hem of his shirt out of his trousers, unfastening the lowest button with an unsteady hand. Eva would tease him too. His breath caught and she felt the slightest jerk of his hips towards her before he mastered himself, his fingers stroking the soft skin of her thigh. Eva arched into his touch as she twisted open another button on his shirt then touched his stomach as it was revealed.

"I didn't think you'd want to see me again," she whispered against his neck.

"Why?"

"Because you're *you*." Eva stroked her way from his stomach to his back and ran her fingertip up his spine. "There must be any number of women flinging themselves at the famous bad boy artist."

"Naturally," he deadpanned, caressing her thigh in answer to her touch. "Didn't you?"

A tremble ran up Eva's leg and she moaned. Once her body had stilled again, she murmured, "I threw myself at the man who pursued me."

"The man who kept your card." He dipped his head to nuzzle against her throat again, grazing with his teeth. "The respectable *Mr Carswell*, sending out for a girl to share his champagne."

Eva sighed with desire, tipping her head back against the satin and velvet cushions. "And to fuck, I hope, Mr Carswell?"

He gave a murmur of agreement and slid his hand a little higher, just enough to brush his fingers over her body. All the time his lips were softly roaming Eva's neck, the tip of his tongue tracing lines of heat over her racing pulse.

She brought her hands away from inside his shirt and trailed them over the front of his trousers, his erection obvious to her touch. But she wasn't going to unfasten him. Not yet. Her touch was so light that it was almost a breath, but she knew it was teasing him to distraction.

Eva sensed rather than heard Daniel's sigh of anticipation. She had the distinct feeling that he wasn't used to being made to wait, that the women in Daniel Scott's life were probably happy just to be allowed past the black suit and the attitude, but she wasn't going to be one of those women, one of what might be many. Sometimes, a man had to face a challenge.

"Is that infuriating, Daniel?" She traced her fingers up from his trousers and unfastened another button on his shirt. He replied with another kiss to her throat and another stroke from his fingers. It was the action of a man who was assured of victory, merely indulging her in her little fancies.

"I wonder..." Eva caught her reflection in his sunglasses, an expression of amused arousal. "Is there anything you wouldn't do to make me unbutton you?"

"I could just please myself," Daniel murmured, but she knew that he wouldn't. Then he lifted his head and smiled. "But I like this game."

"Do you now?" Eva caressed further beneath his shirt and brushed against his hardened nipple as she reached his toned chest. "What if we made a bargain?"

"I'm listening."

"I'll unfasten your trousers and admire that impressive cock of yours, if you…" Eva danced her fingertips down his body again, teasing over the hard shape in his trousers, then danced them away. "If you take off your sunglasses."

Would he? Eva was no longer certain if he kept them on just to rile her, or if something more serious lay behind his game. A barrier deliberately set up between them.

"Are you serious?" Daniel's voice was a whisper and his hand stilled on her body. "Why?"

Eva realised, too late, that she had overstepped the mark. But she tried to keep it light, and what she was about to say was the truth anyway. "Because as lovely as my reflection doubtlessly is, I would rather gaze at your eyes."

He lifted the sunglasses for a second then dropped them down again. "Does that satisfy you?"

Eva shook her head. "No."

At least he was being playful. But he might have a reason to hide his eyes, if he'd been at the coke again.

"What do you think you'll see there?" He kissed her lips softly. "The real Mr Carswell trying to get out?"

"I want to see *you*. All of you." Eva rubbed her thumb across his lip, her eyes going in and out of focus as she tried to look through his lenses. "Is that really such a terrible thing?"

"There's nobody there," Daniel whispered.

"There *is*."

He'd become a brand and people read their own pain into his art. The creator vanished, inconsequential as a leaf in autumn. That was what he meant, surely. Eva had known that feeling herself. All artists did. But there was something dark in his tone, and the opulent room seemed to fall away. Crowding in on them were his paintings. Sometimes bleak, sometimes frightening, tense with anger and fear.

The Daniel Scott Method.

Daniel swallowed. She saw his Adam's apple bob in his throat. Then he asked, "And if I say no?"

"To our bargain?" Eva stroked his cheek. "Well, I can't be blamed if they accidentally get knocked off, can I?"

"I'll make *you* a bargain," Daniel murmured, nuzzling against her cheek. "Are you the negotiating type?"

Caution whispered in Eva's ear, but she ignored it. She passed her hand teasingly over his erection again. "Go on, then…let's negotiate."

"I want to paint you."

Although he was an artist, of all the things he could have said, Eva hadn't expected that. Her cheeks heated into a blush. "Really? I'd *love* to pose for you."

"I've never painted from life," Daniel admitted, still nuzzling kisses to her cheek and lips. Of course he hadn't—she couldn't conceive of any living thing like those strange shapes that lumbered across his canvases. "Nothing real, nothing I can touch."

As the last word left his mouth, he slid his fingers against Eva's body again, just teasing a inside her.

Eva lay there, enthralled by his touch, kissing his hair as he nuzzled her. He was being so gentle, but Eva wasn't convinced that it was only a tease. "Have *you* ever posed for an artist before?"

"Never." He sighed against her skin, then whispered, "I'm not a suitable subject."

"Would you let me try?" Eva gasped as her desire rallied to his touch. "I'd even let you keep your sunglasses on…"

"No." He kissed her with a fierce heat, clearly intent on distracting her from pursuing the topic. And his sunglasses were still on, despite their so-called bargain. Daniel pressed his body closer to her, his free hand cupping her breast through the flimsy blouse, caressing gently.

Eva sighed his name, and in a haze of building pleasure caressed him through his clothes. "How long can you bear to tease? *I want you…*" she breathed. She hadn't anticipated his next move as the hand on her breast slid higher until he lifted his sunglasses, pushing them up into his dark hair. He blinked down at her as his lips met hers again, holding her gaze into the kiss.

The intense blaze she had seen in Daniel's eyes before was softened now. By desire, of course. Answering her side of the bargain, Eva gave him one last teasing touch through his clothes, then unfastened him. She sighed into their kiss as she took his erection in her hand, its heat and hardness promising bliss.

His hand found her breast again through the light fabric and he whispered, "I need to get this out of my system." Then he slipped his finger deep into her body, exploring tenderly.

Eva pressed her mouth to his ear as she moved against his finger. "Do you think you ever will?"

"Not if I paint you. We're bound together." She moaned as his second finger pressed against her, joining the first. "Do you really want that?"

Eva gazed at him, at the gentleness she saw in a face that had been disguised with arrogance. "Perhaps," she whispered. "Would you?"

"I'll leave that for my instinct to decide." Daniel circled Eva's nipple with the pad of his thumb. "But right now the answer's yes."

"I somehow thought you'd say that." Still stroking his erection, Eva unfastened the remaining buttons on his shirt and caressed his torso in long strokes, from his throat down to the base of his cock and back again. "How will you pose me?"

"Something like this," Daniel decided, sweeping his gaze over her. "You recline like an empress, presiding over nations. You caught my eye in the gallery, but this is perfect. This is *you*."

A nervous tremble went through Eva. She was surprised that Daniel Scott of all people would say such a thing about her. But he wasn't Daniel Scott, the bad boy she'd seen in the press anymore. He was Daniel Scott, her lover. "How else could I pose on a big heap of cushions, with a handsome man pleasuring me? And will I be a nude, or will you drape me in something diaphanous?"

"I haven't seen you naked yet," he purred. "How long can you stay?"

"Tonight? I haven't anywhere dash to, and no one to go home to." Eva lifted her head to kiss the end of his nose. An affectionate gesture which she might have bestowed to annoy him three days ago. "I'm all yours, for as long as you like."

Daniel blinked, something in his expression entirely taken aback for just a split second. Whether that was in response to the kiss or her answer, Eva didn't know, and he blinked again, clearing the look from his face.

Then he kissed her, the gentle touch of his lips growing more heated by the second.

Eva removed her hand from his chest and caught him about the wrist as he teased her nipple. She guided it to the hem of her blouse and began to lift it off over her head. "I want to feel you against me," she whispered.

He drew the blouse higher and threw it aside then shrugged out of his jacket and let it fall. Eva caught his gaze, no longer hidden by the Wayfarers, and saw a spark of fresh desire there. Then he sank down against her body, the heat of his naked skin pressed to her breasts. His hand thrust harder and his thumb massaged her, driving her on. Eva drew one arm around him, holding him tight to her as she arched again with pleasure. She still stroked his erection with her other hand, and how they were lying now, it was against her thigh. With little trouble from either of them, he would be inside her.

"Now? I've brought condoms, by the way." Eva wasn't sure what he'd think of the plural, but it showed willing, at least.

"So did I." He jerked his head over his shoulder. "Back pocket, help yourself."

Because Daniel was busy, after all, one hand thrusting against her body, the other arm wrapped around her shoulders to embrace her.

Feeling blissfully wanton, Eva stroked over his firm buttocks and slid her hand into the back pocket of his trousers. By touch alone, Eva estimated there were three or four condoms in there. She produced one, and with efficiency that surprised her, slid it onto Daniel's erection.

Daniel withdrew his hand and reached up for his sunglasses. She knew that he was about to drop them onto his nose again, but he paused, then left them in his hair. Without removing what was left of his own rumpled suit or even Eva's skirt, Daniel shifted over her and the tip of his erection brushed her body. His breath was warm on her throat as he kissed her.

Eva caressed his buttocks again, then grasped them and, with a moan, she lifted her hips up from the bed, meeting his erection and taking it inside her. "Fuck me, darling," she urged. He reached down and caught his arm beneath her knee, lifting her leg high around his waist as he made a fierce thrust of his body, a moan of exertion escaping his pouting lips. Then he dropped his mouth to Eva's, tracing the fingers that had been inside her over their lips.

Eva raised her other leg and looped it around his middle, and with that he filled her completely. She could taste herself, and she could taste him, and she felt the heat of his body all over her, his bare torso pressed against her. She moved against him, more hungry for him now than she had been during that first encounter.

And she could see him, as she had wanted to. Could look into that glittering black gaze, could see the fire there, the passion, and she knew then that there had been no coke tonight. This was Daniel Scott, *Mr Carswell*, and it was intoxicating.

She stroked through his hair, then caught his face in her hands, steadying him and gazing into him. What had he been so afraid of her seeing? She could see nothing to fear, only excitement.

His chest rose and fell with exertion, the faintest sheen of perspiration on his skin. He flicked the tip of his tongue over his lips and whispered, "Didn't I tell you there's nobody there?"

Eva kissed him. "I can see a wonderful man in there. Exciting...funny...*very* sexy... He's just the kind of man I like and I'm so glad I've met him."

"I'm just sorry I missed you at the Tate Modern." Daniel quirked one cheeky eyebrow then thrust his hips again and dipped his head to scatter kisses over Eva's jaw and throat. His mouth moved lower until he could caress his lips over the swell of her breasts, his breath warm on her skin.

"You'll just have to—" A shiver of pleasure ran through Eva and she moaned before continuing, "catch my retrospective at the South Bank!"

"I'll expect a comp and a glass of red at the very least." With that, Daniel drew Eva's nipple into his mouth. His tongue circled the stiffened bud, tasting her, the intensity of his movements increasing. With his head lowered to her body, she could see her reflection in the sunglasses, wanton and abandoned.

Eva tipped her hips back to take him inside her as deeply as she could. The heat of their bodies had amplified the spicy scents of their perfumes. "If you're very lucky, there might be fellatio at the private viewing."

"I haven't forgotten my promise." He drew the tip of his tongue over her nipple. "I still want to taste you tonight."

His energy was electrifying. Most men would be ready to fall into a heap by now, yet the indefatigable Daniel Scott was already planning his later moves. "Good. I want to feel your tongue on me."

"That perfume you wear has been following me around," he told her breathlessly. "You're haunting me."

"I wondered why the bottle was nearly empty!" Eva laughed. She bent her face to his neck and inhaled.

"Mmm...whatever your cologne is, it's divine. It just screams *Naughty artist, exceptional at fucking.*"

"Exceptional at everything," he clarified, touching the tip of his nose to hers. It was a curiously intimate gesture, even given everything they had so far shared. "Though I *think* you had a few notes for me before?"

"Still do." She grinned. Moments later a warmth spread through her, the delicious prelude to only one thing. Eva moaned, "You're making me come..."

His reply was to increase his pace just a little, just enough to push her closer to the edge. Eva felt the change in his muscles too, a tension beneath the skin like a string pulling taut. His eyes had closed with the last thrust, but now they opened again and settled on her, filled with fire.

It seemed that he wanted to see the moment, and Eva was so aroused that he must've seen quite the show. The warmth that filled her flowed like waves, building in intensity until it was almost too much to bear. But at just that moment, it shivered and grew until Eva's sigh turned into a moan, louder and louder as bliss took her over.

Surely it wasn't possible for him to be any deeper inside her than he was now, and Daniel threw his head back. She was vaguely aware of the sunglasses tumbling against her feet and down onto the bed. Then he gave a groan of ecstasy and exertion, each muscle tight and defined as pleasure swept through them and they left the world behind.

Eva clung to him, feeling every last shudder of his orgasm as it faded away. She kissed his face and rumpled his hair, unable to tear her gaze from his. "The desk was fun, but you can't beat energetic hanky-panky on a bed, can you?"

"Hanky-panky?" He gave a soft laugh and shifted onto the bed beside Eva. In the moment before he settled back onto the pillows, Daniel reached out and pulled her skirt down just a little, the gesture as uncharacteristically sweet as it was pointless. There was no preserving Eva Catseby's modesty now, not that she minded. Besides, Daniel was anything *but* modest beside her, his shirt and trousers opened and in complete disarray, sweat glistening on his skin.

"Smoke?" he asked. "Don't worry about the alarm, it won't go off."

"I might have a puff or two, if there's one going." Eva rolled onto her side to look at him. He really was adorable, once he'd allowed her past that egotistical outer crust. Not that she'd tell him that. For a few seconds he frowned, as though trying to figure out exactly what that smile might mean. Then, very slowly, as though his face wasn't used to trying it, Daniel returned the smile.

"Do you—" And she saw again the gesture he had made unconsciously at the party as Daniel brushed his thumb over the tip of his nose. "Or just a cigarette?"

"To be honest, mainly Earl Grey tea." Eva ruffled his hair. "Answer me something. After that incredible sex, what can coke do to top it? Don't you feel amazing already?"

"Are you outreaching?" His tone was friendly, teasing again. "Just say no?"

She grabbed one of the pillows and playfully poked him with it. "I'm just curious, really. I've never, ever done coke. It's an alien concept to me. I smoked a bit of a weed at art college. Doesn't everyone? But coke never really crossed my path."

"It's been"—he drew in a thoughtful breath, then decided—"helpful."

"Ahhh, I see… Helpful in a…" Eva paused. Should she bring it up? But he'd obviously been through something horrible in his time, because where else would all those hellscapes have come from? "I'm not prying, by the way. I just want to understand. Do you mean, in a self-medicating way?"

"I don't give interviews," he informed her carefully, and sat up to retrieve his fallen sunglasses. Into his hair they went, safe again. "So, Earl Grey for the critic. Are you hungry?"

"Champagne and a fag wouldn't go amiss." Eva wished she hadn't said anything. They barely knew each other. Sex was one thing — opening up old wounds was something else entirely. "I haven't had any dinner, actually. Do they do food here, then?"

"Doesn't everywhere if you're paying for it?" Daniel climbed off the bed and dipped into his pocket to drop the handful of remaining condoms onto the table beside the bed. Then he picked up his jacket from the floor. It took a moment of rooting before he retrieved a packet of cigarettes and tossed them across to Eva. She caught it, watching Daniel cross to the bathroom door. "Help yourself. I'll be two minutes."

Eva opened the packet and tapped out a cigarette and a lighter. She sparked up, then got off the bed. The carpet was thick and soft under her bare feet. She pulled a throw from a chair and draped it around her.

How exceptionally decadent this all is.

She wandered over to the huge windows and looked down at the seafront, and wondered if anyone had heard their cries of ecstasy. The bathroom door creaked open and she turned to see Daniel, completely naked now, his feet still spattered with paint. Eva made no attempt to hide the fact that she was taking in the sight of his unashamed nudity.

As she exhaled a cloud of smoke, she said, "Turn around, I want to see your arse."

And of course he did, turning his back to her and resting his hands on his hips.

"What's the feedback from the critics this time?"

Sounding decidedly fruity as she took in his firm, shapely bottom, Eva remarked, "The private view does not disappoint. Classic use of shape and line, boldly reinterpreted for a twenty-first century audience. Audacious. And perky."

And, she knew when he turned to face her again, entirely without the influence of narcotics. So the trip to the bathroom had been just that, a chance to freshen up, not a stolen opportunity to do a line or two. He roamed his gaze over Eva, taking in the skirt, the draped throw, her tousled hair and the slight flush she knew would be on her skin. Then he asked, "Any thoughts on room service?"

As he waited for her response, Daniel retrieved their forgotten champagne glasses and held Eva's out to her again. He was utterly confident in his nudity, in displaying that toned, slightly tanned body with paint-spattered feet. And he still wasn't wearing his sunglasses.

Eva took the glass and passed him the half-smoked cigarette with its smudge of lipstick on the filter.

"Something elegant, or something hearty?" She softly pressed her lips to his cheek. "Have you worked up quite an appetite?"

Daniel took a long drag on the cigarette and exhaled a smoke ring, the expression on his face thoughtful. Finally he decided, "You should choose. We'll get another bottle too."

Eva picked up the telephone, which stood on the table by the bed. No bland production-line plastic phone here — it looked like a brass antique. She flipped through a folder beside it. "Is there a menu, or do we order the most exciting thing we can imagine?"

"You're an artist." His voice was a murmur, his gaze travelling over her again. Then he plucked his sunglasses from his hair and reached across to put them on the table. "Use your imagination."

Conscious of his gaze, Eva reclined on the bed again. She rang down to reception and her call was answered in one ring. "This is room number seven," Eva informed the polished receptionist in a giggle. "We need food."

"And massage oil," Daniel instructed, as though that was the easiest thing for room service to supply. Then he rested one knee on the edge of the bed and reached beneath the throw to untie the bow that held her skirt in place. With a simple gesture from his elegant fingers, the wrapped fabric fell away and he drew it from beneath her.

"Of course," the receptionist replied. "What can we get for you?"

Eva almost dropped the handset. She had never been stripped while talking on the phone before. And — massage oil?

"Hang on," she told the receptionist, and cupped her hand over the phone while stroking Daniel's side with her toes. "You're a saucy one. Won't she ask me what scent?"

"If she does, answer her." Daniel took Eva's free hand and raised her arm to rest on the pillow, carefully sliding her fingers into her hair. Then he gently brought her elbow down a little, relaxing her muscles. He whispered, "Play with your hair while you're talking, the fingers need to be right."

"What are you—?" Eva could hear the receptionist cough politely at the end of the phone. She went back to the phone call, twisting a length of her hair around her finger. Her eyes didn't leave Daniel's. "Hello, sorry about that, I got distracted. Well, could we have something with a cream sauce? A rich one, with wine in it. And poured over pasta, but a delicate sort, like angel hair. And in the sauce…seafood. And as a side order, a fresh baguette with lots of unsalted butter. Another bottle of champagne, too, and…" Eva was blushing, she could feel the heat in her face. "And a bottle of massage oil."

"Any particular scent?" the receptionist asked, just as Eva had hoped she wouldn't.

"That's it," Daniel mouthed, holding up his hand as he reached to discard the cigarette into the ice bucket. He whispered, "Keep your hand just there."

Eva did as he said. "Nothing relaxing," she told the receptionist. "Something spicy and exciting."

Like Daniel Scott.

"Of course!" The receptionist's voice was full of enthusiasm and, not for the first time, Eva wondered at this establishment. As she asked, "Anything else, madam?", Daniel took the throw and draped it over her like a blanket, careless, frowning as he began to arrange it, using it to conceal and reveal her skin in turn.

Faced with what might be an infinite choice, Eva was very tempted to be saucy herself and ask for a blindfold. But she didn't want to lose sight of Daniel, or to cover up his eyes now that she could see them. "No, that's everything. For now. Thanks."

She clicked the phone into its cradle. "Are you posing me, The Celebrated Daniel Scott?"

"When I look at you, what I see is so *right* that I can't—" He raked his hand through his hair and stood back from the bed, his eyes narrowed in concentration. "I can't capture it. As soon as I move your hand, so much as your *finger*, you lose *you*."

Daniel returned to kneel beside her. With a flamboyant flourish he pulled back the throw, leaving her naked again. "Show me Eva Catesby, as she sees herself, at her most beautiful."

"I'm not sure. Does that sound silly?" Eva sat up and looped her arms around Daniel's neck. "I was a life model on and off while I was a student. I got so used to being instructed how to sit or stand or lie that I really wouldn't know how to pose without you telling me what you want. Unless I happen to be doing something else, not thinking about it. Although…"

She lay back down again and drew her arm above her head just as she had done earlier. "There. I did *that* on purpose earlier because I wanted to tempt you with a fine bosom!"

He smiled, and Eva saw the shadow that had settled over his gaze lift. It was as though someone had turned a light on, his whole face losing that look of frustrated concentration.

"That's exactly what I'm trying to capture," he told her, his tone rich with enthusiasm. "Now get as comfortable as you can. You're with your lover, you're sensual and completely free. There's no world out there, there's just *here*. If you want to cover yourself, do. I want you to be you, not a construct by Daniel Scott."

Eva was more than happy to go along with what he wanted. Not that she had to do much. She tilted her hips slightly and drew the throw just over her thigh, making herself no less naked than she had been without it. As she relaxed, she saw the excitement in him, and she wondered if he would challenge his own art by painting from life. But a smiling lover didn't seem to fit into the Daniel Scott method.

Oh, but it's fun to try.

"All right, I'm ready. How's this?"

"Perfect," he breathed. "Don't move."

"Have you brought an easel and paints?" Eva giggled.

"No." He scooped up the folder from beside the telephone and tore a handful of pages from it. "But I have paper and a biro, that's all I need for now."

"I never went to bed with any of the artists I posed for," Eva told him, as she lay as still as she could. "This is new for me too."

"Does it feel different?" He took a pen from the desk, where it had rested beside a small notepad, and positioned the torn pages atop the folder. Then he turned one of the armchairs to face the bed. "Do you think it'll change how I draw you?"

"Yes, it does feel different." She caught herself about to nod and stopped. "And maybe it *will* change how you draw me. Because you've touched me. I'm not an abstraction of shape and colour, but living flesh. You know how my skin feels."

She saw the flash in his eyes as he flicked his gaze across to her again, then he sank down onto the chair and began to work. He was silent, his expression focussed and darkened by concentration.

So this is the Daniel Scott Method in action.

Her thoughts began to drift to the private viewing and the moment he had first spoken to her. How long had he stood there before his approach? She thought of the heat they had shared and she didn't know, couldn't begin to guess, how long this would last. Living with such intensity might be exciting, but surely there would come a point at which it was exhausting.

Eva didn't want to think of that. Instead she lay still, thinking of every painting she had ever seen of courtesans and lovers, models who must have carnally known the men who had painted them.

Long minutes of silence passed, Daniel's gaze flickering back and forth between the page and his muse — not that she would ever think of herself like that, obviously, not for a moment — the nib scratching on the paper as he worked. Occasionally he paused, chewed his lip, tilted his head, narrowed his eyes, but he never spoke. The silence was broken only by the sound of seagulls from outside, the occasional toot of a car horn or shouting voices that drifted up on the breeze, all of it a world that didn't exist for them.

"The light's terrible," Daniel murmured, almost to himself. "We should be in the studio."

Eva's arm had gone sleep and she stretched it above her head. "Why not? I hope you have a decadent chaise longue for me."

"It needs to be a bed." He folded the papers carefully into four and put them on the desk. Then he stood and tilted his head to one side to look at her. "Tell me about your illustrations."

"If you wish…" Eva rolled onto her front, propping her head up on one hand. "They're really not all that exciting. You've probably seen them and you wouldn't remember. But they're out there in the world, decorating articles and opinion pieces, websites and books. Cakes and bees and mermaids and whatever else I'm asked to draw."

"And what about your art?" Daniel sat on the bed beside her. He brushed his fingers tenderly down her hair. "What comes from your soul?"

"All my illustrations have a bit of me in them." Eva leaned into his touch. "But when I get time, or even if I don't, but I can't stop, I paint. Or use charcoal or anything really. Whatever the image needs. It's all a bit scattershot—landscapes or people or just colours and shades. They're for me, really. I sometimes give them as presents, but most of them are piled up in my studio."

"Why?" He brushed a strand of hair back behind Eva's ear. "Do you show them to your kids?"

"Sometimes I do, if it fits in with the theme for that session. They seem to like them!" Eva laughed. "But no one else gets to see them. It's not as if you'll see an exhibition any time soon."

"You know that's not why you're here, right?" His voice held a guarded quality suddenly. "I'm not offering a favour for a favour and I didn't get that from you either. You do know that?"

"I *do* know that. I'm not asking anything from you." Eva felt hurt at the idea that he thought she had only come here to advance her career, or whatever it was he seemed to think. But it must happen to him all the time, being unable to trust people or allow them to get close. "I'm quite happy working as an illustrator, honestly. I didn't come here for anything other than to be with you."

"I've had offers. Always say no." He smiled, that arrogance seeping through. "I didn't think it of you, but in case you're wondering, I did you a little favour this morning anyway."

It went the other way too, of course, as Rupert had made clear on their failed date. Share more than a boring snog with the man who called Eva's art outreach *'art for chavs'* and he might consider exhibiting her work. Eva hadn't been interested.

"I'm glad you didn't think that of me." Eva reached for his hand. Her tone became playful. "But what favour's this? Can you tell me, or is it a surprise?"

"Your gallery-owning boyfriend wasn't too keen on letting a bunch of kids from an outreach group rampage around his gallery. He didn't tell me why, but I know his sort." Daniel raised an eyebrow. Of course he knew the sort, because he had once been just the kind of child that Rupert was now terrified might wreck his precious *space*. *'Council estate rats'*, as Rupert had once sniggered. *'Watch your handbag, Eva, they'll have it off to* Cash Converters *if you blink.'* "If you still want to take your group to my show, they'll find the red carpet rolled out for them."

"Thank you!" Eva kissed his hand. "That's the loveliest thing, Daniel. And... Rupert's definitely *not* my boyfriend."

"You should probably remind him of that." He smiled. "He dropped a pretty strong hint that you had an on-off thing."

"At the risk of spoiling the mood, although it'd take a lot to do that, we went out on one date, and it was not something I wish to repeat." Eva shuddered theatrically. "I won't tell you what he called my art outreach, but I'm sure you can imagine, and he said he'd show my paintings if I went to bed with him! He didn't put it in so many words, but it was very clear it's what he meant."

"I called it right. He *is* a prick." There was a knock at the door and Daniel winked, almost playful. "Sounds like dinner to me."

Eva laughed. "I suppose you're going to answer the door without a stitch on?"

"Except my sunglasses." He rose to his feet and crossed to pick up the Wayfarers, hiding his eyes behind them again. For a moment she thought he was actually about to carry out his threat, but at the last moment he opened the large wardrobe and took out one of two white dressing gowns that hung inside, each embroidered with an elaborate *M* on the breast. As Daniel slid his arms into the sleeves he told her, "I'm choosy about who sees me in white, let alone naked. You might want to pull those covers up?"

Eva slipped under the edge of the bedclothes. "Am I decent now?"

"I hope not." He tied the belt of the dressing gown and opened the door. She heard the sound of rattling crockery, then Daniel stood back to let in a young man, pushing a trolley laden with cloche-covered plates. There was a fresh silver champagne bucket from which the neck of a bottle protruded and two candles in silver candlesticks, their wicks unlit.

With a polite nod of acknowledgement for Eva, the young man pushed the trolley with its pristine white tablecloth covering into the room. He took a lighter from his pocket and sparked the ignition, applying the flame to the candle wicks. Then he told the couple, "We've added some chocolates and strawberries for dessert. Compliments of the house."

He gave the suggestion of a bow, scooped up the exhausted champagne bucket and said, "Have a pleasant evening."

"I'm sure we will." Eva grinned at Daniel. "More champers, Mr Carswell!"

"And my massage oil." He held up a small, dark bottle. "That's for after dinner. Will you join me, Ms Catesby?"

Eva got out from under the covers and took the remaining bathrobe from the wardrobe. She sank into its softness and went over to Daniel. "This is a lovely treat," she said, and slipped her arm around his waist. He dipped his head and pressed his lips to hers, letting their kiss linger as he embraced her.

"Shall we dine, Mr Carswell?" Eva lifted one of the covers to reveal a plate of pasta, just as she'd described. "I like this hotel."

"I suppose I should apologise for the taxi driver," he told her slyly, turning to take the bottle from the bucket. "Did it bother you that he thought you were booked?"

"No, I thought it was funny! Bearing in mind how I was dressed, too." She kissed Daniel's cheek, then said, "He was delivering me to someone with unusual tastes!"

"The notorious Mr Carswell." He replenished the glasses. "Let's eat, and you can tell me all about Eva."

They brought some chairs up to the trolley, and sat at it opposite each other as if it were a dining table. Eva wound a length of pasta around her fork, then she laid it down on the side of her plate. "Before we start, can I make an apology?"

"It's not a husband," he mused. "You're not looking for a quid pro quo and it looks as though you've ordered a great dinner. So what's left to apologise for?"

"For what I said at the private view. About throwing wine in your face." Eva looked up from her plate at Daniel. "I'm sorry. I just felt a bit…vulnerable. I didn't mean it. If I'd had wine, I'd've been drinking it, not wasting it like that!"

"I don't take criticism well." He picked up his own fork, then pushed the sunglasses back into his hair. "Especially when there's truth in it. I know I need to push what I do — I'm hoping a few roots, a home, might help with that. Maybe I need a muse?"

Eva lifted her fork, catching the end of the pasta with her tongue as it began to unravel. After passing the back of her hand across her mouth to dash away any sauce, she asked, "And where will you find one of those?"

"I think it'd be pretty easy to find one," Daniel admitted. "The problem is, what artist would want a muse who applies for the job? Who's yours?"

"My muse? I don't know…" Eva sawed the end off the baguette and tore the golden crust open to reveal the soft white bread inside. "Well, actually, I do know. And you're going to think it's cheesier than this bowl of parmesan. But it's Brighton."

"Is there enough of Brighton for two of us?" He wound his fork into the pasta. "Because I'm not planning to go anywhere."

Eva chewed off a lump of bread and grinned at him. "I'm happy to share."

"Are you happy to visit my place and pose properly?"

"Wow, I'd love to!" Eva dunked the other end of her bread into the sauce. "When would you like me?"

"I can give you my address and number." So the withheld phone number was about to become a thing of the past, it seemed. "Whenever you feel ready, just message me, and if I'm at home, we can start. Or I could click my fingers and see how fast you run?"

He winked again, then put the forkful of food between his lips.

The reckless part of Eva would have willingly volunteered to go back with him that night, but that flash of playful arrogance reminded her that perhaps she was being just a bit too keen. "Let me finish my bees first. Is that okay?"

"And bring some of your work when you do? Not the recipe books, the actual stuff." Daniel reached for a piece of bread. "The stuff that inspires those kids of yours."

"If you really want to see my scribbles!" Eva loaded up her fork again, wondering if she could repeat the dish at home. She pictured Daniel at the island in her kitchen, but pushed the thought away. "By the way... You know that date with Rupert? I didn't really want to go, but Lyndsey is a bit of a matchmaker and...I broke up with someone a few months ago, and she thought she was being helpful. You know how some people are?"

"That's why I don't like *people*. Most of them, anyway." He wound his fork into the pasta again and winked. "*You're* all right, when you're not tearing shreds off my paintings."

Eva slathered another piece of bread with butter. "How long did you stand there behind me, listening to me waffling on?"

"Long enough to hear about the *Daniel Scott Method*. What exactly does it entail though, in your opinion?"

"Lots of being intense!" Eva laughed. "It's a shame, if you'd been there earlier you would've heard me say I love your work..."

"I was so angry," he admitted, pausing to take a sip of champagne, "because you were *saying* what I'd lost sleep *thinking*. Nobody tells you, *change it up*, because nobody sees the repetition in it. I've been around the world, I've spent a fortune *discovering myself* and I've come back and settled straight back into it. So what do I do, Eva? What would you do?"

Eva sipped her champagne, thinking. She couldn't really imagine what being Daniel Scott was like. "You're here now, in Brighton. Why not take a break? You don't desperately need the money, do you? So...just potter about for a year. They won't forget who you are. Learn how to sail a boat, or join a dance class. Find something to do which isn't *being Daniel Scott*. And I bet you'll find your inspiration then, when you're heaving up the sails on a dinghy or spinning across a ballroom."

"Maybe even outreach?" Daniel teased. "The thought of a year off is— Jesus."

"You won't fall apart if you have a rest, I promise." Eva reached across the makeshift table and stroked his hand. "It may even keep you together."

His hand moved up to the sunglasses, but instead of flipping them down over his eyes, he smoothed his fingers through his dark hair. Then he asked softly, "How the hell did a woman who draws dancing cakes get to be so wise?"

"My mum's a hippy, she's always saying things like that!" Eva picked up her drink and took a mouthful. "She said something similar to me when I broke up with Miles. We'd been going out for a while, and he was fun to start with, and he really liked the fact that I'm an illustrator."

Eva sighed and put down her glass. "But people change, don't they? It was as if one morning I woke up next to a different man. He said I just *sat about all day drawing with a crayon*, and he wasn't very nice about outreach when I started to do that either. It made me question what I do, who I am. And Mum said to me, *just have a rest*. I sat in my studio where I'm safe, where I feel most like me, and faffed about, and I felt a hell of a lot better afterwards. So there you go. Take some advice from Mrs Catesby!"

"Will you tell her about me?" he asked. "I don't have a mum to tell, so I'm counting on you to scandalise yours instead. Will Eva's hippy mum worry about you being debauched by Daniel Scott?"

"My mum was debauched by — well, she had quite a wild youth, put it that way!" Eva let her laugh ebb. Daniel's admission that he didn't have a mum made her wonder once more what had happened. It must have been why he was in care. Had she died, or had she been such a bad lot that he had blocked her from his life? "I think she'd like you. And I'm sure she'd be your mum, if you want."

Something changed in his face, just a glimpse of something, but Eva couldn't see what. Sadness? Regret? Perhaps it was annoyance, but she didn't think so. It was lost a moment later when he dropped the sunglasses onto his nose and told her, "She's got her hands full with you already, hasn't she?"

Eva leaned over the table and lifted the sunglasses to peer underneath. "She has big hands, Daniel."

"I hope she's proud of you," he murmured. "Because she should be."

"She seems to be." Eva smiled as she took his sunglasses from his face and folded them neatly beside his plate. He looked down, as awkward as a child waiting to see the head teacher, then he raised his gaze to meet hers and tried a smile, just the slightest curl of his lips.

"Better?" Daniel whispered.

"Yes." Eva went on with her dinner. "You have beautiful eyes."

"And a beautiful lover." He raised his glass. "To you, Eva Catesby, and your bees."

Bashful, Eva clinked her glass with Daniel's. "And to Mr Carswell and his excellent taste!"

It didn't surprise her that Daniel managed to polish off his entire meal, since they'd worked up such an appetite, and he set down his cutlery and decided,

"That almost makes me wish I could cook. I'll let you order for me again."

"I should try to whip that up at home sometime. I'll invite you round for tea, of course." Eva brushed the crumbs off her hands and came over to Daniel's side of the trolley. She put her arms around him and kissed him on the lips. "What were you planning to do with the massage oil?"

He put his arm around her and pulled her down into his lap. "I thought you might like a nice—" Daniel punctuated the words with kisses. "Relaxing. Massage?" The last kiss was long and deep. "Then a bath as Brighton lights up just for you?"

"Yes, please, that sounds perfect!" Eva took the end of her dressing gown's belt and slowly pulled. "Where do you want me?"

"Get comfortable on the bed." He kissed her shoulder. "We'll start on your back and see where we finish?"

Eva stood and let the belt fall, and the gown dropped to the floor after. Daniel's hand stole forward and stroked over her bottom appreciatively, before he told her, "Don't forget your champagne."

Picking up her glass, Eva winked at him. "As if I'd do that!" She climbed onto the bed and lay in the middle, watching Daniel over her shoulder. He picked up the bottle of massage oil and approached the bed, where he knelt beside her. Then he leaned forward and kissed Eva's shoulder again as he unscrewed the cap from the bottle.

"*This* would make a painting," Daniel decided. He poured some of the oil into his palm and set the bottle aside. As she watched, he rubbed the oil between his hands before pressing them to her back, his touch as soft as it was sure.

Eva raised her head, sniffing the air. "Mmmm! Doesn't that smell wonderful? I feel all tingly!"

"It's mutual," he teased, sweeping his hands over Eva's skin. "How does it feel?"

"Great! I feel relaxed, but I also feel…" Maybe it was feeling his hands on her body, or maybe there was something in the oil, but Eva was feeling decidedly aroused and a tremble ran through her. "I'm sure you can tell."

"There's been a few clues." His hands swept lower, massaging the warm oil into her buttocks. His fingers strayed a little farther, sliding between her thighs, and he whispered, "Tell me what you want, Eva."

Eva gasped and clutched at the bedclothes as her body tightened with need. "Kiss me," she murmured. "But not on my mouth."

Daniel shrugged off his dressing gown and bent forward to kiss her shoulder. Then he trailed his lips down her back, dotting soft kisses over her oiled skin. As he did, he continued to caress her body, parting her legs a little more. Yet he still took his time, teasing her until Eva finally felt his lips on the most sensitive part of her.

A deep sigh escaped Eva and she parted her legs wider for him, lifting her hips from the bed as he traced his lips across her. Every nerve in her body was tightened to a soaring pitch. She felt everything, even his breath against her as he moved his mouth on her body, and the gentle rasp of his evening stubble on her sensitive skin.

The sensation was so intense that she clasped the bedclothes tighter as she moaned his name. In response he moved more deeply, his tongue making deep, sensuous strokes against her core. Shivers ran through her, radiating from the centre of her being, reigniting the heat from the oil on her skin. Desire pushed through her veins and she lost all control as she moaned, her breaths shallow as the force of her climax made her buck and shudder against the mouth that still tormented her.

Daniel's response was to simply redouble his efforts, possessing her with every sweep of his tongue. He was an artist in every sense of the word, and he knew his craft well. Through the heat-haze of her satisfied pleasure, Eva's desire grew again, faster this time as she still tingled from her orgasm, and stronger, too, as Daniel took her to a height of bliss that she had rarely visited before.

Even now he didn't stop, and through her ecstasy Eva was dimly aware of his arm reaching up to the bedside table where he had thrown the condoms earlier. She heard the sound of the tearing wrapper somewhere, and if the world outside was still there, it had faded out.

"I want you..." Eva's moan was long and low, barely sounding like speech. "Have me...take me..."

The bed shifted as Daniel's mouth left her, and the next kisses were on her shoulder, tracing along to the nape of her neck. His arm encircled her waist, that strength she'd sensed in him even before they had touched now holding their bodies together. Eva heard him whisper her name as his erection pressed to her, seeking out the place where his mouth had been.

Entwining her fingers with his against her stomach, she tilted her hips just enough for him to enter her. Eva turned her head, seeking his lips for a kiss as he possessed her. He captured his own moan of pleasure in their kisses and trailed their linked hands together, guiding them down over her stomach and lower until together they drove her pleasure even further, their bodies moving as one.

Intense pleasure still rolled through her, like waves across the sea beyond the window. Eva tightened her fingers with his against her body, never wanting to let go. She stirred against him, moving with his thrusts, wanting to repay him the pleasure he had given her.

"Eva," he groaned, breathless against her lips, his hips moving harder. "God —"

Eva's champagne spilt across the bed as, unthinking, she let go of the glass to reach back and tangle her fingers in his hair. "Have your pleasure of me, Mr Carswell," she whispered, as a shudder of joy went through her again. His teeth caught Eva's earlobe lightly and his fingers tightened on her hand, then he was thrusting harder and faster, and she felt the tension in his muscles building and recognized that this meant he was on the edge of his own release.

As his body pressed to hers, his chest against her back and his arms around her, Eva felt cared for and wanted, secure in her desires no matter how wild they became. As his orgasm grew closer, so too did Eva's, stronger and more intense than before because they were experiencing their bliss together.

He gasped her name again, his face pressed tight against his neck as pleasure claimed them as one, and together they soared. They were truly one now, their bodies combining in the sunset.

Eva sank against the bed, the spicy scent of the oil surrounding them making the room's opulence exotic and exciting. They could be anywhere, but Eva only wanted to be in Daniel's embrace.

"That really was rather marvellous," she murmured, and kissed him softly on the lips. His eyes were closed and he trembled when he returned the kiss. It seemed to ripple down his whole body, running through every muscle. "Can I hug you?" she asked.

"I'd like you to," he whispered. "If you want to."

"I do." Eva nodded. "Just a little one."

Daniel turned her in his arms and drew her against him. He buried his face against her hair and whispered, "You're really something, Eva Catesby."

"I could say the same thing about you." She smiled against his cheek, her arms around him, his body sheened with perspiration. "You're magnificent."

"Hugging is..." He sighed, obviously seeking out the word. "New."

"And fun." Eva ruffled Daniel's hair, wondering who could go to bed with him and not want to hold him afterwards. Unless it was Daniel who hadn't wanted any closeness besides the thrill of sex.

"Not very *bad boy*, though." Daniel kissed her cheek. "Promise me you won't tell?"

"Gosh, no. I won't dent your image by letting on that you once allowed a woman to hug you!"

He laughed softly and said, "I could just stay here."

"Me too!" Eva said. "So...have you worked me out of your system yet?"

"Nowhere near," Daniel admitted. "How about you?"

"Not at all." Eva pouted. "I even worked up a sweat in the attempt!"

"Let's give that bath a try." He pecked his lips to her hair and sat up. With another sigh Daniel reached his arms over his head and stretched, perhaps peacocking just a little for her benefit. Of course he knew how attractive he was, from the tousled hair to the paint-splashed feet. He knew and he made the most of it.

"We definitely should." As Eva got up from the bed, she remembered the champagne spill that she had barely been aware of at the time it had happened. She pointed to it. "Ooops! Have I got you into trouble?"

"I'll just have to buy the hotel." He refilled the glasses and put them on the edge of the bath, then pulled back the curtains to reveal the world outside, where a bright moon sat high in the starlit sky. Only when the water was thundering from the taps did he ask her, "We want bubbles, right? Lots of them?"

"Definitely." Eva swirled her hand in the rising water. "And shall we turn off the lights? So it's only the moon and the stars?"

"And what's left of the candles." He picked up a glass bottle from the side of the bath and emptied its dark blue contents into the water. A relaxing scent rose up on the steam and Daniel breathed it in, then told her, "Let's do it."

Daniel prowled across the room and extinguished the lights. All that was left of dinner on the room service trolley now was the bowl of strawberries and small box of chocolates, the hotel's name inscribed ornately in gold against the white. Daniel picked them up and he glanced towards the discarded sunglasses, but he returned to the bath without them.

"Who'll draw the short straw and have to sit on the plug?" Eva grinned. "Me and my sister always fought over that!"

"We could—" He laughed, suddenly bashful, and scrubbed his hand through his hair. "I could get in first and we can snuggle up together if you like? I'm *fast* losing what's left of my bad-boy credentials, aren't I?"

Eva arched an eyebrow. "Don't worry, your reputation is safe with me, bad boy. If anyone asks if we *snuggled*, I'll say, *we enjoyed a frisson skin-to-skin*."

"Did I snort a line off your naked body?" Daniel teased as he turned off the taps. Then he climbed into the water and settled down amongst the cloud of bubbles, looking as angelic as an *enfant terrible* could. "And do unspeakable things to you?"

Eva held her hand out to him as she got into the bath. "*Terrible* things. Shocking things! And I loved every second."

"Tell me about them." He caught her hand and drew her down into his arms, easing her back against his chest. "You might give me some ideas for next time. Or later."

"Oh, it's far too naughty. I couldn't possibly break a confidence and reveal what Daniel Scott..." Eva's saucy tone dwindled away, and she held Daniel's hand. In her jest, she had hit on something which hadn't until then occurred to her. "Are the press going to come after me?"

"The tabloids aren't too fussed about us artists," he assured her, stroking his hands through her tousled hair. "We're not box office, don't worry. Anyway, what if they come after *me* for bedding the woman behind the dancing cakes?"

"Do you know, that *could* be quite the scandal? The baker in question has a very sweet image, and if it became known who her illustrator's been cavorting with...!" Eva laughed, and the water rippled around her.

"I'll illustrate her next one. Monsters from the id on the Yorkshire puddings?"

"Yes!" Eva hadn't stopped laughing, and the water lapped dangerously up against the sides of the bath. "Sorry... I'm going to cause a flood!"

"You've already trashed the bed, why stop there?" He kissed her cheek. "I thought my days of trashing hotel rooms were *way* behind me. Bad boys have to grow up, but we never leave our sunglasses at home."

"So what do you become when you grow up from being a bad boy? A naughty man?" Eva tickled his chest. "I like that...my naughty man!"

"A serious *artiste*," Daniel informed her, swatting at her hands. "*Your* naughty man? Is that your way of trying to get me to share this box of chocolates with you? Are you using me for my sweets?"

Had she said the wrong thing? 'My naughty man' made it sound like they had a relationship, but, in truth, she wasn't entirely sure *what* they had. At least they had each other, though, for as long as the evening lasted. "You're very naughty indeed if you don't share your chocolates with me!"

"Only if you promise to share the strawberries with me in return?" He reached for the box of chocolates and opened it, presenting them to her. "Would you like me to wash your hair?"

Eva brushed her fingertip over the tissue paper covering the chocolates and chose one with a flake of frosted raspberry on the peak of its dark shell. Just before popping it into her mouth, she replied, "Wash my hair? That would be so sweet of you. I've been well and truly spoiled today, haven't I?"

"We all need it sometimes." With that, Daniel cupped his hands in the water and lifted them, letting it rain through his fingers onto her hair. It was oddly decadent, the hot water cascading over her and down as her shoulders as he repeated the gesture time and again, pausing only to eat the occasional strawberry.

As he washed her hair, Eva stroked her toes up and down Daniel's leg, languid and content. The evening was fast ticking away, and she wanted to see him again. "I won't be long with those bees, by the way. We'll see one another again soon."

"Don't go without taking my number." He unscrewed the cap from another bottle and she breathed in the subtle scent of shampoo as he massaged it into her hair. "So you can let me know when those bees have buzzed back to the hive."

"I wish they'd buzz off!" Eva laughed, even though it was hardly the sophisticated sort of humour that Daniel would be used to in rarefied art world circles. "Sorry...that was unforgivable, wasn't it?"

"I *almost* said that!" Daniel laughed, a hearty, silly laugh entirely at odds with *Daniel Scott*. A laugh that didn't suit the man in black. "But I thought, *she'll think I'm cheesy as hell!*"

"It *is* cheesy, but haven't you heard that bad jokes are the new rock 'n' roll?" Eva half-turned towards him and dabbed bubbles on the end of his nose. He puffed out a breath and sent them fluttering into the air, then fixed her with a comically stern look and clicked his tongue disapprovingly. "Oh, I see, Mr Daniel Scott, bad boys don't do bubbles unless they're in champagne!"

"Bad boys," he kissed her nose, "do bad girls."

"*Me*? Am I bad, really?" Eva found the idea hilarious. "I do own two leather jackets though, so I *must* be bad."

"Only two?" He reached for one of the chocolates and popped it into his mouth, chewing thoughtfully. "How about helping yourself to a desk that isn't yours so you can fuck an artist you don't know and knock his Wayfarers halfway across the room? You're very bad, Ms Catesby."

"Now you come to mention it...yes, that *was* very bad, wasn't it?" Eva bit her lip as she giggled. "Do you know, I lost an earring at the private view, and I think it's likely it fell out while we were in Rupert's office. Can you imagine if he finds it, and if he saw what you left in his bin?" Eva snorted with laughter. Maybe it wasn't very kind, but Rupert could take his casting couch and stuff it.

"Was it valuable?" Did she imagine the concern in his eyes? "You could ask that friend of yours if she's seen it?"

"I'm seeing her for lunch tomorrow, so I'll ask then," Eva decided. "I did send her a text, but she didn't mention it. I suppose they're busy fielding calls about your exhibition! And don't worry, it really wasn't expensive. It was just a little silver thing. I've got piles of them at home."

"I made a bad call with Hawley." Daniel sighed. "I didn't realise how much of a prick he was until the contracts were signed. He gives off a weird energy, but I let nostalgia rule my brain. Not like me, but I guess it'll be the making of him and his gallery. Lesson learned. Never listen to nostalgia."

"But at least you *did*, because we would never have met otherwise." Eva stroked her hand up and down his thigh. "But what was it that made you feel nostalgic? I think it's always been a gallery or an art thing, that building. Not much more than a beach hut, really, then Rupert took over."

"I went there a long, long time ago and it stuck with me," he said, his voice growing distant. Then he kissed her again. "So I came back and there *you* were."

Eva leaned back against him, letting her head fall against his chest. "Dissing your work! Could there have been a worse beginning for a—" *Not a relationship. Definitely not that.* "Liaison than that?"

"I like the fire in you," Daniel confessed. "I could feel it from across the room, and I wanted you."

Eva tipped back her head to look at him. "So is that why you were standing behind me? I knew you were attractive because I'd seen photos of you, but nothing could've prepared me for how I felt when we met. It was…instant. This heat between us. And I still feel it now."

"Are you asking if I was checking you out?" he whispered, meeting her gaze. "Because if you are, yes I was."

"It's that dress. Clingy red satin. All the bad boys are drawn to it like a magnet!" Eva wove her fingers with his and slowly ran them up and down his thigh.

"So there are others?" He raised one eyebrow mischievously. "But do they wear vintage Wayfarers in bed?"

"No, I'd have to say that's a first for me!" Eva lay still and gazed out from her post in the bath to the strings of lights along the prom. "I've had a lovely evening with you, by the way."

"I'd ask you to stay, but you poured champagne all over the bed." Daniel's gaze followed hers out into the night. "At least you didn't hurl the TV out of the window."

"I did that last week." Eva smiled, but she knew that bed wasn't for sleeping in. The man who had struggled to take off his sunglasses indoors wasn't about to lie through the hours of the night beside her. He was silent but settled his lips against her hair and wrapped his arm around her beneath the bubbles, holding her protectively. Would he work when he got home tonight to his art deco palace, or take her advice and switch off, let himself sleep safe in the cushion of all the memories they had made tonight? Eva hoped he would choose the latter, but still she pictured him in the vast house, working at the dark canvases of his imagination.

Drunks staggered by, shouting their way along the prom. A siren wasn't far behind. "It's getting late. If I'm going to get those bees to buzz off, I should probably head home soon."

"It's been the best day," he said, the words utterly without guile. "And not the last."

Eva held his hand tighter. She was more to him than a quick, frustrated fuck over a desk, more than an evening in a hotel room. Daniel had talked Rupert, the man he obviously found odious, into letting her bring her art group to his precious gallery. He had invited her to his home. Perhaps, if nothing else, they would be friends.

"And in case you're still wondering," his lips brushed her hair, "coke *can't* top this. Not tonight."

"I'm glad to hear it!" Eva laughed gently. "Just a kiss, before we leave?"

"One for the road." He nodded, putting his lips to hers. The kiss was as tender as it was heated and his arms tightened just a little, holding their bodies close in the moments before they broke for breath. "Take the rest of the chocolates home. Spoil yourself?"

"Thank you, I will." Eva untangled her arms and legs from his and pulled herself up out of the bath, giving him an unparalleled view of her behind as she did so. Another image from their evening together for him to remember in solitude until they next met. She wrapped herself in a towel, drying off as best she could as she watched him still sitting in the huge bath like an emperor.

"Clean feet at last." He lifted one foot from the bubbles and circled it at the ankle. "Throw me my phone from my jacket, I'll send my number and call you a cab. I'm going to walk home. I feel like I need to come down from you before I get there."

He rose from the water and reached for a towel, which he wrapped around his waist. Then he climbed from the bath and gave another one of those peacocking stretches.

'Come down from you.' Eva smiled at him as she rummaged in his pocket for his phone. As she passed it to him, she kissed his shoulder, then began to rub her hair dry with a towel. "I'll dream of you," she told him.

"I don't sleep too much, but I have a feeling I'll be thinking of you too." He tapped his phone screen and she heard her own mobile buzz for a second. "Now you've got my number, so keep in touch? Let's leave the cab until you're ready. No rush."

Eva glanced at the rumpled bed, at the crumbs on the floor around the trolley, at the stacked, empty plates, at the discarded bathrobes, at a smudge of cigarette ash on the carpet. They had shared such pleasure here, and maybe it was best to remember it like this. He was so sweet behind that arrogant outer crust, and Eva's vulnerability flared again at the thought of how tenderly she was beginning to feel towards him. Because what if, once they left here tonight, he didn't answer her calls, or even blocked her number? If this was all they would ever have, she'd tell herself not to mind, and not wonder what could have been. Daniel Scott didn't do relationships, he wasn't the type, and it was silly of her to begin to hope otherwise.

"I don't want to rush off." Water pattered like rain on the carpet as Eva wrung out her wet hair. "But I'm sure you don't want to be hanging about. I'll just chuck on my clothes and…we can say goodbye."

"For now." Daniel smiled, his voice thoughtful. *For now. Will that change when we leave this room and go back to our everyday lives? Is anything about Daniel Scott everyday?* He picked up his sunglasses and unfolded the arms, carefully settling the glasses in his hair. "If your friend asks about her security card... Make it our secret?"

"Of course." Eva had tied her skirt back on and, with one arm in a sleeve of her blouse, leaned her head against Daniel's chest in a half-embrace. "Our secret."

"They're a speciality of mine."

Eva glanced up at his sunglasses, waiting for them to fall over his eyes again, the carapace to close over him once more. She finished putting on her blouse and wondered where her shoes had ended up. "Can I trust you to be a gentleman? I mean, not in everything, of course, but... I won't gossip about you, I promise."

She realised too late that she had said the wrong thing. Daniel's face darkened and he turned away, saying nothing until he was in the bathroom where he had thrown off his clothes.

Then he appeared in the doorway, a clutch of black fabric in his hands, and asked, "Does this mean the painting's not going to happen? Because you don't want people to know that we —"

He threw his shirt across onto the bed and began to dress, leaving the sentence unfinished.

"It's not that. It's not that I don't want people to know, but I'm sure you wouldn't want to think that I'm going around Brighton going into detail about... about..." She gestured to the rumpled bed. "And of course the painting'll happen. I really want to pose for you, Daniel. It was fun earlier, wasn't it?"

"I'm not eighteen." He fastened his trousers and approached the bed to scoop up his shirt. "I don't brag about my conquests and that's not about to change. Don't you trust me?"

"Yes, I do." At least, Eva was fairly sure she could. They had only met twice, even though it seemed as if they had known each other much longer. "I just wanted you to know that you could trust me too."

"If I didn't think that, we wouldn't be here." He held out his hand to her. "If you want this to be another secret, that's what it'll be."

Eva took his hand. One day, would they walk along the prom, arms linked, sharing chips and candy floss? She swallowed down the thought. This was a liaison, two adults driven to distraction by each other. Hoping it might be a prelude to romance was to court disappointment.

"A secret, but not secretive. Not furtive." She squeezed his hand. "Fun and passionate and exciting."

Daniel bent his head to kiss her, then whispered, "Trust me."

There was something in his touch, or his voice perhaps, which made Eva take a leap. "I trust you, I really do." Her heart beat faster as she knew she meant it.

Did he believe her? Was that why the sunglasses remained in his hair, those coal-black eyes unhidden as they finished dressing and prepared to go back to the world outside? Clothed once more in what seemed to be his suit of armour, Daniel casually threw a couple of strawberries into his mouth and retrieved the chocolates from beside the bath. He offered them to her and asked, "Ready for that cab?"

Eva put the chocolates in her bag. "Yes, and I'll enjoy these, thank you."

The car was summoned with a few taps on his mobile phone, then the moment had come, and they left their sanctuary together. The hotel was quiet as they descended the stairs and passed the closed doors with their gold numbers. Behind them, though, were other assignations like theirs being enjoyed? Stolen evenings between virtual strangers, relationships beginning, perhaps even ending? Maybe, but none of them would have this crackling, burning intensity.

Outside, the evening breeze struggled to stir the sultry summer air. Eva put her arm around Daniel's middle, her face tipped up towards him as she wondered if he would kiss her on the hotel steps. "We'll see each other soon."

"Count on it," he replied as a private hire car pulled to a halt in front of them. He pressed his lips to hers and kissed her, before murmuring, "Have a good night."

"And you." Eva wondered how many good nights the man who couldn't sleep or dream might have. She was almost into the taxi when she paused and looked back up at him again. "Thanks for a brilliant time!"

"The best in a long time." He smiled, the gesture one she already knew that he made all too rarely. "See you soon."

Eva responded with a wave and closed the taxi door behind her. She gave the driver her address, and as the car pulled away from the kerb, she glanced back at Daniel again, a dark figure on the pavement like a shadow in the streetlights.

'The best in a long time.' Eva kept that thought in her mind all the way home.

The cab dropped her off in the darkened courtyard and she went into her house. She'd left in rather a hurry earlier and had to go from room to room closing the curtains as she went, but her mind drifted to other things. The curtains in the hotel room, and the feel of Daniel's suit under her fingertips, and—

A blinding flash of light went off inches from Eva's face as she stood before the window in her front room. Her hands clamped on the curtains and she pressed her eyes tightly shut, a vivid afterimage repeating and repeating of a ball of light.

Lightning, that was what it was. But Eva's heart was racing as she finally drew the curtains closed, because she knew that it wasn't lightning at all.

It had been the flash of a camera.

Chapter Four

Eva barely slept. The camera flash sent her checking all her locks twice before going to bed, and she hovered over her phone, wondering if she should tell Daniel.

Who would have taken a photo? As she lay in bed, she pictured the front page of the local paper bellowing BRIGHTON WOMAN IN TRYST WITH ARTIST. No, it couldn't be the press, they wouldn't care. Maybe it was a tourist, as the courtyard did look very pretty with its flower tubs and traditional pebbled walls.

But why take the photo at night? Maybe it was something to do with outreach?

But she couldn't fathom what, other than a parent who'd been cut off from their child. And someone like that was more likely to go for the more direct message of a brick through the window.

Rupert.

Would he? If he'd found her earring and realised it was hers… If he'd seen what was in his bin… Would he have been jealous enough, not to mention creepy enough, to do *that*?

When Eva finally slept, her dreams were voluptuous, a place without unexpected camera flashes, just flesh and pleasure and Daniel. She played them through her mind as she went off to meet Lyndsey, to keep her mind from darker things.

Now it was Eva's turn to wear sunglasses indoors, as she headed into the café. She wanted to keep them on to disguise her bleary eyes.

It was probably nothing, I'm worrying over nothing, she told herself as she chose a table in the café and sat down.

Lyndsey wouldn't be late—it just wasn't in her DNA. True to form, she arrived in the chintzy cafe that was their regular haunt two minutes before the appointed time. Here, among the tinkling crockery and polite chatter, there was no cause for concern, nothing but cheer, and Lyndsey brought more with her. She wore a bright red sundress and a white cardigan, a delicate gold cross nestling at the base of her throat and her usual pearl bracelet around one wrist. Her blonde hair was caught in a high ponytail and she was really as far from Daniel's darkness as anyone could hope to be. The anti-Daniel.

"Someone had a heavy night." She laughed, letting her large handbag slide into the crook of her elbow. "Sunglasses indoors?"

"Of course. I'm the rock'n'roll artist bad girl, haven't you heard?" Eva slid off her sunglasses and put them away in her bag. Lyndsey stooped down and pecked her cheek, then slipped into the empty seat.

"What've you been up to?"

"Drawing bees, that's exciting, isn't it?" Eva thought of Daniel, and saw him wink at her. She grinned. "And you, busy with the Daniel Scott exhibition, I suppose?"

"Oh my God." She picked up a menu. "So, I have to tell you three things about that. You will *die.*"

Eva leaned her elbow against the table, an eyebrow raised. She couldn't guess if these were going to be fairly minor incidents that had flashed up as red on Lyndsey's melodramatic radar, or if something major had happened. "Go on...tell all!"

"Oh my God," Lyndsey said again, widening her blue eyes. "First and most naughty, I never got my pass back from him. Luckily, since I'm in charge of issuing them, only I know that so I won't be disciplining myself. Second and most fabulous, we can't accommodate all the people who want to see the show and we're *bursting* at the seams. Third, wait for it... Are you ready?"

"I am *agog*, Lyndsey. Don't hold back or I might burst!"

"Mr Scott came back to the gallery the day after the opening and went straight into Rupe's office without even knocking. I don't know what was going on because I couldn't hear, and I tried, believe me." She laughed brightly, shrugging off the admission. "But Rupe told me later that Mr Scott had spoken to *someone—*" As she went on, she pointed one French-tipped fingernail at Eva. "And that *someone* had told him about her painting for the poor and he wanted them to be given use of the gallery on whatever day was most convenient for them. You'll never guess what else?"

Eva shrank a little in her seat. It seemed as if she had unwittingly unleashed a nest of angry wasps. *So much for bees.* "Erm...no, I can't guess."

"Well, Rupe was *so* stuck, bless him, because if he said he couldn't and upset Mr Scott, then he might not exhibit with us again, or worse, but if he said *yes*, then what about the ticket holders?" She raised her eyebrows to emphasise the drama. "But Mr Scott, Mr Man-in-Black-Never-Smiles, told Rupert that in return, he'd let us have the show for one more week before it heads off to Paris so nobody misses their chance. Can you believe it? What a doll!"

"He's done all that for my outreach group?" Eva stared at Lyndsey in surprise. She wasn't sure that Daniel would want her to know this. "I had no idea. I mean, he told me he'd spoken to Rupert, but I didn't realise… Well, there you are, then. Bad-boy artist who isn't so bad after all!"

"Not what Rupert says." She closed the menu. "Rupert wants to know how you did it. I won't tell you what he *actually* said because you won't like it!"

"I probably wouldn't…" Eva almost jumped as the camera flash came back into her mind again. "Lynds, did you get the text about my missing earring? Has it turned up at all?"

"Oh, I will tell you because I know you want me to!" Lyndsey laughed, as though Eva had spent ten minutes begging to know what had been said. "He said *care home rat sticking up for his council house cousins.* Isn't that horrid? I think he's jealous because Mr Scott and Rupe don't seem to get on."

"I wonder why that might be?" Eva felt the edge of Rupert's desk against her bare thighs again. She wasn't going to regret it. Rupert had it coming to him. He'd obviously thought she was supposed to have had Rupert puffing away on top of her to get the outreach group into the exhibition. *What a gruesome thought.* And if it *was* him creeping about in the courtyard at night, then he was going to have a very big surprise when he found Eva's foot in his testicles.

"And I turned the office inside out looking for that earring *and* my pass and found—" She froze, eyes widening again, one hand held up. "You know what I found, you rotten, dirty pair!"

Lyndsey dissolved into laughter, then waved the hand she was holding in the air. "I can't even say it. I can't say anything but *afternoon tea*!"

"I wonder where my earring could be?" Eva remarked, feigning innocence. But she couldn't for long, and erupted in a dirty giggle. "It was *amazing*, Lynds. *He's* amazing. He's so...oh, he knows what he's doing, that's for sure. He's such a tonic after Miles, really."

"Let's order our treats, because I have to be terribly serious after that." Lyndsey pouted. "I'm going to actually act my age for once!"

"Shall we order the cake stand and a pot of Earl Grey?" Eva knew the cake stand was one of Lyndsey's favourites, stacked with neat little sandwiches and an array of dainty cakes. "It's on me, to say thank you for looking for my earring."

"Oh, yay!" She gave a little round of applause. "I'll go and order, then it's *serious talk* time."

Serious? Lyndsey headed to the counter, all joy and lightness. What could have gone on in Lyndsey's enchanted world that could be serious?

It would be nothing, of course, it always was. It was one of the joys of being her friend. There was so much drama, without there being any drama at all.

When Lyndsey was settled at the table again, she knitted her hands carefully in front of herself and said, "I need to tell you something."

Of course Eva knew that—it had been Lyndsey who had introduced them, after all, who had been a shoulder to complain on when things hadn't worked out. She was the best sort of friend a girl could hope for. "And I'm so sorry things didn't work out for you and him and I hope you don't mind but… Miles and I are seeing each other, Eva. I wanted you to be the first to know."

Passionate sex over a desk didn't quite seem to be Lyndsey's thing, after all. Nor Miles', for that matter.

"Lots and lots," her friend admitted, blushing prettily. "He's such a lovely friend but so affectionate as a boyfriend. If you can still be a boy when you've just turned thirty-seven!"

"That's so sweet!" Eva grinned. She really was happy for the pair. Miles seemed better suited to Lyndsey than he had seemed to Eva. "I'm glad, really. I worried about Miles, when we split up. I didn't want him to be lonely."

"He's not the sort. I don't think I've ever seen him anything but smiley!"

Eva had, however, but she thought it best to skip over that. If a morning came when Miles woke up and told Lyndsey that she was too bloody cheerful and that arts management was a load of bunkum, then she would see the unsmiley version of the man that Eva had split up with.

"Well, that's good then!" Eva sat back in her chair as their lunch arrived, as twee as it would be delicious. There was something slightly not-twee about picking up one's friend's ex, but Eva dismissed the thought. There'd been plenty of that at art school, and Eva wasn't a dog in the manger when it came to her exes. "I'm happy for you both."

"Are you sure?" Lyndsey's coral pink lips set into a pout. "I know it's not a *best friends* thing to do, but we didn't think you'd mind, and we seem to just go together so well. He's such a little sweetie, far more my sort of man than yours, *she said knowingly*."

"You already knew Miles before I started going out with him, so really, why would I complain?" Eva poured the tea into the floral cups that reminded her of Sunday visits to her grandparents. She knew how Lyndsey took it without having to ask. Sweet and sugary. "And as for Daniel... Well, yes, he is rather different from Miles, but I wouldn't like to say he's *my man*, exactly."

"Hmm." Lyndsey nodded. "So have you seen him again? Are you dating?"

Eva laughed. "Can you imagine a man like him *dating*?" She bit into a delicate triangle of a white bread sandwich and only once it was too late realised she had poked out her little finger. "We...well, we did meet up again, and we plan to meet again soon, but it's not like we're *in a relationship*, or *dating*, or anything like that. We just—" Eva couldn't say or even think the four-letter word in a chintzy teashop like this. "You know what grown adults do. And it's fun, and he's amazing, and we get on really well, but I'm under no illusions that he's about to turn around and call himself my boyfriend or something like that."

"Do you remember when he came on the scene? You must've been at uni, because I was." Lyndsey took a bite from one of the sandwiches. "We went to the Tate to see his first exhibition and wandered around feeling terribly grown up, stroking our chins at the *horror*. No pickled sharks for him!"

"Yes, I remember. *Everyone* at my college was madly jealous of his career taking off like it did, and he even made some people go back to painting after faffing about with rather bad sculpture!" *And now I'm posing for him.* Eva had somehow managed to forget that he was famous. She only thought of him as Daniel, not *Daniel Scott*. "All that darkness, all the intensity. He's hardly going to come here for scones!"

Although, Eva wondered, might he, if she asked? If the gentle version of Daniel was uppermost?

"He has to get them somewhere if he wants them," was her friend's reply. "Just think though, all those famous women who used to race to his viewings and now—" She dropped her voice to a whisper. "Now he's dating my best friend!"

All those famous women. "Well, I'm famous. In Brighton, at least!" Eva said. "And we're not dating, Lynds. By the way…it's probably best not to say anything about it at the moment. I'm sure it's just a passing thing, and he's very private, really."

"Famous Eva, fighting the paps to get to her cucumber sandwiches," Lyndsey teased. "Just you be careful, miss, I don't want my friend upset by a grumpy old artist in sunglasses."

"I made him take them off!" Eva laughed. "He's got such lovely eyes. He can be so gentle, Lynds. Not at all like you'd think from that public persona of his."

"I'm only a lowly PA, I don't get to see that." She took a sip of tea. "And Rupe *definitely* didn't see it."

Eva changed tack. She couldn't be responsible for Daniel coming across as rude or surly. Especially to people like Rupert, who no doubt thought that Daniel should be wringing his hands in obsequious gratitude.

"Do you think paps *will* come after me if they find out?" The camera flash burst in front of her eyes again, and Eva decided she had to say something. "Daniel thinks they won't, but last night… I think someone took a photo of me through my window."

"It'll be a tourist, don't worry. Although—" But she shook her head. "No, nothing."

"I wondered if it was a tourist too." Eva topped up her teacup. She shivered, as if cold fingers were tapping their way up her spine. "Although *what*, Lynds? What were you going to say?"

"Just that his paintings aren't exactly Beatrix Potter. Believe me, we've had some proper loons in to see the exhibition." She sucked in her cheeks. "Questions about whether he paints with blood, *fluids*, you know the sort."

"What are you saying, Lynds?" Eva blinked at her friend, trying to grasp what she meant. Because the implications were horrible. "Do you think Daniel was creeping about outside my house last night?"

"No!" She hooted with disbelieving laughter. "Why would you even think that? Can you *imagine*?"

Eva exhaled, only then realising that she'd been holding her breath. "Thank God for that! But do you think one of his more *intense* fans might have…found out?"

"Probably not, it's probably just me being silly."

"That's a relief!" Eva placed her hand on her chest, panting in theatrical fashion. "I thought I had a stalker for a second!"

"Why would you, though?" She shrugged. "Because you're seeing Daniel Scott?"

"It's an unknown quantity, that's all." Eva ran her gaze over the cakes on the stand, delicate sugar constructions as fragile as butterflies. "I've never been out with—maybe that's not the right way to put it. I've never *been* with someone like him before. Would some fan of his come after me?"

"You'd have to ask him that. Google him, have a look at some of the crazies who like his work." She picked up another sandwich. "They're not all art-loving millionaires!"

"I'm not sure I want to peep into that particular cesspool, thank you very much!" But Eva knew she would once she got home. Just a peek, just five minutes, before finishing off her bees.

"I can't believe you and Daniel Scott—" Lyndsey gave a little shriek. "Oh. My. God."

Eva chuckled. "And you were convinced he was furious with me for what I'd said about his work!"

"Instead you've become a conquest!"

"I'm not his conquest!" Eva wafted her hands, dispelling the idea. "We're not a couple who go on dates, but I'm not a conquest, either. If anything, I suppose in a way I've become his muse."

Lyndsey's eyes widened and she reached for one of the choux buns. "I've never met a muse before! Do you have to pose for him?"

"Oh, *yes*!" Eva grinned. "I suppose it's my fault, really. I did say a change would do his work good. I'm fascinated, really, what he'll come up with. Do you know, he's never drawn a model before? Well, hadn't until yesterday, that is!"

Lyndsey's eyes widened again, sparkling with excitement. "He's already— Let me see it!"

"You can't, he threw it away! The light wasn't right, apparently." Eva chased a small cake around her plate with a pastry fork. "We're going to have another attempt, bless him."

"I hope he doesn't make it all dark and scary." She pouted. "Just imagine. Oh God, are you naked in it? Is he going to show it publicly? Show *you* publicly?"

"Yes, I'm naked in it, but no, I don't know what he'll do with it. You might not even recognise me in the finished piece." Eva sliced the cake in half with a fork and fondant oozed across the plate. "I did life modelling at art college and my bottom appeared in the final show. If he does exhibit it, it won't bother me."

"Then you *will* be famous! All the millionaires admiring your bod!" She laughed. "All the loons too."

"Stop going on about the loons!" Eva laughed. *She'd be okay, she'd be perfectly fine. Loons? How ridiculous.* To distract herself, she took her phone out of her bag and flicked through her messages without looking at them. It hadn't been a loon outside her house. No, just a tourist. "It's only a painting."

The phone buzzed in her hand. Lyndsey laughed and told her, "Here's one of them now! *Dear Eva, get your claws out of my bad boy!*"

"*Dear loon, sod off, love from Eva.*" Eva swiped to see the message and her heart seemed to miss a beat. It was from Daniel. No message, just a photo.

He was topless, almost smiling, his dark eyes smouldering into the camera and his sunglasses in his hair. The black, loose trousers were there again, paint-spattered, on the verge of sliding down his hips. He must have taken the photo in his studio. The light was bright and on the easel behind him was pinned his biroed portrait of her.

Eva ran her hand through her hair, desire flaring in her blood. She glanced up from her phone at Lyndsey. "Wrong number."

"You've gone red." Lyndsey took another sliver of cake and peered over, trying and failing to see what was on the phone. "Is it something naughty?"

"No...not at all! It's a warm day, isn't it?" Eva fanned herself with the menu. "Better let them know they've got the wrong number."

She tapped out her reply.

You've made me wet.

"You're so sweet to do that." Lyndsey reached out and refilled their teacups, but Eva wasn't really listening. She was thinking about those silky trousers and the man who wore them, the toned planes of the body that had been pressed to hers yesterday. Was he working on her painting even now, there in that sunlit studio? Was she taking shape on the canvas of his imagination?

The phone buzzed again.

And you've made me hard.

"Sorry, Lynds. I don't like being the annoying person with the phone, but I just need to—" She replied, *How long can you wait?*

"Is it him?"

Eva was caught off guard. Was she really so easy to read as that? She touched her cheek—her face was giving off heat. There really wasn't any point in lying to her best friend, so Eva nodded. "Sorry."

"You're *so* blushing." Her friend laughed. "Don't say sorry, I love how exciting your life suddenly is. I never thought you'd be one of those *click your fingers and I'll come running* girls!"

As she spoke, the reply lit up the screen. It was an address and the words, *Whenever you can make it, I'll be waiting.*

"I'm not," Eva told Lyndsey as she tapped out her reply.

Tomorrow?

"I bet you will. As soon as you've licked the cream off your scone." Lyndsey blinked then burst into a gale of laughter. "That *was* supposed to sound dirty, in case you're wondering! Rupe says he lives in a *palace*, but when Rupert tried to get an invite, Mr Scott insisted on coming to the gallery. Poor old Ru couldn't even get the address out of him!"

Eva chuckled at Lyndsey's attempt at saucy talk, although it did put an image into Eva's mind involving cream and Daniel's stomach which wasn't entirely unpleasant. "Apparently it's big, yes...*very* big!"

She raised an eyebrow salaciously and roared with laughter.

Lyndsey gave a squeal and stamped her feet on the floor as, in Eva's hand, the phone buzzed again. This time the message was one word, echoing her own.

Tomorrow.

Eva smiled at the phone, then turned it off. "Anyway, you and Miles?"

"Me and Miles?" Lyndsey blinked, all innocence. "Believe me, after a decade of friendship and a few weeks of lovely dates, I've yet to *lick his scone*, if you follow? My mum is super delighted because she had this horror of me hitting thirty-five without a gent, and just in the nick of time…a gent!"

"You've kissed him, though, haven't you?" Eva started to work her way through a cream meringue, waiting for Lyndsey's answer. It didn't help that the meringue's long shape made her think of Daniel again, but she *would* wait. They both would. And how much more intense their liaison would be for the anticipation.

"We've kissed," she confirmed. "Beneath the stars on the prom, with a candy floss to share. I was wearing my favourite white dress and it was like being in a musical!"

"That sounds perfect!" *If your name is Lyndsey.* "What sparked it off, then? If you've known each other so long and only now you're smooching under starlight?"

"Just…" She licked her fingertips clean of cake crumbs, "One of those moments."

"Ah, yes, one of those!" Eva grinned, happy for her friend. "I'm glad something good's come of me and Miles splitting up. We weren't very well-matched, to be honest, but it sounds like you're having a great time."

"We are. Taking our time, but we already know everything there is to know about each other, so…" She beamed a happy smile. "And the best thing is, we can all still be friends! We could double date with Mr Sunglasses!"

"Who knows? Maybe!" Eva couldn't see it happening, but she didn't want to spoil Lyndsey's fun.

"Is he too cool for the pier?"

Eva slapped the table, laughing. "Can you see him on the dodgems? Really?"

"Maybe his paintings would be a bit more chipper if he did." She laughed. "When're you seeing your *hook-up* again?"

Eva had finished her meringue and licked cream off her fingertips. "Tomorrow."

"Oh, so very hard to get? A whole day!" Lyndsey blinked, then opened her mouth, shocked by something. "Those messages? Are they—" She glanced round and lowered her voice to a whisper. "Dick pics?"

"No, they're not!" Eva was scandalised in response. Though perhaps to Lyndsey, dick pics would be exactly the sort of photo that a bad boy would send. "He's wearing clothes, but I'm *not* going to show you! He's just looking…sultry."

"You should draw *him*, play him at his own game." She held out her hand. "Go on, show me. Or is it one of those special *just for us* things?"

"We promised each other we'd keep this private. I don't mind you knowing that something has been going on, but please, Lynds, don't ask for anything more."

"I'm sorry." Her hand moved again, this time to pat Eva's gently. "Of course I won't, just promise me you'll take care? I don't want you to get hurt and we don't know him. His paintings don't scream *well-adjusted*, do they?"

Eva stacked her hand over Lyndsey's. "Now, Lynds, you don't have to worry, honestly, but it is so sweet that you care. Besides, I wonder about his paintings. Maybe he's better adjusted than any of us because he can get all that horror out."

"You know that I love you, my *bezzie*." She squeezed Eva's hand. "Girls have to stick together!"

"We do. We really do."

"And what're you up to tonight if not seeing Mr Sunglasses?"

"I'm finishing off some work. Clearing my desk, if you will!" Eva chuckled. She went to pour more tea, but only a thin splash was left. "So I can see Mr Sunglasses tomorrow, should you wish to know."

"*I* am going off to the big smoke with the lovely Miles to see *Coppélia*." Lyndsey beamed, never happier than when the ballet beckoned. "And tomorrow evening I have to work because we have a late view, so I shall think of you having all sorts of very naughty fun."

"Maybe you'll have some naughty fun with Miles in London. Please tell me he's taking you to a hotel afterwards?" The thought of any kind of bedroom activity with Miles made Eva's lunch curdle in her stomach, but as long as Lyndsey was happy, Eva would cope. Lyndsey didn't answer though. She simply pursed her dainty lips and smiled a knowing smile.

Chapter Five

Eva rang the doorbell. She hadn't replied to Daniel's text, on purpose, to keep him waiting. And she hadn't arranged a time, either, hoping to draw out his anticipation.

Except now, as she waited for him to answer the door, she wondered if that had been such a good idea. Had he gone out somewhere — but where did someone like Daniel Scott go? She could hardly see him nipping down the shops for milk and bread.

She stepped back from the door and looked up again at the vast art deco frontage of the house. *Palace* was the right word. It was huge, with ranks of windows in their original metal frames blinking in the sunlight.

She rang again, but still there was no response. Eva pressed her ear to the door, wondering if she would hear his footsteps approach. But there was no sound from inside the house apart from a steady beat.

Someone, somewhere was playing very loud music.

Eva rummaged for her phone and was about to call him when she realised that if he couldn't hear the doorbell over his music, he was unlikely to be able to hear his phone. She decided to look for a way to the back of the house, maybe to a patio door. She followed the front of the house round to a border of tall pines, and at the side of the house she found a gate. Not a particularly secure gate, as it wasn't locked, and Eva made her way down the shaded path, the music growing louder all the time.

The sun hit her as she entered the back garden, and Eva held her hand over her eyes. The camera flash came back to her again, and she shivered despite the heat of the day. But there hadn't been a repeat last night. It didn't feel as if she was being watched.

Maybe it really had been tourists after all.

On the terrace, Eva spotted the sun lounger that Daniel had lain on two days earlier, and the infinity pool, and beyond that the view of the sea. She was entranced, staring out across the endless rolling blue, but the music still throbbed from within the house, and Eva turned to see a madman in a white-painted room, topless, hurling colours at a canvas.

Eva watched for a moment, seeing the tension in him, the intensity in every muscle as he worked. Then, unable to bear it any longer, she went up to the window and knocked on the glass.

Daniel spun towards the sound, his black eyes unblinking. For a moment he stared at her, uncomprehending, and she wondered if he had fuelled his work with a little of that powder he seemed so fond of. The thought ebbed away when he broke into a smile and picked up a sleek silver remote, lowering the volume. Then he strolled across the studio to throw open the French doors to her.

"Sorry to interrupt." Eva reached up and kissed him gently on the lips. She recognised what he was listening to now. Roxy Music. It made her smile, because it wasn't what she'd thought he was into.

"It's good to see you." She tasted coffee on his lips and something else, chocolate perhaps. "*Very* good to see you."

"Likewise." Eva slipped her arm around his middle. His scent, the taste of his mouth and the heat of his body set desire racing through her again like flame. But Eva tried to resist, even if she wished he'd ravish her on the studio's floor. He ran his hands up beneath her leather jacket and over her back, then caught her lips again for an even deeper kiss.

"Did the bees buzz off?"

"I sent them packing this morning." Eva gazed at him, transfixed, her heart thudding. She stroked his bare skin at his waist, recalling how it had felt to hold his body against hers. "Did you miss me?"

"If I want to preserve my rep, I have to say *no*." He nuzzled his lips to her jaw. "But yes."

Eva kissed him again, exploring his mouth with her tongue. He was erect and she ran her hand over the hard shape, a tremble running through her which he doubtless could feel. "I really, really want you. But do I pose for you first?"

"If we want to get anything done today." Daniel sighed, sliding his hands down to her bottom. "But afterwards, we can relax."

"Maybe it would be best. All that desire in you while you work...you might find a new seam to mine." Eva had meant her remark in all seriousness, but as soon as the words were out of her mouth, she laughed. "That came out wrong, didn't it?"

"I was going to pose you on the bed, but...we'll get nothing done if I do." Daniel jerked his head back into the studio. "But you asked for a chaise longue, so I got you a chaise longue."

"How marvellous, Daniel! Is it antique?"

"Come and see." With his arm around her, Daniel escorted Eva into the studio. It was vast, the walls hung with a half dozen canvases as dark and glowering as those in the Hawley Gallery that vied for space with framed posters for exhibitions that spanned a career and the globe. She glimpsed unfinished sketches and notepads piled on chairs in this, Daniel Scott's inner sanctum. It would be worth a fortune, of course, but that wasn't what drew Eva in—instead, it was the privileged glimpse into the world of a man whom she suspected didn't let many people quite this close.

And amid the organised chaos, resplendent in deep red velvet, was the chaise longue that he had bought for her. Eva could see it was antique just at a glance, decadent and sensuous and the sort of place for a muse to recline.

"Will this do?" Daniel asked, stepping nimbly over an abandoned coffee cup. "I thought it looked very *Eva.*"

Eva beamed. "It's perfect! Can I take it home afterwards? It would look amazing in my front room! I'm not being serious, by the way, but it *is* lovely."

"Didn't you hear what I said?" He looked down at her, his voice hinting at mirth. "I got you a chaise longue. It's not mine. It's yours."

"That's the best present I've ever had!" Eva hugged him. "It's not too bad being a muse!"

"Oh, you're my muse now?" He laughed and held her tight. "Before we start, do you need anything?"

"I wouldn't mind a glass of water. By the way, I brought you a present." Eva glanced back at the antique. "It's not quite a chaise longue, though."

"Something for me?" He stepped back a little, his arms still around her middle. "Go on."

"In a way, it's not really from me, because my mum made it. She made too much, in fact, so…if Mrs Catesby's Boozy Damson Jam is your thing, then —" Eva pulled the jar out of her bag. It was homemade down to the handwritten label and the ribbon tied around its lid. "It's delicious. A hug in a jar."

He took it from her and she saw the smile on his face grow, knew from the sparkle in his eyes that it was genuine. Where the sunglasses were at the moment Eva couldn't guess, but she was glad of their absence.

"Proper homemade food, thank you!" Daniel beamed. "I *hope* you brought some of your work too. We can have a glass of something later and look through it. And eat jam out of the jar, like kids."

Eva nodded. "I come complete with sketch pad today!"

"Water and work first," Daniel instructed. He took his arm from her waist and padded on his bare feet towards a small fridge against the far wall, above which hung a poster for his retrospective at MOCA. Atop it was a coffee machine and kettle and an assortment of mismatched cups and glasses. He took out a bottle of water and filled one of the glasses. "Then fun, jam and a chance to finally see what Eva Catesby can do."

What must it be like to have a retrospective and be so casual about it that it's just there in your studio, hanging above the fridge?

Lonely at times, Eva was sure. But not today. Her gaze alighted on an intricate spiral staircase of filigreed metal that wound its way up and out of the studio, holding all the promise of a fairy-tale beanstalk.

Eva dropped her bag in a corner and, with her back to him, took off her leather jacket, which she hung carefully over the back of a chair. To avoid leaving elastic marks on her skin, and for other reasons to benefit Daniel, Eva hadn't bothered with underwear. She unfastened the row of buttons that marched down the front of her dark blue dress and turned back to face him as her dress fell open.

"Thanks." She took the glass of water from him and drank deeply, aware of his gaze on her. "Are you ready for me?"

"I've been ready since you climbed into that taxi." He stroked his fingertips from her cheekbone to her jaw. "I found my muse."

Never breaking from his gaze, Eva caught Daniel's hand and brought it to her lips. She kissed the palm, then told him, "We'd better get on, hadn't we?"

"Get comfortable." He nodded, then sniffed and gave that telltale rub of his nose. "Today is for finding the pose, getting the look and a few sketches. It's for capturing Eva."

"I rather like the idea of you *capturing* me, Daniel!" *But not so much painting under the influence.* Eva winked as she put aside the glass and threw her dress after the jacket. After slipping out of her sandals, she was left only with bangles on her arm and a delicate silver chain around her ankle. "Do you want the jewellery off too?"

"Yes." Less than a second passed before he said, "No. No, keep it on. I like the way the sun's hitting it.

Do you mind the music? I usually work with it, but I can try without if you like."

"The music's good. Very smooth. I'm surprised you weren't listening to punk, seeing as you're a bad boy!" Eva plumped the cushions on the chaise longue and sat down, her legs stretched across its length, one arm draped over its end. "Do direct me, darling, won't you?"

"We tried that in the hotel and I lost you." He was busy at one of several easels, turning it to face her. "I want to see Eva, not Daniel Scott's version of her."

Eva tapped her fingers on her thigh in thought, then bent her lower leg at the knee, shifting against the cushions to angle her hips towards him. With a clank of bangles, she flung one arm above her head in her favoured bosom-flattering pose, and let her other arm drape loosely over her stomach. The position wasn't too uncomfortable to maintain and she let her head fall back a little against the velvet upholstery.

"And are my eyes saying *come over here and ravish me, you handsome creature*?"

"They're practically shouting it," Daniel assured her. He put a large sketch pad on the easel and said, "Let's see if I can get Eva this time?"

Behind him she could see the biroed portrait from the hotel, sketched out in blue ink on a folded sheet from a hotel information folder. From this distance she couldn't understand what it was that had left him so despairing. Though it lacked detail, she could see the shape of her body, could recognise the features that she saw in the mirror every day. It was clearly Eva, but something about it *wasn't*.

"Thank you for posing for *me* the other day, Daniel," Eva said, trying to move as little as possible as she spoke. He was dressed the same now as he had been in the photo he'd sent. How those loose pyjama trousers stayed up, she couldn't tell. "Much appreciated!"

"I was just showing you your portrait, bad though it was," he replied, his gaze flicking between her and the easel. "If I stumbled into the shot, it was entirely by accident."

"I'm sure it was. How awkward that your impressive torso and lovely eyes should get into shot." Eva giggled. "You looked so smouldery! I was in the cafe with Lyndsey when the photo arrived and it made me blush, you naughty man."

"Did you show her?" He lifted his head and looked at her, his expression unreadable. Then he smiled. "I hope not, or I would've put my Wayfarers on."

"I didn't show her. She wanted to see, but it's private, isn't it?" An itch was developing on Eva's leg and she did all she could to ignore it. "Anyway, I don't think she would have been able to cope with that raunchy look you had in your eyes. Do you know, she's got a boyfriend and they haven't had sex yet? Kissed sweetly on the prom and that's it! Unless they did it last night after the ballet... Sorry, I'm thinking aloud. Do tell me to shut up!"

"What?" Daniel looked up again and blinked, but she saw the same darkness in his expression that had plagued him at the hotel when he'd tried to sketch her. "You went to a ballet?"

"No, Lyndsey did, with Miles." Eva barely moved, barely opened her mouth. She needed to be the best model she could for Daniel, not an annoying chatterbox who kept gassing away as he tried to work. He nodded an acknowledgement then went back to work. In his face she saw the same intensity that she had glimpsed in the gallery, the fiery indignation with which they had exchanged words before and after their tryst on Rupert's desk. This time, though, it was tempered with annoyance, punctuated by occasional silent oaths that he spat at the paper.

The way he worked fascinated Eva. All that pent-up energy. It explained a lot about his paintings, and something about him too. But was he getting his rage, or whatever it was, out or was he winding himself up even more? She wondered what a calm Daniel Scott painting would look like, but her mind couldn't conjure it.

Perhaps the anger she could see in him now was what stopped him from capturing the sense of humanity that he seemed to be striving for and missing in his sketches. The gentle man who had held her and washed her hair had disappeared into the fierce tension of his muscles, the blazing depths of his eyes. If he let that man out a little more, that *Mr Carswell* from The Mallard, if he lit up the darkness around him, he might see the woman he couldn't capture on paper.

Eva's lower leg had gone to sleep. She tried to wake it up by subtly curling her toes, but it didn't work. "Daniel, could I have a quick break?"

"Now?" He sighed and scrubbed his hand through his hair. "Yeah, okay."

"Sorry." Eva got up from the chaise and put her dress on, fastening a few of the buttons so she could stretch out her limbs without losing too much dignity. With her arms above her head to loosen her shoulders, she picked her way across the room to Daniel. She shone him an encouraging smile. "Do you mind if I have a look?"

"Help yourself. I need more coffee." He stepped back from the easel. "Do you want a drink?"

"Another glass of water will be fine, thanks." Eva grinned at him, then turned her attention to the sketch. Without thinking, her fingers sought the pencil and she twirled it like a lazy majorette as she looked at his work. Daniel stroked his hand over her shoulder then padded away, leaving her to study his efforts.

He should've used a lighter pencil, that was for sure. But aside from the heavy layers of graphite on the paper, he had made her very angular. Her bent knee and her shoulder were too pointed, and Eva realised those shapes had come from his anger. All his rage was getting in the way. While he was busy making his coffee, Eva swiftly sketched in around the angles, softening the parts of her body that he had made too sharp. He'd see it, but she'd let him think he'd done it.

Satisfied, she laid the pencil down and perched on a wooden stool near the easel. "Do you feel the sketch is going better today than at the hotel?"

"You can see it isn't." Daniel's voice was clipped, tight, and even with his back turned to her Eva could see the same tightness in his body. He looked tense, like a coiled spring. When he turned and made his back to her with the water and coffee, the tension showed in his face too. He held out the glass of water. "I don't want you to think that I see you like — "

Daniel fell silent as his gaze settled on the page. As Eva took the water, he cocked his head a little, staring at the drawing she had added her own lines to.

"You've *edited* my work," he murmured, then looked at her. "Have you — you've changed this?"

Eva shook her head. "No, not at all. It's all your work." She sipped her water and put the glass aside. "Would you like a shoulder rub?"

"Don't lie to me!" His voice rose in volume with every angry word. "You scribble on my work and tell me I'm imagining it? I know it's fucking terrible, Eva, I drew it! I don't need you to make me a charity case!"

Eva recoiled from his angry words, at a loss to know what to do or say. Any retort would only make it worse. But she had to say something. "I'm trying to help you, that's all! And your sketch isn't terrible, but you're so full of anger when you work. Look, all I did was try to soften the sketch, see? I'm not pointy, I'm rounded, and you should know that because you know how my body *feels*!" She picked up the pencil again, rounding off another sharp limb. "You said to me you'd never drawn from life before. Well, you can't expect it to be perfect straight away. You've got to practice, for heaven's sake. And no one has to see it, do they?"

"You're seeing it!" His anger seemed more pitched than ever. "You're seeing how fucking crap I've made you look! Of course I'm angry. Everything I do in here is anger—"

His hand was clutched around the coffee mug, his knuckles white as marble. She saw the rise and fall of his chest increase and he spat, "There's so much of it in me, Eva, it's— How the hell can I make you look like this? It doesn't even look human!"

"Stop beating yourself up, Daniel! It's not crap. Bearing in mind you haven't done this before, it's pretty good. But can't you channel something else, besides anger? What about desire? You're sketching a woman you've gone to bed with!" Eva couldn't avoid the elephant in the room any longer, and God only knew it had nothing to do with her, even though she knew it might not end well if she broached it. "Or is it the crap you shove up your nose? Is that getting in the way as well?"

"I'm not one of your kids, for Christ's sake! Look!" Daniel wheeled round, gesturing to the walls. "Do you see any *desire* here? It's pure fucking fury! I don't know *how* to channel desire unless — "

He was silent suddenly, the sentence unfinished.

Eva threw down the pencil and it rattled away across the wooden floor. She began to open the buttons on her dress. "Fuck me, then. Here. In the studio, where everything is fury, according to you. Experience *desire*. I don't know. On the floor, among the bits of paper, or over the sofa, or in that chair. Pin me up against the easel or have me cling onto the mantelpiece, but just *fuck me, Daniel!*"

"Not in here." He shook his head and put the mug down. "How can I? I need the anger in here, or I've got nothing!"

Eva's dress fell to the floor and she put her arms around him. "Well, let's go somewhere else, then. But you're feeling desire *now*, aren't you?"

He put his hands in her hair and kissed her with a fierce strength in reply, pressing their bodies together. The desire and anger were both there now, the air almost crackling with it.

"Bedroom?" Eva whispered. He repeated the word in agreement, then kissed her again with that same fevered intensity. His fingers were tangled in her hair, the tension she saw in him making it fiercer than ever. He was so hard, and Eva was so aroused, even though she wondered if she *should* be attracted to his dark energy. But it exerted an invisible pull that excited her too much to ignore.

"I need you," he murmured, his voice hoarse with desire. He took her face in his hands, nuzzling her jaw. "Don't think that picture— That's not how I see you—"

Eva stroked his tense shoulders and swept her way down to his waist, circling her fingertips against the small of his back. "I know you don't. It's okay. Just take me to your bed, won't you?"

Daniel caught her hand in his own and led her across the studio to the spiral staircase. Here he paused again for another kiss before they ascended, leaving the chaotic studio behind.

Eva was so caught up in Daniel that she barely registered the cool decor of his house, as impersonal as a hospital. It must have cost a lot of money to have a designer rub away traces of Daniel's personality.

At the top of the stairs, a huge white room awaited them, with a wall of windows overlooking the sea. The sun was hot through the glass.

Eva tugged down Daniel's trousers and pressed her body close to his, the warmth of his skin against hers. He kicked them aside and took her in his arms, their bodies tight together, every muscle in him taut with that unreachable anger.

His bed was large and untidy, the bedclothes flung haphazardly across it. Eva guided him towards it and dropped down onto the bed with Daniel on top of her. She sank her hands into his hair, kissing him deeply, feeling the strength of him. She wasn't afraid, because his anger wasn't directed at her, but at some distant point in his background that time could not blot out.

He reached his arm around Eva and held her to him. The man in her arms was the man who made those

hellscapes, who blotted out his pain with coke, who couldn't let go of the rage that he wouldn't explain. Maybe he didn't want to be helped, but how could anyone go through life like this?

"*I need you.*" It was a glimmer of light in the darkness, and so were these kisses, this embrace. He wasn't lost.

Between his kisses, Eva whispered, "We need each other, Daniel." She kissed him deeply, aware of his scent and the weight of his body, of his desire for her, and her own for him. She had a vague sense of his arm reaching out to the side of the bed moments before she heard the telltale sound of the tearing wrapper, and all the time he was returning her kisses, possessing and possessed.

Eva ran her hand from Daniel's shoulder to his hand and slipped the condom from his fingers to put it on him. Her hand trembled as desire coursed thickly in her veins, but something else was there too. Tenderness, even at this moment of lust.

Eva looped her legs around his waist and stroked her fingertips down his cheek. "Show me how you see me, Daniel."

Daniel pushed himself up on his hands and met her gaze. Then, without the protection of the sunglasses, he closed his eyes instead as he thrust into her with a gasp of Eva's name. The word sounded desperate, like a drowning man.

Eva moaned as he was inside her once more, but the stakes were higher now. This wasn't a stolen one-off over a desk, or a playful romp in the cocoon of a luxury hotel room. This wasn't only for pleasure, and as Eva thrust against him she realised she was trying to find a dropped connection or a way in. Something that would draw them back together.

"I'm sorry," he gasped, burying his face against her hair. Still his hips moved, hard and fast, every muscle defined beneath her touch. "To draw you like that — I'm sorry."

"Don't be, oh, don't be, darling..." Eva nuzzled his neck, feeling his pulse there, and every fibre of her body trembled for him. She was losing him, all because of a stupid sketch. She was losing him before she really knew him.

Eva ran desperate caresses over his body, stroking, tweaking, tilting her hips to draw him deeper inside her. "You have nothing to apologise for," she whispered, but she wasn't sure if he heard her, or if he did, whether he believed her.

Every thrust drew a cry of exertion from his lips and he stifled them with kisses, clinging to her as though he might be swept away. She had never known anyone be so close and so distant, even as their limbs were wrapped around each other.

Yet Eva's pleasure built, the intensity and sheer visceral power of their bodies' union stoking the most primal of her lusts. She panted his name, and words fell from her lips in gasps when they weren't pressed hungrily to Daniel's. "Deeper... Hold me... I forgive... My handsome..."

His arms were strong around her, his hands on her bottom to lift her hips even higher. They moved as one in the sunlight, fevered and desperate in their embraces. Eva shifted her legs from Daniel's waist and brought them over his shoulders, knowing it would bring him as deeply as possible inside her. She cried out in ecstasy, Daniel's thrusts sending shudders through her. "Together," she said, even though he seemed so far away. "Together!"

"Together," he told her through his groans of pleasure, reaching to seize her hand. He opened his eyes and looked down at her. His eyes were blazing, filled with intensity, darker than any of his paintings at their core.

Trepidation struck Eva, but it melted away almost at once as she tightened her fingers around his. She couldn't fear the darkness inside him. It was part of him, and it drew her to him.

"I'm sorry," he whispered again, and she knew then that he hadn't heard her words of forgiveness at all. Or more likely, he wouldn't allow himself to hear them.

"I forgive you," Eva whispered, but the last word left her mouth on a sigh as, with a tightness and sudden release, her climax possessed her. As bliss swept through her, Eva was aware of brightness, an infinite kindness, an embrace, which came almost close enough to reach, and ebbed away. Even as she felt Daniel's orgasm claim him, she knew that it wouldn't be enough. That tension was still there, his eyes closed tight as though to keep tears from falling. Then he threw back his head and let out a cry of exertion, filled with passion and fierce with heat.

What the hell can I do?

Eva combed her hand through his hair, not speaking but whispering gentle sounds to him, an attempt at comfort which couldn't work. He'd survived whatever horror it was that had taken him into the darkness, and she couldn't stand by and watch it destroy him. But she hadn't a clue where to start.

Very gently, Daniel slipped Eva's legs down to the bed. Then he sank down into her arms, his body wracked by a shuddering sob.

Eva pressed her lips to the top of his head. "Daniel...please tell me. Is there something I can do? I'll help you, darling, but I don't know how."

"I didn't look at your work." The words were a whisper and another sob shuddered through him. "I need to look—"

"You can, but..." Eva wondered if it might be a useful distraction for him, to take his mind off whatever had consumed him. "I can go and fetch my sketchbook, if you'd like to see."

Daniel nodded but still he clung to her, his embrace tighter than ever. That he needed help was clear, but she didn't know how. It wasn't cocaine, though, of that at least Eva was sure.

"I'll bring some water up as well. I think we could both do with a drink!" And something stronger than water, too, but Eva wasn't going to let him get drunk on her watch.

"Please don't ever tell anyone," Daniel whispered. "You deserve so much better than this."

"I don't tell tales," Eva reassured him. "You were so sweet and gentle in the hotel, you melted me. I know you've suffered, Daniel, and I know you do still... I'm not angry with you for what happened downstairs. Really, I'm not."

She wasn't going to tell him that everything was all right, because it demonstrably wasn't. Empty platitudes were a waste of time. But she kissed him and playfully ruffled his hair. "Mmm... You look good after a ravishing, Daniel Scott!"

"You're so—" He lost the word in another sob, then managed a smile. "You made the drawing better, but you didn't have to lie. Don't ever think you do."

"Would you rather I'd said, *I like the energy, but maybe make me a little less pointy*?" Eva took his hand and laid it on her stomach, a part of her body that was very far from pointy.

"Rather than change it and pretend you hadn't?" He stroked her stomach gently. "How can I learn anything if you don't show me where I've made the mistake?"

"I'm sorry. I thought it might work subliminally." Eva cupped his jaw in her hand. "You were working so hard at it, it seemed like the best way to help. I won't do it next time, I promise." *If there is a next time.* She ghosted a kiss to his lips. He returned it with a sigh and closed his eyes again, sinking against her.

"Sketchbook," she reminded him in an affectionate whisper, and carefully slipped out of the bed. Eva crossed the room and paused at the top of the stairs to see him lying there, calm now, but his tension hadn't abated. She followed the curve of the stairs and was back in the mayhem of his studio again. Her bag was where she had left it on the floor, so she collected it up along with a bottle of water and headed back up to his bedroom again. She wondered what he'd think of her work. They were only sketches, after all.

He was lying so still. Eva took her sketchbook out of her bag and laid it on the pillow beside him. "Daniel?"

Only then did she realise he was asleep.

Eva lay on the bed beside him, her arm loosely around him. Drained from what had passed between them, she felt the pull of sleep.

I'll only have a snooze, that's all. Just a snooze.

Chapter Six

A breeze stirred Eva awake. Someone must have opened a window, but she hadn't. As she opened her eyes, she was disorientated until she remembered where she was. Daniel Scott's house. In his bed. She smiled at the thought until, as sleep reeled away, she remembered what had happened.

And realised she was alone.

And as the breeze stirred again, she noticed that it carried with it the smell of burning. Perhaps that was one of the perils of living so close to the beach in summer, putting up with barbecues and campfires as people stretched their days out into the evening. Yet something in the air seemed to be crackling, that same horrible tension she had sensed in Daniel earlier. From the studio downstairs, she could hear the sound of what seemed to be frantic movement, as though someone was moving furniture.

Struck by a sense of foreboding, Eva got up. As she had left her clothes downstairs, she pulled the sheet off the bed and wrapped it around herself. Her ears primed for every sound, trying to second-guess what Daniel was up to, she went to the top of the stairs.

"Daniel? Is that you?"

"Stay upstairs!" Daniel shouted. Even his voice sounded somehow wrong, pitched and forced. "I'm cleaning the studio up a bit! Having a clear-out!"

"Would you like a hand?" Eva's reply was falsely bright. Her heart hammered. *A clear-out? What the hell is he doing?* She picked her way downstairs, careful not to trip on her makeshift dress.

Daniel appeared at the bottom of the staircase. He wore the pyjama pants again, his eyes hidden behind the dark lenses of his sunglasses. In his arms was a pile of sketchbooks, so many that he seemed barely able to hold them.

"Go back to bed!" he instructed with too much cheer, his words tumbling over themselves. "You look beautiful. Go to bed and I'll be up when all this mess is cleared!"

Eva shook her head as she continued on her way downstairs. "No, I don't want to go back to bed. And besides, you've perked up. What are you —? What are you *doing*, Daniel?"

From the bottom of the stairs, Eva could see the studio. It looked as if a whirlwind had passed through it, leaving a clear path between what had been loose paper, and wreckage everywhere else. On a glass-topped table — because, of course, what else? — Eva saw a mess of white powder, streaks of it, the little that remained from what Daniel must've put up his nose.

Eva stared at him, but all she saw was her reflection in the lenses of his sunglasses, a wild woman wrapped in a bedsheet, her hair in a tousled frizz. "*Why?*"

"I lit a fire." He said it as though it were all the explanation she needed. "To clean it all up. I used to have a mum once, did you know that? You didn't know. I was so bad, so *rotten* that she killed herself to get away from me. Can you believe that?"

Daniel laughed, the sound high and not quite normal.

"I was a real bad boy back then!"

"Jesus Christ, Daniel. What the hell are you saying? Can you *hear* what you're saying?" The smell of the burning was drifting through the doors, and with one hand to keep her toga from slipping, Eva grasped at the pile of sketchbooks in Daniel's arms. "I don't believe you! I don't believe that any mother would do that! They wouldn't do that and leave you alone in the world. They *wouldn't!*"

"Guess what? She did!" He relinquished the sketchbooks to her and wheeled around, gesturing to the studio. "I'm going to get rid of it all, the way the world got rid of me. Throw it on a bonfire. I'd throw myself on after it if I wasn't such a fucking coward!"

Eva stood there, stunned, her mind so busy processing what he was saying that she couldn't find any words. So that was why he had been in care? Because his mother had taken her own life, and he'd spent all these years blaming himself.

"You were a child, Daniel. You can't blame yourself for what your mother did. Children do it all the time. If their parents split up, they'll try to justify it, they'll think, *Last week I broke a plate and Mum was furious, that's why they're splitting up.* But you're an adult now, Daniel. Surely you must realise it *wasn't* your fault!"

"It was nobody else's, was it?" He reached out as though to touch her, but snatched his hand back before they made contact. "That's why I chose Brighton, because we only ever had one holiday, and we came here and she took me to this crappy little gallery and I fell in love with the paintings and— It's your mate's now. Looks different, Mum wouldn't recognise it."

"So that's what you meant by nostalgia?" Eva set the armful of sketchbooks onto the floor. Tentatively, she held her hand out towards him. "That's lovely, Daniel. It's a lovely memory to have of your mum. I'm sure she'd be so proud to know that you went back there to exhibit your work. Out of all the places that would've shown you, and you chose the one you went to with her. Did she— Was she an artist too?"

"She was a cleaner." Daniel twined his fingers with hers. "And she worked in the off licence at the end of our road and she wanted more for me and I ended up—"

He fell silent, looking down at their hands.

"You ended up successful, and lauded the world over, and—and she must be looking down on you now, so pleased." *Pleased?* Eva's glance fell to the remains of Daniel's cocaine binge. She tucked the sheet a little tighter around her.

"They put Mr Carswell away for a long time." He whispered it as though confiding a great secret, then put his finger to his lips. "And when they went back to let him out, he was me."

Despite the heat of the day, Eva's veins were filled with ice. Was this what cocaine psychosis looked like, a man accusing himself of his mother's suicide, whose sense of identity has utterly slipped? Carswell... Carswell... That name sounded so familiar, but Eva couldn't place it. Something sinister was attached to it, but it was the drugs making him think he was someone else.

"You're Daniel Scott, you're a very well-known artist, and you're my...my friend. And I-I think you need help, Daniel. You're manic. You're not making any sense." Eva edged around him until she could grab her dress and her jacket from the chair. She hadn't a clue where her shoes had ended up. "I'll—I'll just nip back upstairs and get changed, then we can hop in a cab, and go to the hospital, and they'll look after you. They'll know what to do."

Because I don't have a fucking clue.

"You look terrified," he observed. "Are you frightened of me? Why would you be frightened? I'm cleaning the studio, that's all."

Eva struggled into her dress and dropped the sheet from around her. Buttoning her dress, half-turned from him, she made for the stairs. "Of course I'm terrified! You're like Dr Jekyll and Mr Hyde, only the wrong way round! Everyone loves a monster these days, don't they, that's the side you show, but the tender side, the affectionate Daniel Scott. He's hidden away."

"I don't want to frighten you, I wanted you to be happy and us to be—" She saw him bite his lip, then he lifted his sunglasses and showed her his eyes, the pupils wide and bloodshot. When he spoke again, his voice rose in volume with every word. "Can you see? There's *nobody* there!"

"You're going to the hospital. I'm going to ring for an ambulance." Eva tried as best she could to keep her voice level and calm, but inside she was screaming. Nothing in her life before had prepared her for this. A happy childhood with a hard-working dad and an earthy mother, art college and friends, a reasonable career and the odd romance here and there. She should never have got involved with Daniel Scott, she should never have gone to meet him at the hotel and she should certainly never have agreed to come into his home.

"I don't need an ambulance, I won't be in the fucking papers again!" he shouted. "Bring your kids to my work, Eva, say something nice about me and tell them *never* to end up like this. Promise me that?"

In a tone that was so cold it surprised her, Eva said as she retreated upstairs, "Oh, I will, Daniel, don't worry about that. You're no fucking role model for my kids."

"I know that!" he bellowed after her. "But I'm fucking good at what I do, whether you think so or not! Follow the money, make sure you tell them that!"

Blinded by her tears, Eva pressed her forehead to the cool glass of his bedroom window and sobbed. Everything hurt and she had no idea what to do. But she couldn't stay here a moment longer. She picked up her bag and went back downstairs again, steeling herself for whatever great act of destruction he would be committing now.

At first she thought that the studio was empty, but, as she rounded the bottom of the staircase, she realised her mistake. Daniel was on the chaise longue he had bought for her, curled up into a foetal position, his body shuddering with sobs, his skin glowing with perspiration. Apart from the trembling he was unmoving, the air eerily silent after the rage.

Eva crouched beside him and touched his hair from his sweaty face. "I'm ready to go now. Look, if I call an ambulance for you, I'll wait with you until it comes."

"Just go," he whispered. "Go home. You don't need this shit from me."

Eva messily wiped the back of her hand across her face through her tears. She noticed her sandals peeping out from under a sheet of paper and shoved her feet into them. "I just wish there was something I could do."

"I'm better on my own," he said flatly. "I'm sorry I couldn't— I just wanted to draw you."

"I know you did. Goodbye, Daniel." Eva got back up to her feet and backed towards the patio doors to head outside, where the evening was full of the singed smell of the bonfire. As she reached the door, Eva turned back. She wasn't sure he'd hear her from that distance, but she said it anyway. "I almost fell in love with you."

Eva's drive home was uneventful. Every traffic light she met was green. No one beeped at her, no pedestrians wandered into the traffic, and yet it seemed wrong, as if it was mocking what had gone on in that house.

She had a short walk from the garages to the mews courtyard, and was relieved to let herself into her home. The first thing she did, as she had done ever since the night of the camera flash, was to draw the curtains of her front room, but as she did, she noticed that the vase she'd on the windowsill was now on the coffee table.

She hadn't put it there. Or had she, when she was dusting? Though Eva couldn't remember the last time she'd done any dusting.

Eva went into the kitchen to make a cup of tea, but in here, too, something was off. The mug tree seemed to have been turned one-hundred-and-eighty degrees. The washing-up gloves she had hung over the tap were lying neatly on the draining board. The cookery book she had left on the stand wasn't the one she had seen there this morning.

Or perhaps it was?

Upstairs, her shampoo was standing in the middle of her shower tray, when it should have been in the wicker basket on the shelf. She wouldn't have left it there. She just wouldn't have.

Now, Eva's heart began to pound, unease leaking from every pore.

Someone had been in her house.

Cold with fear, Eva went into her studio. A stack of photos of bees which had been on the left side of her desk was now on the right.

And her bedroom?

The door creaked so loudly when she opened it that Eva had to suck back a scream. The bed she had left in a disordered heap that morning had been carefully made.

Who would do this? The same person who had taken a photo of her through the window? A loon, was that it, as Lyndsey had said? Some fan of Daniel Scott's who had found out about their liaisons?

"Well, it's all right now, don't worry!" Eva shouted, hysteria in her voice, as if whoever had done this was still in her house. "It's over… It's *over*!"

Eva's mobile screeched into life in the sudden silence. She jumped as though someone had laid their hand on her shoulder. Was it Daniel, miraculously returned to his senses, or worse, the police or someone from a hospital with bad news? Was it whoever had been in her house whilst she wasn't?

Lyndsey's name flashed up on the screen, and Eva gasped with relief. "Lynds! Thank God it's you!"

"Hello, lovely lady, I thought I'd just ring and see how things were going with Mr Sunglasses!" Lyndsey sounded as bright as ever, and behind her, Eva could hear piano music tinkling. It was all so normal after the day from hell, so welcome. "What's wrong?"

"Everything!" Eva was crying again, leaning against the wall because her legs would no longer hold her up. "I don't think I'll be seeing Daniel again, and…and… I'm certain someone's been in my house!"

Putting it into words made the situation sound ridiculous, because who would believe her? Wouldn't it be more likely that Eva was losing her memory? The door hadn't been swinging in the breeze when she'd arrived.

Whoever had done this must've picked the lock.

Or they had a key.

"What? Phone the police, we're coming over." The phone was muffled but she heard Lyndsey call, "Miles, someone's broken into Eva's house! I need you to drive us over to her!"

"Will I see you in a minute?" Eva knew she sounded as wheedling and pathetic as a small child, but fear had left her exhausted.

"A bit longer than that, but no more than half an hour. Now call those coppers!"

Chapter Seven

Two police constables arrived at Eva's house not long after she rang. They had, they said, been in the area anyway. Although they didn't put it into words, Eva knew they were dubious about her call. Nothing had been stolen, no doors or windows had been forced, and *was she certain she hadn't left the shampoo in the middle of the shower, and couldn't she have moved the vase herself and forgotten?* The camera flash, they assured her, must've been lightning.

"Call us if anything else happens," they told her. Eva nodded.

Just as she was showing them to the door, the noise of a car engine in the courtyard heralded the arrival of Lyndsey and Miles. Lyndsey trotted across the yard in her ballet flats, her arms outstretched to Eva as she stood in the door.

"Lovely, are you all right?" She caught Eva in a hug, then asked, "Will you find whoever's been in here?"

One of the constables, a young man with a square jaw and a no-nonsense buzzcut, smiled at Lyndsey. "We'll look into it, madam," he told her, and they headed off to their patrol car.

Eva hugged Lyndsey back. "I'm sure they don't believe me, and now I'm even doubting my sanity. Am I imagining things, Lyndsey?"

"You can come back with me tonight." Lyndsey put her arm around Eva's shoulders and steered her back into the house. "Thank God you weren't in! Did they break a window, or force the door? Have they left a terrible mess?"

Miles appeared, locking his car with one press of his key ring. He nodded hello to Eva, and Eva raised her hand in a small wave. It was awkward, but not as awkward as it could have been.

"No, I don't know how they got in." Eva rotated the door handle as if that would somehow issue an answer. "The only explanation, other than me losing the plot, is that they had a key. But that can't be it. They must've picked the lock."

"You'll want to change the locks, then," the ever-cautious Miles suggested. He was wearing a long-sleeved T-shirt, which was just like him. He'd wear it on a hot day with the sleeves rolled up, ready to roll down the moment there was a chill in the air.

"If Eva and I head back to mine, will you sort all of that out?" Lyndsey asked her new beau. "New locks and a chain and all of that sensible boyish stuff?"

"I'd be happy to." Miles ran his hand through his short, dark blond hair, his gaze fixed on Lyndsey's. With an effort, he glanced up at Eva. "I'll drop the new key over to Lynd's for you. We used a lock-fitting company at work recently, I've still got their number, so I'll give them a bell. Don't worry, girls, I've got this in hand."

So efficient, so helpful. Regret stabbed at Eva that she couldn't find a man like him attractive, but was drawn instead to someone as impossible as Daniel.

"That's so kind of you, thanks. I really appreciate it."

"Pack up a bag and you can drive us back to my place," Lyndsey instructed. "Leave the man's work to the man, whilst we girls demolish a bottle of Prosecco and have a good old chinwag?"

"Thanks, Lyndsey, you're such a good friend."

"The sister I never had." She grinned, squeezing Eva's shoulder. "Now go and get your bits together. Prosecco awaits!"

Chapter Eight

Miles phoned to tell them that the locksmiths were still at Eva's house. It was nine o'clock at night, and tears of gratitude rose in Eva's eyes at the effort that people were making to ensure she was safe.

Eva tucked her feet up under her as she and Lyndsey poured another prosecco. Snuggled in a pair of pale pink pyjamas covered with a collage of smiling teddy bears, Lyndsey had settled for the night as easily as a girl having a sleepover. She took a sip from her glass and asked, "Now, I've deliberately not asked for a bit but…what happened with Mr Sunglasses?"

"I don't know how much I can say, really…" Eva shook her head. "His childhood must've been unbelievably bleak, and it's left a horrible scar. Not a visible one, but… Well, it's obvious from all those paintings of his, isn't it?"

"So you've split? Properly?" She pouted. "Before my double date?"

"I wouldn't say split, exactly. We'd never really been *a thing* to split." As Eva spoke, she was washed with a sense of loss for something that could have been. "And no, to be quite honest, you wouldn't want to him on a double date. He can't go out in public without all that rude nonsense. It's messing him up, it's like he keeps forgetting who he is. Does that sound weird?"

"Massively so," her friend admitted with a comical grimace. "Is he on something? Or just a bit mad? Artists can be a bit mad sometimes, you know."

Mad enough to think they'd been broken into when they had just moved their own shampoo?

But Lyndsey wouldn't mean that, Eva knew.

"I shouldn't say this, really, but it'll hardly come as a surprise." Eva sighed. "He does coke. Somewhere in Columbia there's an entire hillside dedicated to churning out the stuff just for his personal use."

"Don't they all?" Lyndsey frowned. "I just think it's a shame, because you seemed so happy when I saw you the other day. He probably won't make old bones, that one, but what a legacy to leave behind."

"I hate myself for walking away from him, but I just didn't know what to do. He really scared me. All this business about—" Eva put her glass down on the table. "He blames himself for what happened to his family. It's a child's logic and he can't see around it."

"Go on, tell me." Her eyes grew wide. "He doesn't *have* a family, does he? All that secretive stuff about being in care, did he tell you more than that?"

Eva clasped her hands in her lap. The burden of what she knew weighed heavily. She needed to speak to someone, and Lyndsey was surely one of the only people she could trust. "You must promise, you must swear to me on your mother's life, that you won't repeat this to *anyone*. If the media found out... It could destroy him, Lyndsey, and he's already so fragile."

"I swear on my dear old nutty mum!" She pressed her hand to her breast. "And I can keep a secret."

Eva snuggled against her friend, resting her head on Lyndsey's shoulder. "He told me that his mother committed suicide."

"Poor lamb! Is that why they put him in care?" Lyndsey hugged her with one arm. "I think we all just assumed he had no parents from the off!"

"He said he was such a bad child, such a naughty child, *rotten*, he said, that his mother took her own life. So I assume that was why he was in care, because there was no one left to look after him, but the way he described it, it sounded like more than that. As if" — Eva sat up again, and drummed her fingertips on her thigh. She knew it sounded melodramatic, and she wondered what on earth Lyndsey would make of it — "as if he'd been put away. I don't know, in an asylum, or a prison."

"Oh my God, how awful!" Lyndsey shuddered theatrically. "But some of those homes were the worst, weren't they? All those scary nuns and what have you! It was probably just some hellhole place. You don't go to prison because your mum tops herself!"

"There's certainly horror stories around about what went on." Eva felt nauseated. She really shouldn't have left him, but what could she have done? He hadn't wanted her there a moment longer, hadn't wanted her to help him. She would've made everything worse just staying there. "I have no idea if he really was *bad*, or if he blames himself in that way children do. If she was struggling emotionally, a child could do anything and it would set her off crying. It's not a huge leap for a child to go from that to *I made my mother kill herself.*"

"No wonder he's a bit of a loon then," Lyndsey decided. "Do you think — might *he* do something to himself? It might be bad blood."

Bad blood… Tops herself… Eva was relieved that Lyndsey had gone into arts management rather than counselling.

"I hope not. I should ring him, really, and see how he is, but the thought went out of my mind with all that business at home." Eva let the bubbles in her prosecco burst on her tongue before she swallowed. "I can try, can't I? And if he doesn't want to speak to me, he doesn't have to answer. I'll feel like shit, to be fair, but I'll have tried. And I *am* worried about him."

"Are you still bringing your little monsters to the gallery? Rupe'll be rubbing his hands!" She sniffed, then shook her head. "But action plan, sis I never had. What to do if Sunglasses doesn't answer? He might be sleeping it off. Maybe leave it for the morning?"

"You're probably right. In fact, I should probably leave it until midday, because he's going to have one hell of a headache when he wakes up!" Eva was almost able to smile. "Do you have his agent's number, or his manager's, or someone like that? His people, whoever they are? I might have a word with them, just in case. They must know what he's like."

"Here's an idea. Why don't you not ring him at all, let him stew, and I'll ring his people tomorrow?" That was why she needed Lyndsey in her life, Eva was reminded. The voice of excitable common sense. "And when it's all calmed down in a few weeks, you can just give him a friendly little call and say hello?"

"Yes, that sounds like a plan." Eva grinned now. "I'm so tempted to just delete his number off my phone, in case I have one glass too many one night and do one of those horrible ugly-cry phone calls. How embarrassing would that be?"

"Why would you make a call like that?" Lyndsey frowned, as though she couldn't wrap her head around the concept. "Do people really do those? It's like people who get drunk and embarrass themselves, or like Mr Scott, I suppose. Drugs are for losers, as I've *always* said."

Eva laughed. "Are you seriously telling me that you never get upset? What if Miles scooted off with another woman, wouldn't you get drunk and ring him up and cry down the phone and tell him he's a horrible bastard? Would you *really* never do that?"

"Would I humiliate myself?" She grimaced. "*Never.* I'd find other ways to make his life miserable, but I wouldn't make myself look pathetic in the process. Even unicorns have nasty sharp horns, lovely!"

"How would you deal with it, then?" Eva hugged one of the cushions to her chest, laughing at the thought of what Lyndsey would do in the name of vengeance. "Are you a prawns-in-the-curtain-lining sort, then?"

"Trust me, you don't *want* to know." Lyndsey laughed. "Let's have a cupcake!"

Chapter Nine

Eva ticked off her list. "So we're okay for squash and biscuits for the kids, and if the weather's nice, we can go out on the terrace for some hands-on. As long as there's plastic down, we shouldn't make a mess."

Rupert winced and leaned back in his seat, knitting his hands on the desk in front of him. "I suppose you need a prayer room? One-legged single parent transsexual on hand? Someone with a skinny dog on a string to make them feel at home as well?"

Eva slapped her notebook down on the desk. She hadn't slept very well, because the thought that whoever had been in her house had got back in competed in her mind with an image of Daniel, wild-eyed and tragic. "What the hell is wrong with you, Rupert? I thought your grants depended on community work, and here you are sneering about it!"

"I *love* my community. My community is wonderful old dears and young families where Dad works in the city. My community *isn't* chav rats and council house scallies." He shrugged one shoulder. "And Daniel bloody Scott acts as though he's got me by the balls. Which he *has*, annoyingly, and tells me that your work is valuable, he was once a boy from the tenements and all this Dickensian guff! Children are trouble. They're messy and light-fingered, so you watch them!"

At least Daniel admired her work with the kids. That was something, even if she hadn't heard from him and wouldn't ever again. Talking the children through his paintings was not going to be easy, but Eva would do her best. She couldn't disappoint them by denying them their rare day out.

"Think of the local media. Haven't you got someone from the paper coming down to get some pics? The altruistic Rupert Hawley grinning with some paint-covered kids might make the second page."

"Well, that's true." He reached out to throw his gold-plated fountain pen onto the table. "On an entirely unrelated note, Lynds mentioned you'd had a break-in. Bad business for a girl on her own."

Eva rolled her eyes. "It's great fun being a woman. If you're not feeling threatened in your own home, there's always some chap just waiting to mansplain it for you. Thanks a lot, Rupert. Yes, it is a bad business for a woman on her own, but I'm not going to be scared into living in some sort of fortified women's-only commune."

"Bit of an overreaction!" He blinked. "I didn't hear anyone *mansplaining* anything, just a friendly fellow offering support to a girl in a spot of bother! I hope you're not going to start biting the heads off those little borstalites of yours."

"I'm not biting off anyone's head. It's just that I..." *Could* it have been Rupert? Eva met his steely gaze.

Would he have taken a photo through the window and somehow got inside her house, solely to mess with her head because she'd turned him down? "I don't really want to discuss it, but thank you for your concern."

"I'm only a short drive away in the Jag," Rupert told her smoothly. "If there's any more trouble, you give old Rupe a shout. It'll be no problem to dash over and sort it out. A knight in pinstripes aiding his swooning damsel and asking nought but a kiss!"

Eva raised an eyebrow. Did he not understand the word *no*? "I'll pass on that, thanks all the same. Erm... So... I think we've covered everything for the visit, haven't we?"

"Pass the kiss, go straight to go and collect two hundred pounds!" He narrowed his eyes and swept his gaze over her. "Or collect something even tastier. I shall see you and your chavs anon. Remember, though, be a good girl and keep their sticky fingers off the paintings!"

Eva held up her hand. "Rupert, you need to stop this. It's so unprofessional for you to talk to me like that."

"You can't reconstruct me, I'm afraid." He laughed, slapping his thigh. "I'm entirely unreconstructable. What's wrong with some old-fashioned chivalry?"

"I don't remember Sir Lancelot being a perv, Rupert." Eva picked up her notebook and went to the door. "Goodbye!"

"Cheerio!" he called. "Culture Minister's up for lunch to discuss my community work. I'll mention you and your chavs!"

Eva didn't comment as she couldn't trust herself to be polite. She went along the corridor, fanning herself with the notepad, only now realising that she'd managed to stand in Rupert's office and not think about what had gone on there between herself and Daniel.

But now that it was in her mind, she was aware of a blush rising to her face, and every abandoned moment with him came back to her. Those thoughts would have to rest, though, would have to be scrubbed away, because Eva needed to speak to Lyndsey before she headed home.

She knocked on the door of Lyndsey's office and from within heard the friendly, "Hello! Come in!"

Eva was relieved to see her friend again. She hurried round behind Lyndsey's desk to give her a hug. "We're all set for the kids coming tomorrow!"

"How fantastic! Squash and buns at the ready, Captain Catesby!" Lyndsey gave a Brownie salute. "Have you given Rupe a list of what you need? I'll make sure it's all done and ready."

"Yes, it's all here. You may as well have this, actually." Eva tore the top sheet from her notepad and passed it to Lyndsey. Her friend glanced down at it with a nod and put it atop her keyboard.

"Consider it done."

"Great." Eva should really leave, but she was hovering, wanting to ask but not wanting to know the answer. "Did you — you know, ring up Daniel Scott's... y'know...?"

"I did indeed. I was tactful, I said he'd been taken unwell and someone should look in on him." She held out a paper bag of chocolates. "And they didn't seem at all surprised."

"Hardly comes as a shock, does it?" Eva spiralled a length of hair around her finger, as if she was a little girl again, then took one of the chocolates. "Erm...and *have* they been to see him? Has anyone even heard from him?"

"I haven't heard back and, to be honest, I don't expect to." Lyndsey shrugged and popped a chocolate into her mouth. "They'll get him back up to speed, marbles all regained, and off he'll go until the next time. Poor lamb."

"It's as if he doesn't want any help." Eva bit into the chocolate. It was so light that it disappeared in seconds. "I said I'd call an ambulance, that I'd get him to hospital somehow, and do you know what he said? He didn't want it getting in the media again!"

"He's never been in the media for anything other than making tons of money and hanging about with obnoxious rockers and airhead—" She pressed her hand to her mouth. "Well, you know. *Enfant terrible* and what have you. In the media *again*?"

"I haven't followed his every move, so I really wouldn't know." Eva wafted her notepad back and forth in the warm air. She didn't want to know about his *airhead* anything. He'd been with so many women before, but had any of them tried to help him?

"Well, I don't mind admitting that I had a good old Google when I found out about him coming to Brighton." She took another chocolate. "Give him some space then send him a little message. I *still* want my double date!"

"Oh, Lyndsey!" Eva laughed. "It's not going to happen. A double date or even…or even he and I even speaking to each other. It's over, and it was fun, and in the end it was awful, and I have to move on."

Chapter Ten

Like a cheesecloth-clad incarnation of the Pied Piper, Eva led her outreach kids into the Hawley gallery. The large automatic doors glided open and she and her group left the warm summer's day for Rupert's state-of-the-art air conditioning. Eva rounded them up in the foyer and a hush tried to descend over them. The surly children at least were quiet, but the excitable ones, the motormouths who couldn't keep still, fidgeted as Eva addressed them.

"So, we're really lucky today! The artist whose exhibition is on here at the moment has made a special arrangement with the gallery owner so that we can visit. At the end, we'll write some thank you notes to him." Eva would be surprised if she managed to get thank you notes from half of them, but it was the thought that counted, after all. "And as I explained before, we can look at the paintings, but we have to stand *this* far away," she held her hands a metre apart, "and we mustn't touch them. Right. Are we ready?"

"Or would we rather," a familiar voice suddenly called, "get as close as we possibly can and feel the paint under our hands? Let's not just look at them, let's live them. Get our jammy hands on the canvas and make it all a bit less *sensible*."

Him.

The man she had given up.

Eva turned towards the door into the gallery space and there he was, clad in his black suit and his black shirt, sunglasses over his eyes. Her breath caught in her throat as all Eva's desire for Daniel returned, heating her blood. But she had to ignore it.

Before she was able to form a coherent response, one of the children shouted, "Oi, mister, you've forgotten your sunglasses!" And all the other children laughed.

"Jayden, don't be rude!" Eva couldn't interpret the expression on Daniel's face. Had he changed since their last encounter, or was he still on the verge of rage? The last thing she needed was for Daniel to erupt in front of the children. Some of them saw enough of that at home. "Sorry…he's only pulling your leg. Bit of a joker."

"What's your name?" Daniel asked Jayden, his voice calm. Was it the prelude to a storm?

"Jayden," the boy replied, scuffing his dusty trainer across Rupert's expensive carpet.

"Well, Jayden, when *you're* nearly forty, you'll totally get why I'm wearing sunglasses. I'm trying and failing to look younger than I am." Daniel pushed the Wayfarers up into his hair. "Mind if I trail along?"

The red, bulging eyes that Eva had seen a few days earlier were gone. There was still that intensity there, but softened somehow. Eva could hope that he had changed, that he wasn't on the coke today, that the monster was contained. "No, I don't mind at all. Seeing as you—"

She waited by the door and waved the children through into the exhibition space. Three of them whooped loudly as if they were on a roller coaster.

Eva rested her hand on Daniel's arm. "I'm asking this as a friend. Are you okay now? I mean…you look better. I've been worried."

"Can we talk afterwards?" His voice was gentle, his gaze meeting hers. "I know you might not want to—"

"I'd like that. I really would." Eva stroked her hand down to his wrist. "I wish I hadn't left you like that. I'm so sorry, I—"

Maya, one of the group, tugged Eva's sleeve, half-dragging her away in her excitement. "Miss, Miss, look at the paintings, look! They're so big! Look, Miss!"

Eva glanced at Daniel.

"Are you going to introduce me to our guests?" he asked, then added with a mischievous look, "Miss?"

Maya was now towing Eva with all her might, and Eva laughed. "Come along then, Daniel, you can join our group! Maya, you don't mind, do you?"

"No, Miss, no, I don't mind. Miss, look at the paintings!"

The last time the gallery had been packed with people, it had been filled with grown adults who were seven sheets to the wind and who had barely seemed to care what was on the walls. Today, half of Eva's group were standing about looking up at the canvases, while the other half were doing laps around the room and trying out cartwheels.

"Do you want me to blow your cover, Daniel?"

"Yeah." He nodded. "Because I want them to ask me questions and tell me what they think."

"Right, then." She flashed Daniel a smile, then extricated herself from Maya and clapped her hands. The children almost stopped and paid attention. "I told you we were very lucky today, didn't I? Because not only have we been allowed to see the exhibition, but who do you think has come to talk to you today?"

A hand shot up at once and Eva nodded. "Yes, Jake?"

"Your boyfriend, Miss!"

The children laughed and Eva wished she was standing on a trapdoor which at that moment would open beneath her feet. "Well, today, we have Daniel Scott with us. And do you recognise his name?"

Another hand shot up. "Kieran?" Eva asked.

"He's the painter, Miss."

"That's right!" Eva's children failed to look starstruck. They appeared to have never heard of him, until seeing his name on the front of the building ten minutes ago. "So...everyone, this is Daniel Scott."

Daniel took the sunglasses from his head and folded them into his pocket. He seemed far more at ease here than he had been with the great and good at the launch, no posturing or silent brooding in the face of the children who found him so underwhelming.

"In a minute, I need to try and get all your names straight," Daniel told them. "Then we'll have a look around and you can tell me about the art you do and I'll tell you about mine, and we'll see if we can learn from each other. Ask whatever you want to ask, touch the paintings if you want to, and if you just don't like them, I'll live with it. But Eva — *Miss Catesby's* put a lot of work into getting you this visit, so make the most of it. Deal?"

The children nodded, but Kieran, Eva noticed, didn't move. He only stared at Daniel, rigid. From experience, Eva knew this wasn't a good sign, as Kieran was apt to have meltdowns and the prelude was usually blank stiffness. She put one hand on his shoulder but he didn't respond.

Maya stood in front of Daniel, toes nearly touching, her head tipped back as if trying to see to the top of a tall building. "Why are your paintings so big?" she asked the man who never gave interviews.

"I don't talk all that much," he replied, looking down at her. Then he dropped down to his knees, reducing that seemingly unbreachable distance between them to nothing. "But when I work on a big canvas like this, I feel like the whole world can hear me shouting. Does that make sense?"

Maya frowned, as if she was thinking, then her mouth fell open and she nodded. "Big is the same as loud!"

Kieran shifted under Eva's hand, so she stood aside and left him be.

"It is for me." Daniel nodded. "When I was a kid nobody ever listened to me, no matter how loud I shouted. They didn't start listening when I kicked off either, but when I painted, suddenly they did."

A nod ran through the children like a Mexican wave, and Eva smiled at Daniel. He was the perfect person to speak to her kids.

"I'm not standing—kneeling—here as someone who had it all, because I had nothing. Never passed an exam, kicked out of school, never went to uni," he went on. "I didn't even have a mum and dad, didn't have a home, none of that. I didn't have a Miss Catesby either. It doesn't mean that's the end of it. Things aren't always great, but never think that's it. Never think at your ages that you're done. You're *never* done."

Daniel's words managed to reach all the children. The ones who had been excluded from school, the ones whose families were chaotic at best, or nonexistent. The ones who the police had already had stern words with. They drew nearer to Daniel, a step at a time. But Kieran hadn't moved.

Jayden put up his hand. "Mister, what was your first painting of?"

"Call me Daniel," was the reply. "It was a painting of Brighton pier, done from a memory from when I was little. Not great, but not bad. I put a stormy sky above it and whipped the waves up high. The more stormy I made it, the better it made me feel."

At last, Kieran nodded. But whether that was a good sign or not, Eva couldn't tell.

"What's your favouritist painting in all the world?" a girl called Sam asked.

"It's the pier again." Daniel smiled, his expression warm. "No storm this time, but a perfect blue sky and waves that you just want to dive into, and there among them, mermaids. I've seen the sketches and studies and I can't wait to see the finished painting. It's actually by Miss Catesby. I hope she won't mind me telling you about it."

A dozen little faces turned to meet her, and Eva realised where her sketchbook was. She had left it in Daniel's palace.

"That's very kind of you, Daniel, but...it's only a scribble!"

"It's not a scribble," he confided to his new friends in a stage whisper. "Throw me those questions. Anything you want to know, that's why I'm here!"

"Do you like dogs?" Clara asked.

"Love dogs." Daniel laughed. "And now I'm settled in Brighton I hope to get at least a couple of rescue pups. Maybe I'll teach them to paint!"

"What's your favourite colour?" Wai asked.

"Royal blue, like my car."

The inevitable question to follow this, from Angel, was, "What's your favourite car?"

Eva decided not to step in and demand that all their questions be about art. It was enough that the children, who were usually ignored or told to shut up, felt able to speak to an adult who was important but unknown to them. Seeing how natural Daniel was with them, how patient and how interested in them, Eva hoped that somewhere beyond his anger and the drugs, there would be peace for him.

"This one!" He took out his phone, tapped the screen a few times and held it up to display a photo of a sleek royal-blue sports car, chrome gleaming in the sunshine and a white stripe bisecting the long, low bonnet. "My AC Cobra. It's outside, so if anyone's into cars, I'll show you when we're done."

Eva wasn't sure that the liability insurance ran to sports cars, but several of the children were murmuring with interest.

"How do you choose what to paint?" Jake asked. "Have you done a painting of your car?"

As Jake only ever painted cars, his question didn't come as a surprise.

"I don't really choose," Daniel told him. "It's more I get a feeling that tells me, *paint this*. Just now when I was waiting for you guys I was standing outside and, just for the hell of it, I did a quick sketch of the car for the first time. I'm doing some experimenting at the moment, drawing things around me a bit more, things I can see and touch."

Eva caught his glance and smiled.

"Can we see? Can we see?" The children's voices united in a chorus. Never mind that they were the envy of many with their private view and Q and A, they wanted to see Daniel's sketch of a car.

All except Kieran, who had taken himself off to look at the paintings. He paused before each one, tracing the paths of the paint over the canvas with his finger.

Daniel took a small spiral pad from his pocket and handed it to Jake.

"Pass it round, have a look through," he told them. "There's the car and some beach sketches, that kind of thing. Pretty rough, but it's all part of creating art."

The children gathered around Jake, who stood in their midst like a king presiding over the sketchbook. Eva approached, ready to supervise, but she kept a cautious eye on Kieran. If he had an *event* now, he might put his fist through a priceless artwork.

Daniel rose from his knees and strolled across to stand beside Kieran. For a long time he was silent, then he asked, "How would you do it differently?"

Kieran shrugged but went on stroking the textured paint. Then he chipped a piece off with his fingernail. "I'd do that."

The world went into slow motion. Eva couldn't believe what she'd just witnessed, and was waiting for Rupert to appear with security guards to hurl the lot of them out.

"Why that piece, though?" Daniel pressed his own fingernail into a corner, leaving a crescent impression in the canvas. "Why not there? What does it do to the painting for you?"

Kieran lowered his chin to his chest. "Dunno. It's just better."

Instinct.

"Do you paint?"

Kieran nodded. "In Miss Catesby's classes."

"What kind of thing do you do?"

"Stuff," he replied. "Miss Catesby shows us pictures and we just sort of paint."

"Works for me," Daniel told him. Then he turned back to the group, watching them leaf through the pages of the book.

Eva tapped Daniel's shoulder. She'd meant it platonically but it was impossible to forget what had happened between them.

"We're doing some hands-on outside on the terrace. Do you want to join in?" She smiled at Kieran. "Do you want to come outside as well?"

Eva didn't want to leave Kieran to his own devices with the paintings, but he seemed fascinated by them. "You can come back and see them again before the exhibition ends."

"Come and fling some paint around?" Daniel offered, accepting the sketchbook back from Jake. "These aren't going anywhere."

"Yeah, all right!" Kieran smiled at this, and, out of his vision, Eva gestured to Daniel the universal sign for *phew!*

Eva shepherded the children outside. As ever, some of them got stuck in straight away and were already crayoning and sticking, whereas others were distracted, and the sea view caused a sensation. Why that should be when most of the children had been born on the coast, Eva couldn't understand, but perhaps it was because they were seeing it from a new angle.

Daniel paused beside her, his hands in his pockets as he watched the children. He turned to Eva and whispered, "Tell me you painted that pier and the mermaids? It's not just a few studies?"

It was odd, being out here with Daniel again in such different circumstances. All that lust. And standing here with him now, Eva had to convince herself that she didn't feel it anymore.

Even though she did.

"I started it, but I never got round to doing much more than a pencil outline," Eva replied. "Why do you like it so much?"

"Because I want to believe this place is magical." He looked out to sea. "How much would you want if I were to commission it from you?"

Eva spluttered with laughter. "You are joking, aren't you? You want to commission my bosomy mermaids?"

"It's not a joke." Daniel turned his attention to her again and smiled. "Name your price. I want it hanging in my house."

Eva ran her hand through her hair, self-conscious in his presence. She hadn't a clue how much her work was worth, or how much she should charge a man who had once been her lover. "Erm…a hundred?"

"Let's talk size and money later? When you're ready to make a deal and name a serious price." He chuckled and strolled away to join the children in the midst of their artistic chaos.

Eva followed, just in time to stop Maya from painting her own face.

"But they do it on the beach!" the child protested.

"We're not on the beach," Eva reminded her.

It was just as well Rupert and Lyndsey had remembered her instruction to put several yards of plastic sheeting out on the terrace, as a pot of glue and several painty brushes had already fallen off the table. Eva crawled about trying to tidy up, and from under the table she could see Daniel's progress as he went round the table from child to child. Or, at least, the progress of his legs.

She thought suddenly of those paint-splattered feet of his, of the shared intensity of his work and their sex and how she would never see any of that again.

But they weren't enemies, and that was something at least.

Eva could hear Daniel fielding more questions, everything from cars to collage, and answering each with the same patience and enthusiasm as the last. The man who had nothing and now had it all.

Eva came out from under the table and found herself at Daniel's feet. "Enjoying yourself?" she asked him as she got up.

"Having a great time," he told her, busy sellotaping several large sheets of paper together to form one big surface. "And about to give a demo of action painting. You're teaching them well!"

"Big is the same as loud!" Eva laughed. "Go on, they'll love it."

"Will you hold my jacket? Careful of the Wayfarers." He winked and slipped out of his black jacket, holding it out to Eva. She draped it over her arm.

"Your sunglasses are safe with me, Mr Scott."

"Call me Daniel," he replied playfully. Then he rolled up his sleeve and spread the taped paper out on the plastic covering. As he went to work, flinging paint with abandon, she was reminded of that last afternoon when she had found him in his studio, a man possessed and out of control. Now he was anything but, his movements just as free, but without the edge of desperation. There was a joy in it instead, almost a dance here beneath the cloudless summer sky.

What had happened after she'd left him? Had the ambulance come? Had someone calmed him?

One by one the children stopped what they were doing to watch Daniel, some giggling, others cheering him on. Kieran watched in silence.

"We don't have to paint pictures," Daniel told them as he threw down the colours. "It's about making your mark on the paper, however you *choose* to do it. Art doesn't have to follow the rules. Who wants to try?"

"Me, me, me!" the children shouted.

Eva touched Keiran's shoulder and whispered. "Have a go, Keiran, show Daniel Scott what you can do!"

Keiran didn't say a word. He nodded to Eva, then raised his hand.

"There's time and paper for everyone," Daniel told them. Then he spotted Kieran and raised his eyebrows, nodding the boy forward. "Come on up, Keiran, fling some paint for us."

Keiran, one of the oldest of the group, had developed the awkward, surly shuffle of a teenager. He came forward, stooping, his uncut hair in his face as if it were a disguise. He'd been labelled as *difficult* and *challenging*, descriptions which had equally been used to describe Daniel's art.

"Can I use my hand?" Keiran crouched down by the paint and swirled his finger in it.

"Definitely!" Daniel enthused. "You're the artist, follow your instincts."

Keiran grinned up at Daniel. A grin, from Keiran? Eva had never seen one before. The boy sank his hand into the bright blue paint – not just coating himself in it, but it seemed that he was feeling the texture of the paint as well. Then he jumped up to his feet and flung a handful of paint across the paper. He laughed at the blue spatter then got on his knees – Eva hoped the paint would wash out easily – and crawled across the paper, smearing the paint this way and that with his hand.

Daniel's gaze was fixed on him, utterly transfixed as he watched the boy work. When Eva saw the change in his face this time it wasn't a veil of darkness descending, but one of inspiration. There was no careful planning in any of it, just his precious instinct.

Keiran next plunged his hand into the red, but something flashed in his eyes and instead of throwing paint with his hand, he picked up the tin and hurled its entire contents at the paper. It splurged across a blank corner of the paper, and Keiran was back on his knees again, completely involved in his task as if no one was watching. He homed in on a spot where the blue and the red had met and he swirled patterns in it, creating purples where they hadn't existed before.

"Can you help the others get some paper together so they can start?" Daniel whispered to Eva, still watching Kieran. "I don't want to stop him."

"Nor do I!" Eva replied. "Okay, kids, we'll all make our own big sheets of paper and we can join in!"

The children cheered and set to work taping together sheets of paper with an industry that surprised her. They helped one another, some tearing the sellotape while the others held the paper flat. With so many large sheets, it was impossible to stay on the plastic cover protecting Rupert's sainted terrace. Eva ignored the spills. She'd get a mop out herself if she had to, and it would probably all dissolve when it rained anyway.

"Do what you need to do," Daniel told the others as they laid out the paper. "And don't worry about splashing paint on your clothes. If anything gets spoiled, I'll make sure it's replaced. Get creating!"

Daniel Scott had unleashed mayhem, and Eva loved it. She joined in, taking off her shoes and smearing her feet in paint, then walking backwards and forwards across the paper, making shapes with her toes. The paint squidged like wet sand under her feet and she hadn't a clue what the shapes and colours on the paper represented, other than joy.

Even the quietest children took part, crouching on the edge of the paper and doodling with their fingers, some braving themselves to use their whole palms. The loudest flung themselves in with glee and covered themselves and the paper and Rupert's terrace with broad rainbows of paint.

Daniel wasn't watching anymore but working. He stood back from the table with a thick wedge of paper in one hand, the pencil he held in the other moving back and forth across the page. His gaze flickered from the scene to the drawing, and across the bottom of his black trousers, a rainbow of coloured paint shimmered where he had been caught in the crossfire.

Jake and Maya grabbed Eva's hands and made her walk about with her painty feet on their paper, but Daniel fascinated her as he worked and she looked over her shoulder at him. The intensity was still there, but there was no anger on the surface now, all his energy focused on his work.

"Eva. Miss Catesby." Daniel glanced up from the page and gestured to her. "When you've got a minute, can I borrow you? No rush at all."

"Of course, as long as we don't leave the terrace, though." She linked Jake's and Maya's hands and crossed the patchwork of paper and plastic sheeting to Daniel. Shielding her face from the bright sunlight, Eva smiled at him. "And what can I do for you, Mr Scott?"

"I've drawn a picture." He pressed the drawing secretively to his breast. Then he smiled, as bright as the sun above. "And it's given me a crazy sort of idea. So I need to run it past someone with some common sense."

"Are you sure you've chosen the right person to ask?" Eva waggled her paint-covered toes at him. She didn't mind being silly. They weren't lovers anymore, and the playful side of him that she now saw didn't deserve to be met with seriousness.

"Hmm." Daniel narrowed his eyes and looked down at her foot. "Now you put it like that, I'm not sure there's much common sense in that foot of yours."

"I'd say very little at all!" Eva glanced at the paper. "But...go on, I'm curious."

"I'm learning to draw from life." He shifted the page just a little, though not enough to show her what was on the surface. "So I drew all of you as you were painting. It's rough and ready but...no sharp edges." With that, he passed the paper across to her. "Be kind?"

Daniel had captured in pencil the energy and mayhem of the painting class, and indeed, there weren't any pointy limbs. It was from life, but with the spirit of the afternoon in every line.

"I love it!" Eva told him. When she thought of how upset he'd got himself when he'd tried to draw her, tears rose in her eyes, but she brushed them away. "Have I got paint on my face now?"

"Only a little bit." He pressed the pad of his thumb to her cheek and brushed it gently. When he withdrew his hand, she glimpsed a smear of red paint on his skin. "So, this outreach you do. Who funds you? Are you council or charity or—?"

"A mixture of things... We get some money from the council, some from grants that I have to go and look for and apply for, and fight other people to get. We had a very kind local artist who left us a legacy in her will... People donate money from time to time." Discussing money made Eva feel uncomfortable, but he'd asked, after all. "We use a subsidised room in a community centre, and I hustle a bit to get art supplies cheaper... It's difficult. I should really have been networking with the other artists at your show, but they can see me coming and I can see they're thinking, *Here comes Eva with her begging bowl*. I know by now who's receptive, and they chuck the odd bit of money at me if I ask nicely!"

Daniel nodded thoughtfully. "So if I stick my sig on this and send it to auction, I could give the money raised to you guys and that'd help? I just want to say sorry...sorry for— You know why. And what you're doing... I never had anything like this, and it's important to these kids."

Eva's tears overflowed and skidded down her cheeks. If he'd offered her a cheque, she wasn't sure she could have accepted, though she couldn't explain why. "That's such a wonderful idea, Daniel. I don't know what to say, really. Other than *thank you*. Sorry, I'm blubbing everywhere. I'm happy, really."

"Don't cry." He put his arm around her shoulder and gave a platonic squeeze. "I'll ask my agent to get things going, whip up the interest so we make you a few quid."

Heat went through Eva at his embrace, and she tried very hard not to think about it. "It'd be a really nice advert for the group as well. Might make it easier when I have to get my begging bowl out!" Although she might not need to for a while if Daniel's sketch attracted even a tenth of what his work usually fetched. "I might be able to take on more kids—if I had an assistant— there's only so many children I'm allowed to take at once, you see. I could pay a student from the School of Art. And, oh, imagine if one day we had our own premises, and an exhibition space to show the children's work, and we could have a pottery kiln, and what if we could do dancing and drama and music as well? And... Sorry, I'm getting a bit ahead of myself, aren't I!"

"It does no harm to dream." Daniel smiled. "And I didn't make you pointy this time. I made you soft."

He remembered how I felt.

The heat redoubled and Eva fanned herself with her hand. "Sorry... It's a very warm day, isn't it? Maybe it's time to get the juice and biscuits for the kids. Would you like juice and biscuits, too? I think the bar's closed, unfortunately!"

"Give them a few more minutes. Let them be in another world for a bit longer?"

"They do look busy, don't they!" The children were showing no sign of getting bored, and no surface seemed to have escaped the messy splatter of the paint. "I didn't expect to see you. It's a nice surprise."

"I only intended to return your sketchbook, but—" He shrugged and ruffled his hand back through his hair. Then he looked up at the blue sky and blazing sun and reached into his pocket for his sunglasses. "Do you want to borrow these while I find your juice?"

"You were too tempted at the thought of flinging paint around. Daniel Scott couldn't resist!" Eva winked at him. "Actually, I wouldn't mind borrowing your famous sunspecs, if you wouldn't mind."

In a pantomime of ceremony, Daniel unfolded the arms of the Wayfarers and positioned the sunglasses just so on her nose. Then he handed her the drawing and said, "I'll be back. Don't go anywhere."

Eva took the picture and was about to respond, by instinct, with a kiss on his cheek. She stopped herself, but not soon enough to prevent her lips from brushing the air an inch from his face. "I...erm... I'll stay here, don't you worry!"

Daniel left her with a smile, standing out there on the terrace amid the chaos, those much-photographed Wayfarers shielding her eyes just as they had shielded his on so many occasions. The drawing she held would make such a change not only to these children, but to the others who would follow them. Whatever she and Daniel had lost—had never really *had*—it didn't change *this*. It didn't change the fact that out of the mess and the misery and the lost chances, something good was going to be made.

Some of the children came up to Eva, keen to show her their pictures. They were so proud of their bright, chaotic daubs, and Eva congratulated them all.

In a conspiratorial whisper, she told the children, "You've all done really well today, and hasn't Daniel been great? So when he comes back outside, hold up your paintings and we'll all shout *thank you* to him."

It was a couple of minutes before they had a chance to put the plan into action, as Daniel could be glimpsed through the enormous windows, strolling back along the gallery hallway. She could see the bright paint on his black clothes, the expression of peace on his face as he looked out at the sea. Then he pushed open the door and stepped out onto the terrace.

"Thank you, Daniel!" The shout was so loud that it even startled the noisy seagulls, who squawked and wheeled away over the sea.

Eva came forwards and gave Daniel a hug—a platonic one—and admired the view of dripping artwork that the children were holding up to show him. "Thank you!" she added, not quite so loudly.

"Thank you," he whispered into their hug. Then he stood back just a little, just enough to address the children and shouted, "Thank you, artists! You're all amazing!"

Daniel reached into his pocket and retrieved his mobile. "Everyone gather round Keiran's *massive* painting and hold your work up so we can see it. We need a photo to commemorate this amazing day!"

The children scrambled to get into position around Keiran, and Keiran was almost smiling in response. Eva shepherded the more nervous of them into the shot, and signalled to Daniel that they were ready. He fiddled with the phone screen and stood it up on one of the refreshment tables with the care of a man building a house of cards. Then he hurried across to the group and stood beside Eva, his hand brushing hers.

"Smile!" Daniel commanded brightly. "Three... two...one!"

The phone clicked to the countdown and a sound effect of a camera shutter signalled that the photograph had been taken.

The camera flash.

While the terrace was busy once more with energetic children who had struggled to keep still for the photo, Eva froze, blinking as if the camera flash had gone off through her window again. Unease took possession of her, and she tried to supervise the children, pushing away her discomfort and trepidation with effort.

Her locks had been changed. No one could get in unless she invited them. Whoever it was would give up and get bored. And if it *was* one of Daniel's obsessed fans, they wouldn't be bothering her anymore. Eva and Daniel were not, nor could they ever be, anything to each other now besides friends.

"Biccies!" Lyndsey emerged into the sunshine carrying a tray. On it were two large jugs of orange juice, whilst a carrier bag dangled from her wrist. Eva saw a momentary flash of panic in her friend's eyes at the state of the terrace before she was smiling again. At the table she began to unload the bag's contents, taking out plastic cups and packets of biscuits. "Nice shades, Eva!"

Eva lifted them from her nose and grinned. "Just call me the bad girl of the Brighton art world!" The children made a beeline for Lyndsey, and Eva plunged in. "Form a queue, that's it, there's plenty for everyone."

"I need to sign that," Daniel realised, gesturing to the drawing. "So we can raise a fiver or so at auction."

Eva showed it to her friend. "Lynds, look, quite different from Daniel's usual style. I bet even you would like this!"

"Oh my God, that's adorable!" She gave a little round of applause then whispered, "Bosomy you!"

"He's drawing from life." Eva passed the paper back to Daniel. It was true, the bosoms were quite something. "No need to embellish what nature bestowed so...erm... enthusiastically!"

"I'm an artist." Daniel's arrogant demeanour returned for Lyndsey's benefit, and he put the paper down and signed his name in the bottom right corner. "A slave to my instinct."

"Of course, Mr Scott." Lyndsey beamed, watching as he passed the drawing back. "And we're all so glad for it!"

Eva furled the drawing and popped it down the front of her dress. "It'll be safe, don't worry!" She gave Daniel a wink. "Orange squash? Seeing as you're driving..."

He frowned and said, "Can we make that the last joke about me getting wasted? I'm not going to spoil anyone's day, that's not why I'm here."

"I didn't mean that. I was only joking. About adults having to drink kids' stuff." Eva picked up a cup of juice for herself, and shivered as if the sun had gone in. It was all too clear that there wasn't any way to come back from what had happened.

"I happen to like juice." He patted her shoulder and picked up a cup before mingling amongst the children again, his attention focused on their pictures.

"Thanks for sorting this all out, Lynds." Eva watched him for a moment, then looked away. "And don't worry, I'll tidy up the mess! It's definitely been worth it. The kids have had a fab time."

"Rupe's going to go through the roof if they missed the plastic." Lyndsey cringed. "But we can unleash Mr Sunglasses on him! He can go feral!"

"Feral?" Eva lifted his sunglasses into her hair. "He'll arrange for a team of industrial cleaners, I imagine. Then send Rupert the bill!"

"Good luck!" Lyndsey laughed, taking a bite from a biscuit. "But a good time was had by all, and what's better than that?"

"Exactly."

The children were clamouring for Daniel. They'd always remember this afternoon. Eva nudged Lyndsey. "We should do it again!"

"With a million-pound-a-canvas artist on tap? We absolutely should!"

"I'm surprised Rupert didn't arrange for a photographer..."

"They didn't think it was big enough news. We didn't know Mr Scott was—" Lyndsey fell silent as Rupert practically flew into the terrace, a harried man carrying a large camera around his neck in tow. He looked at his previous terrace, his mouth gaping, then Lyndsey said, "Nick of time!"

"Can we get a little piccie for the press?" Rupert oozed sincerity, wringing his hands again. "Mr Scott, if you'd let me know you were coming, we would have been far better prepared!"

"We had paints and paper." Daniel shrugged, cool again in the face of Rupert's grovelling. As he spoke, Rupert wasn't looking at him, though, but at the paint-drenched Kieran. "That's all we needed."

"I'm actually not sure... We need permission from the parents and responsible adults before we start photographing children for the newspaper. Some of them" — Eva lowered her voice, while the children whooped and laughed behind her — "some of them are under the radar, if you know what I mean. They've moved here for their own safety, and we don't want a violent parent tracking anyone down from a photo they've seen wrapped around their chips."

"One of Mr Scott and me then?" Rupert decided. "The artist and his exhibitor?"

"Wouldn't it be wonderful to get Mr Scott and lovely Eva?" Lyndsey suggested, pouring out more juice. Rupert's eyes narrowed, his lips thinning at her next words. "The outreach angel and the bad boy?"

"I'm a bit too grubby to be an angel!" Eva laughed, but she took off the sunglasses and passed them back to Daniel. "And Daniel's not all *that* bad."

"Can I get you in front of your artwork?" The photographer gestured to Daniel, who put the sunglasses in his hair. He gestured the couple towards Kieran's painting. "It's really cool, by the way. I'd buy it if I had a spare mil!"

"You'd have to talk to the artist who painted it," Daniel replied, offering Kieran the hint of a smile. "It's not a Daniel Scott piece."

Kieran scraped his hair out of his eyes and grinned at Daniel.

Eva patted Kieran's shoulder, and the teenager blushed. "There you go, Kieran, I said you were talented!"

As Rupert looked on, his hands thrust into his pinstriped pockets, the photographer shot a few snaps of Eva and Daniel looking appropriately platonic. In front of the camera the sunglasses came down again, the smile one that exuded enigmatic cool, a far cry from his friendly demeanour with the children.

Once the photographer had finished, Eva convened the children to start tidying up. But their attention spans couldn't quite stretch to that, as she knew, and most of them, yelling at the tops of their voices, were running up and down the terrace, across the unprotected areas in their bare, paint-covered feet. She could feel Rupert's rage, but while the photographer was still there, she doubted it would erupt.

Because won't that make an amusing image for the front page?

Daniel went from child to child, saying his farewells and thanking them, reminding those who cared about such things to stop by his car as they left. When he reached Kieran he extended his hand and said, "You've inspired me today. Thank you."

Kieran took Daniel's hand and executed a several-part shake which ended in a high-five, and Daniel didn't miss a step. "No, I never. You were great! I had loads of fun. Thanks, Mr Scott."

"Eva," Rupert whispered her name. "We'll need this cleaning up before you head off, I hope you're not in a rush!"

"I'm sure your friend from the paper — " Eva caught his eye and gave him her smile that she used whenever she needed more paint for the children, "would consider a photo of your good self wielding a mop a photo-op not to be missed."

"I'm sure he would, but alas, that's not to be!" Rupert grinned, showing sharp white teeth. "But I'll make it up to you with dinner if you don't have plans."

"No, thanks, Rupert!" Eva replied briskly. She turned away from him, gathering the discarded plastic cups and dropping them into a bin bag. How clear did she have to be that she wasn't interested?

"A glass of something sparkly them?"

Daniel began picking up empty cups and biscuit wrappers too, throwing them into the bag. As he passed Rupert he told him, "I'd let it go, if I were you."

She saw realisation dawn in Rupert's eyes, realisation of something that would never be. Then she saw a flash of something else, annoyance or jealousy, and he said, "I need the paint gone too."

"Blame Banksy," Daniel muttered, turning his back on the gallery owner as he went on working.

The parents and grandparents, foster carers and older siblings of the children were beginning to arrive. Eva could see them through the glass panels of the gallery, peering through the door from the foyer. Daniel went out to greet them in his paint-spattered trousers, his sleeves still rolled to the elbows, jacket thrown over his arm and his sunglasses in his hair again. She saw tired faces become smiles as he moved among them, saw mobile phones go into pockets and knew that he was singing the praises of the children. At Kieran's mother he paused for longer, the conversation more involved, and before they parted he took out his phone and punched something into it, which she looked at with a smiling nod.

"Right, the children will be off our hands very soon, Rupert, never you worry," Eva assured him.

"Oh God, what now?" Rupert was looking into the foyer, where Daniel was gesturing to him. Without another word he hurried inside to meet his troublesome guest of honour.

"Poor old Rupe," Lyndsey pouted. "All he wanted was a date!"

Eva sighed. "Lyndsey, I just don't... He's so insistent and I really don't want to be pestered. I've said no more than once. I don't want to go on a date just to shut him up, because it'll only encourage him." Eva scraped at a lump of drying paint on the table. "He's a bit creepy, Lyndsey, don't you think? What if… He couldn't have got hold of those spare keys you've got for my house, could he?"

"Oh, Eva, how could — "

"Don't you worry about cleaning up!" Rupert was all benevolent smiles as he opened the door. "Wonderful news about the auction, I'm happy to give you a bit of foyer space. I'll see that this all gets tidied, and the next time you see these marvellous pictures those dear little kiddies have done, they'll be on display!"

Who was Rupert trying to please? The millionaire artist, the man from the press, or the woman who kept saying no? It didn't matter though. Rupert was, despite himself, helping the children in the outreach group, and Eva was grateful for that at least.

"Thank you, Rupert…" Eva smiled at him as she rounded up the children and delivered them to their parents. Several raised eyebrows met the paint-covered children, but whatever Daniel had been saying to them meant no one blew their stack at her. As well they might have done under any other circumstances. She was supposed to look after them while in her care, not induce anarchy and destroy the children's clothes.

"Lyndsey, could you point me towards the cleaning cupboard?" Eva glanced at the plastic sheeting. "It's mop time."

"Rupes just told you not to worry about cleaning." Lyndsey frowned. "So don't."

"Are you sure, Rupert? That's very kind. I thought you—" *Were bloody furious about the mess?* Something had been said, that was for sure. "Well, that is good news. Thanks!"

"I'm just going to get some more snaps," he told her smoothly. "Leave the mess to Lyndsey, she's going to call someone. Lyndsey, I'll speak to you about it when I'm done with the photographer, until then stand down."

With that he was gone, leaving Lyndsey to shrug. "I wonder what Sunglasses said."

Eva was balanced on one foot, to put her shoes back on. The paint had dried and her shoes were old, and she certainly didn't look elegant, but she didn't care. "I have a vague idea... Daniel wants to auction his drawing for outreach! The money'll make such a difference, and I wouldn't be surprised if he's convinced Rupert to hold the auction here, in return for not nagging about the mess."

"We could go for our double date afterwards!" Lyndsey hugged herself at the thought of it. "Miles and I finally get to sit down with Daniel Scott, face to face!"

"I wouldn't get your hopes up, Lyndsey. I *think* he and I might be friends, but..." Eva shook her head as she picked up her bag. "He's really engaged with outreach, and that's brilliant, but don't mistake his enthusiasm for anything else."

From somewhere nearby, a sports car engine growled into life, as though a fighter plane was taking off somewhere. It was a throaty roar, and Eva knew instinctively it was Daniel's car. Was he leaving without—

"He didn't say bye," Lyndsey tutted. "That's a bit rude!"

Eva swallowed down her disappointment. He'd wanted to talk to her about something, but now she'd never know what. "Like I said, there won't be a double date. Or any other kind of date for that matter."

Her phone beeped an incoming message. Rupert, probably, begging for another date. Or telling her to clean up after all. Not Daniel, either way.

"I'll see you soon, Lynds. Let's meet up for lunch in the week sometime?" Eva hugged her friend and pecked her cheek. "Thanks so much for helping out with the outreach session today. Good biscuits, too!"

"And I can tell you about me and Miles," was her meaningful reply. "Things have moved on! I need to go and find Rupert, though, so I'll say bye-bye."

The unread message beeped again and the car engine revved, followed by a loud toot of the vehicle's horn.

Eva swiped the screen on her phone, and a message appeared from Daniel.

Do you want to join the kids for a photo with the car? We need miss Catesby.

An invisible thread tugged at Eva's chest. "I've got to go, Lynds, but wow, good to hear things are developing!" *As long as I don't get too much detail.* "Take care—we'll arrange something. Bye!"

Eva went at a trot through the gallery and out of the front door, where Daniel was waiting with his car. She'd seen it on the way in, but hadn't taken much notice of it. Now, though, she looked at it as if for the first time. A classic sports car, surrounded by children.

"Yes, Mr Scott? I'm required?"

A cheer went up from the children and adults alike and he called, "Come on, we need an epic selfie. Can I rely on you to send it out?"

Eva opened the camera app on her phone. "All right, everyone. Smile!"

Daniel held out his hand and laughed. "You're *in* the photo, come on! Rely on the tall bloke to take it?"

"Oh!" Eva dropped her phone into her bag. "Where do you want me, so to speak?"

"In the middle, boss lady." He stood aside to make space, and with a bit of arranging and squeezing to fit everyone in, Daniel finally took out his own mobile. Only then, in the image on the screen, did Eva see that Jake held Daniel's sketch of the car, his face as proud as his dad's, who was posing showily in the driving seat. Daniel held the phone above them and said, "Biggest cheesy grins please?"

"Cheeeeeeese!" The word echoed around the plaza outside Rupert's gallery. A dozen excited children beamed for Daniel's camera. He took a few shots then lowered the phone.

"Miss Catesby'll make sure you all get a copy," he told them. "And when the paintings are on display, I'll see you back here for a proper artist's showing."

Eva stood aside so that the children could say their goodbyes to him. Perhaps she should have headed home, but she wanted the chance to say *something* to him, to dispel the feeling of unfinished business that hung in the air. Only when they were alone did Daniel ask, "Did I do okay?"

"You were brilliant! Really, you're a natural with them." A breath of sea breeze blew a length of hair across Daniel's brow, and Eva resisted the temptation to brush it aside for him. "I don't suppose you'd like to do another session with them? When you can… They'd love it."

"I intend to. We're going to have an exhibition." He smiled. "I promised Rupert the arsehole that I'd sort the cleaning costs if he let us put the paintings the kids did up in the foyer. Don't worry about those that have to be anonymous, there won't be any names unless their parents say yes to it. I promised him the auction too, so it all stays local. I want people to see the work you're doing, and that won't happen in a London sale room."

"I don't know how to say thank you, really I don't." Eva picked at the dried paint around her fingernails. "I've been doing this for four years, and today was the first time that someone really grasped why I do it."

"I'm going to go home, order a pizza and crawl around in paint, inspired by Kieran." Daniel laughed. "But before I do, can I give you a lift anywhere? I haven't been drinking or doing anything I shouldn't, you can trust me."

"I walked here, seeing as the day was so nice, but I wouldn't mind a lift home. I suppose all this paint doesn't pose any qualms for you, does it?" Eva couldn't help but smile at him, or at the thought of being near to him, even if it was only for the five minutes it would take for him to drive her home. "Wouldn't want to destroy your upholstery!"

"I have an understanding man at a good car wash." He smiled. "I drew you today, didn't I? I did it."

Eva produced the furled drawing from her cleavage. It was warm from nestling against her body. "You did. It was really good. You are feeling better now, aren't you? I was so worried, and you did seem so much happier today."

"Fancy sharing my pizza?" Daniel blinked, his gaze hopeful. "I promise not to burn anything today."

Eva nodded as she got into his car. Platonic pizza was a good sign. She'd just have to forget how attractive she found him. "I'm really hungry, actually. All that art has worn me out!"

"I'm the world's worst cook. I live on takeaway and cheese." He closed the car door and walked around to climb into the driver's seat. "And you're— Have you been all right?"

"More or less." Eva smiled at him. She had missed him, and she barely knew him. "I was worried about you, and I... Something happened, and I suppose I should tell you, but it can wait."

"I heard what you said as you were leaving."

Eva bit her lip. "I don't know why I said it." But she did know, because it was true.

"No one's ever said it since my mum." He pulled out into traffic, the sun beating down on them in the open-top car. "So even someone like you saying *nearly*, that meant a lot to me."

"I shouldn't have said that and walked away. It wasn't fair." Eva tucked her hair behind her ears as the air rushing past began to exert its own haphazard styling decisions on it.

"But nearly's pretty close." Daniel smiled. "I'm sorry you saw me like that. Believe it or not, it was the jam that did it!"

Eva laughed. "Oh dear, did you get a particularly potent jar?" She brushed her hand over his where it lay on the gearstick. Serious now, she asked, "Did it stir memories about your mother? If it did, I'm so sorry. I was thoughtless."

"You weren't to know. It would've been her birthday, I was feeling a bit weird and—" He glanced at her. "Shall we get some bread or something, try the jam later?"

Eva bowed her head. "Oh, Daniel, I can't begin to… No wonder you got into a state, you poor thing." She glanced at him, his hair blown back from his face by the wind. "We could get some bread, if you like. Or just eat it out of the pot with our fingers!"

"Let's do that. It'll be pudding!" They drove out of the town and along the coast, the horizon opening out, the ocean disappearing into a distant haze. Sunglasses weather, though he wasn't wearing them. "But I'm sorry, Eva. I just wanted to say it and for you to know I mean it."

Eva nodded. "Thank you, Daniel, I know you mean it. Seeing you with the kids today—they're not daft, they know when someone's insincere, and they really took to you. And how you got Kieran to smile, I'll never know!"

"I see a hell of a lot of me in him. Maybe he knew that?"

"Maybe he did. He's been excluded from school a couple of times for causing trouble, but from what I've heard from his mum, it's how he reacts to the other kids picking on him. You know what they can be like. Horrible and then *calm down, mate, it's just a joke!*" Knowing she could trust Daniel with a confidence, she told him, "His dad's in prison and the other kids read about the case in the papers, and—you can imagine. He's got so much pent-up rage inside, and when he's painting, it comes out."

"He's got a real talent, that's why I wanted to talk to his mum. She was so proud of him." He glanced at her. "And those kids today, I saw myself in every one of them. If there's anything I can to help with your work, I want to do it."

Eva took a deep breath. It was a lot to ask a man as successful as Daniel, who no doubt had more demands on his time than she could ever understand. "Well, there is one thing you could do. It's not about money, just—can you give up a couple of hours on a Saturday to help me run the class? Not every week, I understand that—you're very busy, I'm sure—but even just once a month, it'd be great. I know the kids would love it."

"You're amazing, I hope you know that. I'd love to," he replied, his tone as warm as the sky above. The vast palace that was his home swam into view through the summer haze and as the car drew close, the gates swung open with a quiet electric hum. "And I still want my mermaids."

"What if... What if I give you your mermaids in exchange for a donation to my outreach group?" Eva combed her hands through her messy hair. She wished she'd brought a brush. Heading into Daniel's palace looking like she needed a good bath seemed wrong. Bohemian, certainly, but wrong. "You decide the price. I can't. I'm rubbish at that sort of thing."

"It's got to be worth a few grand?" He turned off the ignition and climbed out. "I went away the morning after I last saw you. I haven't been home until today so it's a bit of a mess in the studio. Nothing got burned in the end. I just stayed on your chaise longue until the sun came up, then I hit the road."

Eva got out of the car. She adjusted her dress, and tried vainly once more to remove the tangles from her hair, discovering in the process yet more paint. "Where did you go, or shouldn't I ask?"

"I went up to Middlesbrough, where I lived before—" He shrugged. "Lost the accent a long time ago. I haven't been there in thirty years, so I just wanted to see Mum's place, my old school, try and exorcise a few old devils. I'm not going to get better in the space of a week, but I didn't think I'd live to see the dawn, Eva. And I don't ever want to think that again, it was like drowning."

"You've been through a lot, Daniel." Eva had given up on tidying her hair. It was an insignificant matter when held up against a man's life, a man's sanity. "If you'd like a hug, a platonic hug, you need only ask."

"It's not very *bad boy* to admit you're going into drug counselling, so I'd love a hug." He ruffled his hair, a few flecks of paint fluttering from it. "Then let's get the pizza ordered and settle in for some painting."

Eva held her arms out to him and embraced him tightly. "You're not bad in the least, Daniel. In fact, you're quite lovely."

"Do you fancy crawling about in some paint?" He hugged her in return. "I can lend you something to wear."

"Sounds like fun, as long as you don't mind me borrowing your shower before I go home!" Eva rested her head against his chest. She didn't want to let him go. Perhaps she was imagining it, but she had the idea that he felt the same because he was clinging to her too, his cheek resting on her hair. Eva whispered, "I'm easy with the pizza, by the way, although I do insist on pepperoni."

"And a bottle of red," he murmured. "Just the one, though, don't worry."

"Sounds good." Eva at last let him go. "Wine and pizza. Sounds like a good way to spend the evening. And in excellent company, too."

Daniel unlocked the door and stood aside, letting Eva into the vast, white foyer. An alarm was beeping, and he paused to tap a code into a keypad just inside, silencing the sound. A staircase swept upwards and Daniel headed for it, telling her, "Make yourself comfy in the lounge, I'll be back with clothes to paint in. I'll phone for food too!"

The lounge, so it appeared, was next to Daniel's studio, with the same view across the sea. The decor was very white, and Eva wondered how they'd manage to eat pizza and drink red wine in the room without creating another mess. She didn't want to sit on the vast white suede sofa, even though it looked incredibly comfortable. The room smelled of new furniture and new carpet. A huge television screen watched her from across the room, and Eva thought back to the burglar alarm. Having all this money and the big house was one thing, but did it mean very much if it was empty? She turned her back on the impersonal, blank space and instead gazed out at the sparkling blue sea beyond.

"Food's on its way, and I don't have many clothes suitable for a girl like you." Daniel stood in the doorway, wearing those by-now-familiar pyjama trousers, a black T-shirt pulled over his body and his sunglasses in his hair. "So I hope a T-shirt and shorts'll do?"

"Should do!" It was a far cry from her red satin dress that he'd once found arousing, but they were beyond that now. Though she couldn't help the shiver that ran through her as she remembered the sensation of his mouth on her body.

He held out the bundle of clothes to her and said, "The bathroom's first on the left, if you want a bit of privacy. I'll grab the bottle and we can start work while we wait for the food."

"Thanks." Eva grabbed the clothes from him and followed his directions to a huge shower room. Self-conscious in the white, clinical space, Eva changed quickly into the clothes he had lent her. She took a scarf from her bag and used it as an impromptu belt, then knotted the T-shirt to one side to stop it bulging around her middle. She tied her hair up into a topknot and flakes of dried paint fell out and speckled the immaculate white mat.

Eva was laughing by the time she got back to the lounge. "I look like I'm going to a festival! Can I borrow a tent?"

"Now *you're* the one who needs someone to wash her feet," he told her tenderly. "You look lovely. I wish I looked like that when I'm dressed for work!"

Eva danced a little jig. "I'm filthy, but it was fun! So…what do you propose we do now?"

"Wine's open. I've laid down a few sheets, so I propose we see what we can do with Keiran's inspiration. A word of warning, though. I didn't tidy up before I left so the studio's a mess." He reached out and brushed a fleck of colour from her cheek. "But I'll get it cleared up another time."

"Mess is good." Eva nodded.

Once she was in the studio, the memory of what had happened there rushed back to Eva. Loose paper still littered every surface, canvases were tipped over, and the stack of sketchbooks had slithered across the floor. Broken glass crunched underfoot and Eva realised something was missing.

The glass-topped table that had been smeared with coke was nowhere to be seen, apart from a twisted metal frame.

"So are you... Have you given up the coke, then?"

He turned to look at her, and for a moment she felt a flash of recognition from somewhere, but not of Daniel Scott, of a photograph or — something in the paper, probably, back from when he had blazed onto the art scene. A younger man, coal-black eyes glaring from a photograph she had forgotten.

"This morning, I went to see someone," he told her. "A counsellor with one of *those* client lists, so he's used to discretion. It's going to be a long road, but — I've been a fuck-up for too long and coke's a big part of that. I lost you, Eva. It's a lesson I won't forget."

Eva fidgeted with some paintbrushes — expensive ones, which had known rough treatment. She held them up one by one to the light, examining their bent bristles. "I wanted to help, but you've got yourself help now, and that's all great, and look, I'm here, and you're here, and we're going to eat pizza and drink wine and make a fantastic mess."

"I've even covered your chaise longue." And he had — a clean white sheet had been draped over it before the paint throwing began. In front of the vast windows, side by side, Daniel had laid down two more sheets and a selection of paints. Beside them was a bottle of wine, two glasses already poured. "I thought sheets would do for now? So, I guess we just follow Keiran's lead and plunge in!"

Eva grabbed a wine glass first and took an unladylike swig while getting a feel for the materials. Then she put the glass aside and sank her hand into the paint.

"Are you going to go Full Keiran and lob the whole tin?" She pulled out her hand and flung out her arm, letting the blue paint arc away from her onto the sheets. "Bloody hell, that feels good, doesn't it!"

Daniel laughed. He took off his sunglasses and threw them onto the safety of the covered chaise, then dragged his T-shirt up and over his head. This was no attempt at seduction, she knew, but a prelude to making an almighty mess of paint.

"I don't know what the pizza guy's going to think." He laughed and dipped his hand into a pot of bright red paint. "But I order from them a lot, they're not easily surprised."

Then Daniel flung out his arm as though throwing a discus, sending a shower of red over a pristine white sheet. He gave a cry of celebration and took another handful, flinging that after the first.

Barefoot now, Eva dipped her toes into the paint and kicked the blue colour, which sprayed the floor before ending up on the sheet. "Oh, good Lord, sorry!" But in her head, that kick had been aimed at whoever it was who had been in her house, whoever it was who had photographed her through her own window. Whoever it was who wanted her to be scared.

"Why? This is great!" Daniel picked up a pot of yellow paint, a colour she couldn't recall seeing too often in his dark works, and hurled a wave of it across his impromptu canvas. Then he dropped to his hands and knees and, just as Keiran had, crawled through it. As he did, he said, "What did you want to tell me before? What happened?"

Eva paused, her hand in a pot of green paint. "Do you have any odd fans, Daniel?" She took her hand out and sprayed the sheet, and Daniel, with the paint.

"Only, I don't know who else it could be. Other than…" *Rupert.* Eva shook her head.

"Probably, but none that jump to mind. Nobody sending me their toenail clippings or anything iffy like that." He glanced at her, frowning. "Why, what's up?"

"Someone took a photo of me. Through my window, I saw the flash. After I got home from…" A smile crept to her lips. "From the hotel. And when I got home after…after you drew me, someone had been in my house. Moved things about. Made my bed, would you believe. I wasn't in a fantastic frame of mind, and thought I'd imagined it, but I know I hadn't." Eva attempted a laugh. "I *never* make my bed!"

"Why would a fan of mine do that? They wouldn't even know you existed, let alone where you lived." He rose to his feet, his bare chest speckled with red and yellow, his hands and trousers a riot of the colours. "That's bloody horrible, and after the crap I'd just put you through, you must've been terrified. Can I do something? You changed the locks, put an alarm in, all that?"

"Yes, Lyndsey and Miles came over and helped sort out the locks. I've got an alarm already, but I must've forgotten to set it when I left. I *did* remember today, though!" Eva stirred a pot of paint with her finger, then drew a line along the edge of the sheet. "I'm just worried in case — what if it's Rupert? Making my bed just seems…weirdly intimate, do you know what I mean?"

"There's something about him with you, the way he looks at you." Daniel walked over to Eva, leaving a pattern of red and yellow footprints on the edge of her sheet. "And I'm not saying that out of jealousy, it's just — *something.*"

"He keeps asking me out, and I keep saying *no* and he says these things that are just *lewd*, really. Sexual favours in exchange for him helping me out." Eva drank some more wine, hoping to dislodge the bitter taste in her mouth. "Other than not go anywhere near him or his gallery, I don't know what to do. And he's so important in the art scene down here. If he makes up his mind to crush my career, then he will."

"Except now you're painting with triple Turner Prize winner Daniel Scott, which makes you considerably more difficult to crush," he told her dryly. "He seems the sort to resort to frightening someone, probably hoping you'll cry on his shoulder and make him a hero. I'm sorry about paddling all over your sheet, by the way."

"I'll paddle over yours, if you like!" Eva laughed. "It's good to talk about it. Lyndsey sounded horrified when I suggested it might be Rupert. But it's such a relief to hear you agree. Not that I know what to do, really. I've told the police, but it's weird lying in my bed and thinking…someone was in my room, and I have no idea who they were."

"And there's been nothing since?" He frowned. "Say Lyndsey told Rupert that you'd had the police out and then it stopped. It's a bit too much of a coincidence, isn't it? He's not going to risk getting arrested, and I know she's your mate, but she doesn't seem like a girl who avoids drama to me."

Eva rolled her eyes. "That woman *loves* drama. She even sees it where it doesn't exist. The idea that I have a stalker has given her far more entertainment than you can imagine!" Eva picked a cloth up from the floor and wiped her hands on it. "I don't mean that nastily, she was really concerned, but knowing Lynds, she'll be dining out on it for months."

"Did they break in or unlock the door?" He dipped his toes into the blue paint as he was talking, then pressed them to the sheet on which they were standing.

"No sign of a break-in. That's why I asked Lynds if it could be Rupert, because she's got spare keys for my house, and he could've helped himself to them out of her handbag or her desk or anything." Eva wished she could hug Daniel again, but two hugs in one day didn't seem very platonic. At the scent of his cologne, the memory of their bodies moving together returned to torment her.

"Or it could be her." Daniel glanced over Eva's shoulder. "Pizza's here, they know to come to the side."

He touched her hand fleetingly, a gesture of friendship or comfort, then strolled over to the doors where she had entered in what seemed like another lifetime, leaving her with the ridiculous suggestion that Lyndsey had been making her bed and moving her shampoo.

Why the hell would Lyndsey do that?

Unless it had something to do with Miles. But Lynds had Miles now. She didn't need to stalk Eva. And Lynds was hardly the stalking type. There wasn't a more normal, level-headed person than Lynds.

When Daniel closed the door and returned to her, he was carrying two enormous pizza boxes, which he set down on the floor beside the wine bottle. When he lifted the lids she saw first the promised pepperoni then, in the second, a vast garlic bread. Not quite the meal they had shared in the hotel, but no less welcome.

"I didn't mean she was trying to frighten you." He knelt down beside the boxes, extending one leg to dip his toes in the red paint. "But maybe, I don't know…a joke that backfired? Something like that?"

"I see…sort of." Eva gratefully sat down with a wine glass in one hand and a greasy slice of pizza in the other. "I hope that's what it is, I really don't want to have a stalker!"

"My money's on Rupert." He dabbed his toes this way and that on the sheet. "Are you all right there? You know you can stay over here if you want, though I'd understand if you didn't after what happened. But you can."

"That's really kind of you." Eva wondered if she could get any sleep if she was in the same house as Daniel. How would she not lie awake and lament their failed liaison? "To be honest…heading back later this evening does worry me."

"So don't head back." He pressed his bare foot to her shin, leaving a smear of red paint there. "Stay with me."

Eva retaliated, tickling his ankle with her blue-painted toes. "Thanks, I'll take you up on that, and I'll head home tomorrow in daylight!"

"I don't regret anything that happened between us." Daniel took a sip of wine, then another slice of pizza from the box. "I've never been so alive, such intensity, without drugs or booze, just— I regret the end, but I don't regret what we did. You're amazing, Eva, never think otherwise."

"You're so sweet!" Eva laughed gently. She fell silent, but only for a moment, because his words had freed hers. "I don't regret it either. I keep thinking of you, I keep remembering—all the time. I try not to, but I can't help it."

"I don't know what it feels like to be in love." He looked down, his voice quieter when he spoke again. "I'm no good with words, sorry. I miss you."

Eva almost dropped her glass in surprise at what he'd said.

Was that almost a declaration of – ? No, it couldn't have been.

"I miss you too." She put down her glass and threw the crust of her pizza into the cardboard lid, then brushed her hands against her borrowed shorts, leaving crumbs and paint in their wake. "Hug?"

"So long as you don't mind the paint on my hands?"

"Not at all." Eva pushed herself across the floor, half-skidding on the loose paper, and put her arms around him. She whispered against his neck, feeling the warmth of him on her lips. "Shall I tell you what love feels like?"

"Yes please," Daniel replied in a murmur as he wrapped his arms around her, cradling her against his chest.

Eva heard his heart beat where her ear lay against him, could feel his pulse in his throat and the strength in his arms and the longing in his embrace. "It feels like this."

The steady thud of Daniel's heart leapt and quickened at her words, then she felt his lips against her hair. It was so gentle that for a moment Eva wondered if she'd imagined it, but there it was again, the ghost of a kiss.

"Is it too late?" he murmured.

"No, it never is." Eva stroked his cheek, leaving a stripe of paint. "I love you."

"I love you," he replied, barely even a whisper. "And I don't want to lose you again."

"You won't." Eva tipped up her head. "Give me a big garlicky kiss, my darling man."

Daniel laughed, then put his lips to hers and granted her wish. All of that desire, that longing that she hadn't been able to push down, came flooding back. They couldn't be apart. From that first time in the gallery, they had been heading here, to this moment.

Eva tangled her fingers in his hair once more, sighing into their kiss at the familiarity of the touch. She had missed this, she had missed everything about him.

"I'm a mess, but I'm working on it," he confided with a smile in his voice, stealing another gentle kiss. When he spoke again there was that arrogance she had first glimpsed in the gallery once more, as infuriating as it was exciting. "And at least I'm a sexy mess with vintage sunglasses."

"A *very* sexy mess!" Eva caressed her way across his bare chest. "I want you to know that I'm here for you, Daniel. I won't turn tail and leave you again, not when you need someone there."

He replied with a kiss, his hands sliding up into Eva's hair. It was hungry and filled with fire, that same heat with which they had possessed each other in Rupert Hawley's office. The same heat that Mr Carswell had shown for the woman he'd summoned to his hotel room.

Eva trembled with answered longing, her body opening up to his. She kissed him with all the passion she had thought would have to be hidden away forever, but now it was freed.

"When I was a kid —" Daniel drew in a breath and a shiver ran through him. His hands were still in her hair when he drew away just a little, just enough to be able to meet her gaze. "I need to tell you something, Eva."

Eva cupped his face in her hand, gazing at him. She thought back to the last time she had been in this room, and Daniel's insistence that he had been so bad that his mother— "Darling, what happened? Tell me, I won't judge you."

"It wasn't just *care*." She could feel the effort it was taking to force every word out, for the man who never talked about his youth to tell her his secrets. "I was a bad kid—really, really bad. Do you know what it means when they say *secure children's home*?"

Eva nodded. "When I first started the group, one of the kids had been in one. For a few months. He'd fallen in with a bad crowd."

"I was in one for eight years."

Eva's hand began to slip from his face, but she brought it back up again, even though her mind was whirling. It was years ago, but what had he done to be in a children's prison for eight years? "No wonder there's all the darkness in your work... But you wouldn't be out if you hadn't changed, would you? You were so good with the kids today, you *must* have changed."

"I came out when I was eighteen, and in twenty years—*twenty years, Eva*—the only thing I've done, the only person I've hurt, has been me." He looked so desperate, so lost, and she caught a glimpse of that odd familiarity again, of something she had seen before. "I've never told anybody before, I'm not supposed to tell you, but— If it changes how you feel, I'll understand. But I love you, and I swear to God, I'm not the same person."

"It doesn't change a thing. I've fallen in love with *you*, with a wonderful man," Eva told him. "And it means so much that you trust me enough to tell me. I told you I wasn't going to run away, and I'm not. I see it all the time in the outreach kids." Eva's laugh was gentle. "Right little sods, some of them, but people *can* change if they're given the chance."

"I didn't do everything they said I did, but you must hear that all the time." He offered her a weak, sad smile. "And when you're ten years old and they're telling you that you did, it's easier to just nod and say nothing. I spent a long time saying nothing at all to anyone, and I saw that in Keiran too."

"He was caught shoplifting, and you can imagine what happened, with his dad in prison and the bullies at school. He did it because he thought he was helping his mum." Eva rested her head on Daniel's shoulder. "Will you be a friend to him, Daniel?"

"I talked to his mum afterwards about what I saw in him, that raw talent. She was really proud." Daniel kissed Eva's hair. "But if I'm going to help him, he needs to play his part in that too, and that means no more trouble with the law. He has to behave to make the best of his talent, I have to stop shoving crap up my nose to make the best of the amazing luck life's thrown at me in the last twenty years. And you're the most amazing of all of it."

Eva caught his hand and twined their fingers together. "Daniel... You *have* been very lucky, though it's not undeserved. You're such a talent. And I'm lucky too, that we found each other. Because I care about you, and I want to be with you, and I really do love you, darling."

"Say it again," he whispered, just a hint of playfulness in his words. "I like hearing it."

Eva deliberately pouted her lips, her eyelashes fluttering like a coquette's. "I love you, darling. With all my heart."

"And I promise you won't lose your arrogant bad boy." Daniel pressed his lips to her and growled, "Because I *still* want to fuck you."

Eva laughed a throaty chortle. *This* was one reason why she loved him, that he could be so tender and yet still so utterly filthy. "Good, because I want you to! Let's get this thing off…" She brought their joined hands to the knot on her T-shirt. With one rough tug at the fabric the knot gave way, and together they lifted the top over her head and cast it aside. Daniel slipped his arm around her and pulled her body towards him, his chest firm against the softness of her breasts.

The straps of Eva's bra slipped down her shoulders, and as they kissed he slid her bra off completely. Eva stroked Daniel's torso, down to his waistband, and slipped her hand inside to encircle his erection. He clearly wanted her as much as she did him.

"Do you ever wear underpants?" She giggled.

"What're underpants?"

"You're about to encounter some under these shorts!"

"I always thought ladies wore *lingerie*," Daniel teased in a flamboyant, rolling purr. He untied her impromptu belt and unthreaded it from around her. "Don't spoil it for me now."

"Ladies wear lingerie if they know in advance that a chap intends to—" Eva gasped in anticipation of his touch, and helped him to bring down the zip. "Except I'm not a lady."

"You are," he told her. "And I love you."

"Touch me," Eva breathed as the unfastened shorts dropped from her hips. He slipped his hand lower, letting it rest on her bottom as they kissed again. It was almost reverential, the heat in his skin mirrored in her blood. Eva wriggled free of her knickers and returned to stroking Daniel's erection inside his loose trousers. It didn't matter that they were surrounded by the debris from their pizza, or that they were on the paper-strewn floor, or that they were streaked in paint. Nothing mattered besides them being together.

"I thought I'd lost you." His voice was a desperate whisper. "And I wanted you to see— I wanted to be a man worth loving."

"And you are."

Eva brought his trousers down lower, revealing his erection. "Lie back, darling, there's something I need to do."

Daniel did as she instructed, pillowing the discarded T-shirt behind his head as he settled back onto the paint-spattered sheet. She saw the rise and fall of his chest quicken in anticipation. Eva straddled his legs and kissed him on the lips, then traced her way over his chest, down across his stomach, aware of every twitch of his body as she trailed her mouth lower and lower, finally reaching his erection. She kissed him from its base to its tip, then—for the first time—gently took it into her mouth, running her tongue around its ridge, before sinking down onto him.

His whole body seemed to answer, from the sigh of pleasure on his lips to the arch of his back and the feeling of his elegant fingers tangling in her hair. Eva heard her name as a whisper that became a soft moan, as her lover gave himself up to her touch.

Eva rose and fell on him, all the time stroking with her tongue, loving him. She had never been fond of the act, but now it made sense and seemed the most natural way in the world to show him how much she loved him. There was nothing forceful in the way his hand rested in her hair, stroking, and all the time she could hear his gentle groans of pleasure, the sighs of joy that her touch was drawing out. Eva held him, caressing his skin in small circles as she went on pleasuring him, until she thought there was a telltale movement in his hips.

She raised her head and gazed into his dark eyes. "Darling, do you want to come?"

He nodded and whispered, "I'd love to."

"Then you shall." Eva smiled at him, then licked the entire length of his erection before taking him once more into her mouth. She moved a little faster against him, and as she still made love to him with her lips, she reached up to stroke his hardened nipples. Daniel's back arched up and he gave a cry of pleasure. His fingers were against her hair again, and she felt the surge of power in his body before he orgasmed, surrendering to Eva's touch.

Eva gave his softening cock a final kiss, then lay beside him, her head on his shoulder and her arm over his chest. "I hope that wasn't too bad!"

"It was amazing," he assured her in a soft voice. "And I'm covered in paint, but it's worth it."

Eva pressed a brief but loving peck on Daniel's lips as he drifted in his calm glow. "I'll have to make you homemade pizza one day. It's amazing, I promise. I mean, I know that sounds terribly domesticated, doesn't it, and you have glitzy parties to go to here and there, but won't it be nice to come home to an Eva Catesby special?"

"I've never used the oven in this house, I live on takeout," Daniel admitted, patting one hand against his toned stomach. "When I remember to eat at all. Are you determined to look after me?"

"It's about time someone did." Eva hugged him. "If you'll look after me?"

"I promise to try." He slipped his arm around her waist, strong and protective. "But I might get it wrong sometimes. I'm still learning."

Eva propped her head up on her elbow. "We all start somewhere, don't we?"

"How would you feel, Miss Catesby, about letting a paint-covered *enfant terrible* make love to you?"

"Oh, Daniel…" Eva kissed him again. "You'd make me the happiest woman alive."

"I need to find my wallet," he admitted. "Lots of paint in here, not so many condoms. Give me two minutes?"

Eva kissed his shoulder as she sat up. "Two minutes. Starting now." She grinned.

"Back in one," Daniel laughed, leaping to his feet. "Don't go anywhere."

He crossed the studio to the door and opened it. Only then did he pause and call, "Love you!"

Eva got up from the floor and wandered over the vast windows. She stood, looking out across the patio and the swimming pool, but the trappings of Daniel's wealth didn't interest her. The view of the sea caught her attention, the clouds that had begun to swell on the horizon as the evening came on, the colours that shimmered and changed before her eyes. It was a fantastic view for an artist. For anyone who wanted to be reminded that the world, despite its horrors, was still capable of astonishing beauty.

"Tell me what you're thinking." Daniel's voice was a whisper at Eva's ear as he slipped his arm around her. Then he pressed his lips to the nape of her neck. "You look really peaceful."

"I was just thinking how beautiful this view is. Always changing." Eva pointed. "See? That cloud over there was golden a minute ago, and now it's pink. Then it'll be purple…then…" She turned in his arms. The light had given everything in the studio, even Daniel, a delicate golden sheen.

"I know it's early days for us." He raised one hand to brush Eva's hair back behind her ear. "But one day, when you're ready, we could make this *our* view?"

"Maybe…" Eva hadn't thought that far ahead, but the fact that he seemed to see something permanent, or at least lasting, in what they had, made her happy. "I'd like that."

"Our studio." He smiled tenderly, his dark eyes reflecting the golden summer light. "I missed you every day."

"I missed you too. I kept wondering what you were doing, and I worried that… I didn't know if I should ring you, so I asked Lynds to speak to your people. You don't mind, do you?" Eva wondered now if that had been a good idea, but she had been lost as to how to help him. "Nothing specific. She told them you hadn't been well, and would they check on you."

"I can't promise you a miracle recovery, Eva." Daniel kissed her cheek. "My life's not been one I'd wish on anyone. I promise you, though, whatever it takes, I'm going to get better. I'm going to see a doctor

Catherine Curzon & Eleanor Harkstead

tomorrow, someone who works with this therapist I'm seeing. I want to be here when you need me."

"Anything you need me to do, just say, won't you?" Eva nuzzled his neck. "Whether you need hugs or space or a naked woman posing on your chaise longue, just tell me."

"Right now, I just need you." His kiss was deeper this time, his tongue softly stroking hers as they sank together.

Eva gasped, her blood heating with passion and tenderness. She caught one leg around his and his rejuvenated erection pressed against her. "Here?" she whispered. "Against the window?"

"Right here," Daniel murmured, putting the wrapped condom into her palm. Then he lifted her other leg around his waist, holding her as though she were weightless. Eva tore the wrapper with her teeth, then slipped the condom onto him. She looped her arms around his neck as she gazed at him, feeling safe and loved in his arms. And very aroused.

He was still her bad boy, Eva knew, even if the darkness, the veil that swallowed Daniel Scott, had lifted enough for him to reach out to her. This wasn't the bad boy who snorted coke and stared out through bloodshot eyes, unseeing and uncomprehending, but the man who loved her, the man whose *badness* was about to be very good indeed.

"Let's go back to our hotel," he purred as his erection pressed against her, teasing. "Would you like that?"

"Oh, yes, to that room, or perhaps we could explore another?" Eva said. "I want you inside me, your wonderful hard cock."

"Every room," he decided, a hard thrust bringing their bodies together. "And we'll fuck like this in every one of them."

"We will, hard and deep and —" Eva's voice was lost in a moan of pleasure at feeling him inside her once more, his powerful thrusts and the hard shape of him. She tightened her legs around him as he pressed her back against the cool glass of the window. Without the sunglasses between them she could see flecks of amber deep in his eyes, glowing and bright in the light that reflected off the ocean beyond the glass. What those eyes had seen Eva couldn't guess, but now they were seeing only her, his body devoted to bringing them both to pleasure. The man who didn't know what it was like to be in love was finally finding out.

"That's it, that's it…" Eva sank her hands into his hair. She felt so connected to him, so close, so utterly in love. His lips were as soft as his body was hard and they moved as one, perfectly in sync in each other's arms. The thought of them being apart now, of them being anything that wasn't *this*, seemed ridiculous. They were two halves of one, and she would be there with him for the road ahead.

What was urgent and fierce in their thrusts was loving all the same. All that hectic energy in her lover and in herself came together now as their shared heat and passion, and their breathless pleasure. They needed to make this new memory here, to banish the fire and fury of the night they'd parted. Now the studio was a place not of misery but of joy, of love and connection. Now she would think of it not with dread, but with love.

Ripples of joy ran through Eva, increasing moment by moment with each thrust, each sigh, and every thought of how much she loved Daniel. She wasn't going to hold back—she couldn't have done so if she'd tried—and let desire build in her, ready to sweep her away.

"I love how you feel," he whispered hoarsely, his breath hot against her lips. "Everything about you, it's—it's pure instinct."

"Me?" Eva gasped. No one had ever said that to her before, but if anyone should know about instinct it was Daniel. "You're so passionate—in everything you do. I'm addicted to it."

"I think that's love," he whispered, kissing her again as his muscles tensed, his climax racing towards him with the same breathtaking speed as her own.

Eva held him even tighter as the ripples in her body turned into a surge and her peak took her with an intensity that stole her breath, leaving her only able to murmur her lover's name. And all the time he was beside her, joined with her, in body and soul. For a few seconds they clung to each other, then Daniel carried Eva to the covered chaise longue and they settled there together. He quickly scooped the sunglasses onto the ground, saving them from an uncertain fate.

Her orgasm has been so intense that she still shuddered from it, and, drunk with pleasure, she embraced him. "That really was something! I love you, darling."

"I love you." He kissed her forehead, the touch soothing and peaceful. "Miss Catesby."

Worn out, Eva lay back on the chaise longue, relaxing into the soft cushions with Daniel's body against hers. She closed her eyes, feeling his heartbeat and the warmth and the closeness of him as she drifted off to sleep.

Chapter Eleven

When Eva awoke, the room was bathed in a warm amber glow. She turned over to embrace Daniel only to find herself alone. In an instant her mind filled with a hundred different scenarios, each worse than the last, and she sat up, looking around the studio for the white powder, the booze, the —

"I didn't want to wake you." Daniel smiled over his shoulder then stepped back from the wall towards the chaise longue and asked, "What do you think?"

"It's me," Eva murmured. "You've drawn me onto the wall!"

She first kissed him, then, his hand in hers, Eva went over to the wall to touch it. "You drew me while I was asleep."

"No pointy bits, no sharp angles." He smiled. "Just curves and softness. The woman I love. Do you like it?"

Eva traced the gentle lines. "You've made me look beautiful — but would you mind me adding something? I'm asking your permission, I won't dive in."

"Do whatever you need to do." Daniel handed Eva the pencil, but she caught the slight deflation in him, the hint of a sigh. Then he straightened his back and told her with more confidence, "I'll keep trying until it's right."

"Oh no, I don't mean that. I mean — will you sit on that stool over there for me? And angle your head… Like this?" Eva tipped her head slightly to the right, knowing how the light would fall across his face.

As naked as her, he crossed to the stool and sat down, following Eva's instructions. When he'd angled his head, he asked, "Like this?"

"Yes, that's perfect." Eva rested the tip of the pencil against the white wall. Keeping her eyes mainly on him, rather than on her pencil, she drew him. Her lover, the structure of his face set off perfectly by the angle of the setting sun's light. He was wonderful to draw, and she laughed as she sketched in his disordered shock of hair in sweeping pencil arcs. "That's it. You're very good at modelling, very still!"

"There's a very good reason for that. It's not very noble, though," he teased. "It's because I've got your gorgeous bottom to admire while I do."

Eva skipped over to him and tapped him on the forehead with the pencil. "Naughty!" Then she kissed him and went back to her drawing. The minutes passed, and finally Eva tucked the pencil behind her ear and stepped back from her work. "There we are! What do you think of that?"

Daniel rose to his feet and approached the wall, their joint mural uniting them in each other's arms. He caught his arm around Eva's waist and lifted one hand, pressing his palm to the drawing.

"You know what was missing from my work before? What the drawing needed?" He pressed a kiss to her hair. "It needed *us*."

Eva laid her hand over his against the wall. "It did. And you know, I'm perfectly happy to pose for you again. Just name the date."

"My next exhibition, I can see it now." He laughed. "*Eva* by Daniel Scott!"

Eva picked up another pencil and signed her name. *Eva Salome Catesby*.

Imagine, the famous Daniel Scott, with another artist's signature on his wall.

"Salome?" He added his signature to hers. "Is that — Really?"

"There's the one who went to the tomb on Easter morning with the Marys." Eva put her hand on her hip in a seductive pose. "And there's the *Bring me the head of John the Baptist!* Salome. Just think, I'm named after two tempting ladies!"

"I think I prefer to think of you just as *Eva*," he decided. "And at risk of endangering my 'difficult artiste' credentials still further, how would you like to go on a date with the bad boy of British art one day?"

"A date?" Eva laughed and wrapped her arms around him. "I really never thought of you as the dating type! But yes. Why not?"

"You're covered in paint." Daniel combed his hands through Eva's hair. "Like you've just stepped out of a canvas."

"Maybe I have!" Eva wrapped a length of her hair around her finger. There were clots of paint between the strands. "And maybe so have you."

"You've found me out. How about a swim to wash the paint off?"

"Well…that pool of yours is very tempting!" Eva held his hand. "Shall we?"

He stooped down and retrieved his sunglasses from beneath the chaise longue. "You'll need these, if you want to achieve peak *difficult artiste* status."

"Oh, I'm *extremely* difficult!" Eva put his sunglasses on and pouted. "I don't give interviews, I just paint."

"And as we know," Daniel turned the key in the French windows and pushed them open into the warm evening, "I missed you at the Tate Modern. Next time, Ms Catesby, perhaps?"

"I'm very in demand… I couldn't say when I'll next be at the Tate. New York beckons. Paris. Tokyo." The patio's slabs were warm underfoot and there was no hint of an evening chill in the air. Eva held on to the pool's metal steps and dipped her paint-encrusted toe in the water. The colours began to dissolve. "I hope your pool filters are robust!"

Daniel stood on the side and watched her, his body still stained with the bright paint, his hair in wonderful disarray. He looked so peaceful, so utterly at ease that Eva could hardly believe this was the man who had curled up on the chaise longue and sobbed just a few evenings earlier. She had less trouble seeing her Mr Carswell in him, though, confident and handsome, that same aura of sheer sex that she had been unable to resist on the museum's terrace evident all over again.

"It's nearly as warm as a bath!" Eva braved herself to go down the steps until her feet were on the bottom rung and the water had almost risen to her shoulders. It lapped against her, and more of the paint sloughed off. "Come on in, Mr Scott-Carswell!"

"You look like one of those *bosomy mermaids* in your painting," Daniel observed. "A siren in a painted sea."

"Maybe you should paint me as a mermaid!" Eva turned on the steps and pushed away from the side, coasting through the water until she reached the other side of the pool. She slicked her hair back and spouted a jet of water from her mouth. "I could paint you as a saucy merman."

"I like that. What colour would my scales be?" Daniel climbed nimbly into the water and around him. As the paint dissolved, she saw a cloud of red and yellow, with a swirl of blue from his feet. He turned to await her reply and reached up to hold the steps. Muscles tensed beneath his skin, toned and defined, and the glint in his eye told Eva that he knew it too.

"Your scales would be silver and shimmery, reflecting all the colours in your ocean home." Eva began to swim across the pool to Daniel, laughing as she went. Today was like a holiday.

"When you paint my commission, put us both into it?" Daniel swam out to meet her in the middle of the pool. He caught his arms around her before finishing the thought. "A merman and a mermaid, swimming together beneath the pier."

"I'd love to! They won't be doing anything saucy, will they?" Eva raised an eyebrow. "Though that could be arranged, in a special *private* version, if you'd like?"

"Something vast and oceanic and romantic sweeping right across the bedroom wall?" Daniel raised his hand above the water and gave an expansive gesture in the air, showering them with droplets. "Get rid of some of this bloody *white*. It's like being in a hospital sometimes."

"I'm glad you've said that. Your house is lovely, but make it more personal and it would be even lovelier!" Eva slipped one arm around his shoulders, while swirling the other in a figure of eight to keep afloat in the water. "Shall we paint your bedroom together?"

"Why stop there? I don't know if an entirely white house does much for a bloke's sense of inner calm. I need some colour." Daniel tightened his arm around Eva and piloted them safely back to the edge of the pool. "What you said about some time off, I'm going to try it and see what happens to my art. Maybe we'll see a bit more colour there too."

"Turquoise and yellow and pink, rather like your pool!" The water had changed from blue to a kaleidoscope of colours as the paint had washed off their skin and swirled and merged around them.

"Art's everywhere you look." He reached out and pushed the sunglasses into Eva's hair. "I hope you tell your kids that. I saw so much wonder in them today, Eva. They reminded me what I got into this for. You were right, I need to move forward."

"I always thought you were brilliant, I just wanted you to be *more* brilliant because I knew you could be." Eva clung to him. "I'm so glad we met. We'll have so much fun, you and I."

"I don't know how easy the next few months are going to be while I try and get my shit together," Daniel told her honestly. "And all this stuff from the past, I know it's a lot to take in, but I love you, and I *have* changed. I've still got some work to do, but I'll get there."

"I know you will," Eva said. "And whatever you have to go through, it won't be alone, I promise."

"Is it too early to go to bed?"

"No! It's nice to go to bed when it's still light outside, it feels terribly decadent." Eva propped the sunglasses up in Daniel's hair. "We've got that wine to finish…and there's plenty we can do to amuse ourselves."

"Would you like me to wear my sunglasses and you can ravish me?" His voice, an exotic purr, now grew brighter. "Then we can eat jam and look at your work together, before a bit more ravishing."

"I vote for as much ravishing as possible. Ravishing, loving and jam!" Eva rubbed the tip of her nose against his. The warm water of the pool and Daniel's strong arms wrapped her up in happiness.

Daniel reached up and flicked the Wayfarers down onto his nose. Then he growled, "Let's go to bed."

Eva tipped back her head and laughed at the raw sex in that growl. "Carry me? I don't want you to let me go."

Daniel scooped her into his arms and together they ascended the flight of blue mosaic steps up onto the patio. She snuggled against him as he carried her into the studio, kicking the door closed behind him, then out into the foyer and that sweeping, film-star staircase.

"I'm not risking spiral stairs," Daniel admitted with a laugh. "I'm not that confident."

Eva gazed up at the staircase, swinging her feet with the excitement of a child. "We should be accompanied by an over-the-top string arrangement and a chorus line!"

"We wouldn't be naked then, though, would we?" With another kiss, he whisked her up the staircase and into the bed where she had woken alone after their frantic, desperate coupling. There was no desperation this time, though, as Daniel laid Eva down on the rumpled covers, his lips barely leaving hers. He settled beside her and, drawing the duvet over them, left the world behind.

* * * *

Time passed by somewhere, but Eva and Daniel barely noticed. Nothing beyond the bedroom mattered. As the light faded over their joined bodies, the room sank from golden to blue. The shadows that had begun to lengthen as they finally fell into a doze had been banished by a lamp's soft glow when Eva opened her eyes to find Daniel still at her side. He was snuggled deep in the duvet, her sketchbook open in his hands as he looked through the pages at the work she so rarely shared.

"Evening," he whispered with a smile. "Did I wake you?"

"No, it's the evening, it's when I'm most awake!" Eva glanced away from her sketchbook. "Don't laugh too much, will you?"

"I raided the kitchen for jam while you were sleeping and found more wine." He turned a page of the book. "I don't laugh at anybody's work, especially when they're as good as you."

"Jam and wine!" Eva piled up the pillows and sat up against them, but she was still embarrassed to see him going through her work. "I don't really settle on a style, do I? Pastel sunsets one minute, charcoal leaves the next, mermaids and the pier following close behind! I really couldn't decide on that— Ink, I thought, but if you want it painted…"

"I want you to do what your instincts tell you." He turned another page. "So long as I get my mermaids."

"Very well…" Eva half-closed her eyes and thought of the beach and the salty sea breeze in her hair. "I might do it as a mixture, the pier in oils because it's supposedly the real world, and the mermaids and mermen in watercolours, because they belong in the sea."

"If you want to use the studio here as inspiration, treat it as your own." Daniel closed the book and reached across to the bedside table. "Jam?"

Eva grinned as she reached for the jar. "It would be the best place to paint a picture like that, wouldn't it! Thank you, Daniel. As long as it won't distract you, having someone else working in your studio?"

"Probably," he admitted with a shrug. "But maybe I'll put my black and purple away and get out some colours if you're there to keep me company. I need a bit of a shake up, as some annoying would-be critic with an amazing bum told me at my Brighton launch."

"Did they now? And just how amazing was this bum?" Eva laughed, and dabbed jam on the end of his nose then kissed it off.

"It was so amazing that I drifted over to impress her with my artistic prowess just in time to hear her listing my professional deficiencies." He sucked in his cheeks and pouted. "But I forgive you."

"So you were going to chat me up?" Eva bit her lip. "Whoops, nearly ruined that, didn't I! But yes, you have forgiven me, *several* times."

"I wasn't going to chat you up, I was going to let you be dazzled by my presence and fall into my manly embrace," Daniel deadpanned as he popped a jam-coated fingertip between his lips. "So it's worked out just as planned, Miss Catesby."

"Oh, you think so?" Eva grinned as she circled her hand around his wrist and pulled his finger from his mouth, licking off what remained of the jam. In reply he gave her a devilish look, dark eyes glittering.

"I'm sure of it."

"I only wanted to go to a private viewing." Eva nuzzled against his neck. "I wasn't expecting to end up in your bed, covered in my mum's Boozy Damson Jam! But as it happens, it's not a bad old turn-up for the books, is it?"

"And my first date in a long time." Daniel set the jar aside and took her in his arms. "I'll wear black and sunglasses, like a real rock star. How does that sound?"

"I love it!" Eva laughed. "And what shall I wear? My red satin dress again? Or something else equally flattering to my rear?"

"The red satin. And I'll book us a room at The Mallard, *Mr Carswell and guest*?"

"Mademoiselle Sirène!" Eva giggled. "What a wonderful first date we'll have. Do you have anywhere in mind? Dinner somewhere?"

"I don't know the place, so you choose. Daniel Scott and Salome has a ring to it, doesn't it?" He grinned, giving her a deliberately arrogant wink. "My name can usually secure a table."

"Shall I send a taxi to collect you?" Eva quirked an eyebrow. "A mystery drive. Maybe they'll think you're my male escort for the evening. You come highly recommended by some woman called Eva."

"I hope she gave me a good review. She's a demanding customer."

"She's saucy, that one." Eva was not ignorant of the fact that Daniel was getting hard again, and she caressed him. Neither of them would sleep much tonight, but it didn't matter.

Chapter Twelve

The sun was already rising. Eva had no idea what time it was, but it must have been early. Too early. But something had woken her, prompting her wide awake, poised for unknown danger.

There it was again. That sound. A voice, distant, murmuring.

Daniel, his eyes screwed shut, his head jerking against the pillow, his face sheened with sweat. His body was rigid, as if cramping in every muscle, his hands balled into fists against his chest. His eyes opened wide, wild, then closed again, and she wondered for a second if he had taken something, but somehow she knew that he hadn't. This wasn't cocaine.

Eva wasn't sure what to do. *Never wake a sleepwalker.* She knew about that, but she couldn't just lie there as Daniel was tormented by whatever horror was so real to him beneath the pall of sleep.

And so, tenderly, Eva placed a light kiss on Daniel's face. It seemed to make it worse for a moment, then she slipped her arm around his shoulder, gently embracing him.

She pressed her mouth to Daniel's ear. "It's all right, you're safe, I've got you."

A shiver ran through Daniel's muscles and Eva went on whispering, consoling, bringing Daniel Scott back.

The change, when it came, was almost shocking in its violence. Every muscle untensed for one second then grew taut once more, and Daniel flipped onto his side. He snapped into a tight ball and clung to Eva as deep, silent sobs wracked him.

Eva rocked him gently, hushing him as if he were a frightened child.

"I'm sorry." Daniel's voice was small, broken. "I don't sleep. I woke you."

"I was awake anyway." It was better to tell a gentle fib. "The sun's coming up."

He nodded and snuggled closer. "I love you."

Eight years in a children's prison. Is that what it did to you?

Or was it something else, was Daniel trying to reach back through time and save his mother from her own hand?

"I love you too." Eva stroked his hair. "Can I get you something? A glass of water?"

"One of those hugs of yours?"

"As many as you'd like, darling." Eva held him against her, caressing him, whispering gentle words. "Whenever you need them."

Chapter Thirteen

After being in Daniel's house, her own home seemed small and cluttered. But it was homely, that was the main thing. And, as far as Eva could tell, nothing had been moved.

Eva sat on her sofa with her laptop on her knee, trying to decide on a venue for their date. Somewhere exclusive, or quirky? Elegant or trendy? But her search was constantly interrupted with thoughts of *him*, of Daniel. They had made love and cuddled, and made love again. She had lost count of the number of times their bodies had been brought together, and even his night terror couldn't spoil her memory of the time they had spent with each other.

What a scar to leave behind, though. Despite his wealth and his success, inside Daniel Scott there was still a terrified child.

Eva opened another tab on her browser, which was already crowded with what felt like every restaurant and bar in Brighton.

Daniel scott middlesbrough

Nothing came up, other than a suggested search for a show of his at the Baltic in Gateshead. Maybe whatever he had done that had landed him in prison had been forgotten by the Internet? It had been a long time ago, after all, twenty years. Maybe it hadn't even made it to the Internet.

Carswell middlesbrough

Eva jumped, her laptop nearly skidding onto the floor, as her screen filled with pictures, with words, with a name. *Lee Carswell, The Middlesbrough Monster*

How could she have not realised?

Child A, as he had first been named, who had pushed a little girl off a cliff, and her body had never been found. The embargo on naming an underage suspect had been lifted as soon as the boy had turned eighteen and been released. And renamed. Though that new identity had been hidden from almost everyone, much to the gnashing-teethed fury of the press. It was an *extraordinary case* and in the name of *public interest* the media had printed the wide-eyed boy's mugshot, taken eight years earlier, under the banner '*MONSTER*'.

Which was what Eva had called Daniel on the day he…he was bad, so bad, and as Eva scrolled and clicked, she found a photo of his mother. An attractive woman, with Daniel's dark hair, posing in a snapshot taken in a garden that was about to burst into bloom. Only one newspaper had claimed that she had been hounded to death by the press, but the public had been out for blood — *bad mother, bad son*. No one cared that she had died of alcohol poisoning.

School photos of the blonde and pretty Emily Shaw smiled out from newspapers, and her parents had cried on the television about the death of their little angel, killed by a feral child who had been raised by a bad mother. A spokesman from the coastguard had described their fingertip search for her, but the currents there were too strong, they had said. The body had been carried out to sea.

And Eva hadn't been allowed to play outside for the rest of that summer.

The case had cast a shadow over many childhoods. In Eva's Foundation Year at art college, someone had attempted an Andy Warhol-style repeating print of Lee Carswell's mugshot. They had called it *The Beast at Large* and it had sent a shiver down Eva's spine.

But the shiver hadn't been fear of the boy, but fear of a panic that could whip up sane, level-headed people to call for a return to the death sentence for just this one case, calling on the state to kill a child. That, Eva knew, was the real monster.

Mr Carswell. The mysterious figure in black, his eyes hidden behind dark lenses, the boy who had –

At Eva's elbow, her mobile buzzed. The screen lit up with a simple message, sent from the man who had stolen her heart.

Missing you, mermaid. Xxx

Eva cradled the phone. How could she tell him that she knew? But she couldn't hide the knowledge from him. She closed down her browser, the screen showing her desktop image of the outreach children holding up their paintings with Daniel smiling in the middle of the picture.

She passed her hand over her eyes, tears building as her heart thudded heavily.

Missing you, Mr Carswell. Can I ring you? Xxx

And the reply took seconds.

Anytime, Miss Catesby. Xxx

Eva pressed the icon of the green phone and it began to call. Her throat tightened, but she couldn't risk sending him a text. What if it came out wrong? It was bad enough that she had researched him, but if he hadn't wanted her to know, would he really have kept calling himself by his real surname?

"I'm painting," Daniel said merrily as soon as he answered. "In sunglasses."

"It's a lovely day again. I bet the sun's really bright in your studio! Good light for painting." Eva folded an arm across her stomach. Could he hear it in her voice, that she knew? She could picture him in those loose pyjama bottoms, which he had put on that morning when they had finally got out of bed.

"You know you could come over and make the best of it if you want? There's room for another artist in here."

"I need to put some washing on. Water the plants." Eva knew how feeble that sounded. There was no point in dithering, she would have to say it. "Daniel…I… I don't know how to put this, exactly."

There was a long silence from the end of the line and she pictured him in his studio, waiting, suspecting. Finally he said, "Go on."

"I'm sorry, darling. I was just curious, that's all. You said you'd been to Middlesbrough, and I couldn't find a Daniel Scott there. And then I tried…" Eva's voice caught in her throat and turned into a sob. "I should've remembered, I don't know why. It just didn't occur to me."

"What are you —" She heard him swallow, his voice a sudden rasp. "What?"

Eva's tears flowed now. She could well be on the verge of losing him all over again. "I love you, I really do. More than I've ever loved anyone. This doesn't change anything. I want you to know that."

She closed her eyes, but dancing before them were the pretty young mum and the frightened boy and the beaming schoolgirl.

There was more silence, and this time, Daniel didn't break it. Just as he had after his arrest, Lee Carswell was refusing to speak.

"Do you want me to come over, darling? Sod the washing, it doesn't matter." Eva was now a snivelling, snotty mess. She staggered from her lounge up the stairs to her bathroom, searching for a packet of tissues. "Darling, are you still there?"

"What do you want me to say?" Daniel asked in a whisper. "What should you have remembered?"

"That name, Carswell. Your real name." Eva sank onto the landing, the packet of tissues torn open, her eyes sore from where she had rubbed them. "I know who you really are. At least, who you were."

"I... Can I see you?" His next words were quicker, betraying a hint of panic. "You don't need to worry, Eva, I'm not — I won't hurt you. I just want to see you."

"I want to see you too. And I know you won't hurt me."

"Should I come over there?"

"You can if you like. I'll get the kettle on." Eva got back up to her feet and headed downstairs. "There's still some of my mum's rock buns left, if you'd like one?"

She heard Daniel release a long breath, then he said, "I'll see you really soon. I love you, honestly."

"I know," Eva whispered, and with infinite care typed out her address. She heard the sound of him moving the phone, pictured him reading the message, there in that bright studio.

"Please don't tell anyone," was all he said.

Eva occupied herself by washing up her grandma's teapot and choosing a plate for the rock buns. She wouldn't allow herself to think of anything else, because as soon as she paused, the faces came back to her. The dead women and the little boy. She set everything up in the front room and stood in a gap in the curtains, watching for the man she had called *Daniel*, holding her vase without a clue where to put it. She had moved it, and so had an invisible, unknown hand. But she knew without a doubt that it hadn't been Daniel who'd come here.

From outside came that jet engine roar a few seconds before the car itself appeared, top down, paint job gleaming in the coastal sun. He was wearing the sunglasses, of course, and when he left the car she saw that Daniel was still in his paint-spattered pyjamas and black T-shirt, his feet bare. He pushed the Wayfarers into his hair and headed for the door at something that wasn't quite a run, but wasn't just a walk.

Eva rushed to the door, opening it before he could knock or ring the bell. She hugged him despite the vase in her hand, and covered his face in kisses.

"Darling…" she whispered.

"I'm sorry." He sank into her embrace, holding her. "I'm so sorry, I couldn't tell you."

Eva closed the door behind him. "It's okay, it's okay…honest. Will you —?" Eva was struck by the oddest sensation, as if he was too big for her arms. She was hugging a man, then suddenly a boy, the child in the mugshot. She almost dropped her vase. "I really need to put this down. Sorry. Just…rearranging the ornaments."

He nodded mutely, then drew back and gazed at her through large, dark eyes.

"It was so long ago." Eva stroked his cheek. That face… She saw the crass attempt at the Andy Warhol print again. "*You* weren't a monster. *They* were."

"I used his name, *my* name, because —" Daniel took the vase from her and set it down on the carpet beside them so he could embrace her again. "Lee never got a chance to grow up. I thought — I felt as though you and me had a connection and I knew it wouldn't last because I'm fucked up and — It was a way to let Lee have a moment of happiness. To close the door and be with a woman like you, just once, just to let him breathe one last time."

Eva rested her head on his shoulder. She tried to speak but was convulsed with sobs. "I'm so sorry for what happened to you. I can't begin to — I can't bear the thought that you think your mother took her own life because of you. Darling, it was *them*, all those people who want…" She took his hand and twined it tightly in her own. "Now look here, Mr Carswell-Scott. I love you. Whatever your name is, I don't care. You do know that, don't you? I love *you*."

"I'll tell you all of it." He pressed his face to her hair. "But if it gets out — There was nothing weird about using *Carswell*, I just wanted to hear the name and it not be followed by a pack of lies about me and Mum."

"I won't say anything, you can trust me." Eva scuffed her fingers against his cheek. "It's your name, you have every right to use it."

"It's not me, though, not anymore." He kissed her forehead. "Can we sit down, maybe?"

"Come on in." Eva led him into her front room. She indicated the sofa to him and held up the teapot. "Sugar? Milk? I can't offer a slice of lemon, I'm afraid. How terribly unsophisticated."

"Builder's tea," Daniel admitted, sinking into the sofa. It was a valiant effort at jollity, but she could see tears sparkling in his eyes. "You can take the boy out of Middlesbrough but he'll still want builder's tea."

Eva poured milk into a mug decorated with a photograph of fireworks shooting above the pier. She added the tea, then offered Daniel the sugar bowl before pouring a mug for herself. "Help yourself to a rock bun."

It was odd how normal this seemed. On the surface, at least.

"What do you want to know?" Daniel picked up a bun, though he didn't bite it. "Where do I start?"

"Start wherever's easiest for you." Eva sipped her tea. It was too hot, but she swallowed anyway. He nodded but said nothing, then held out his hand to her. It was a plaintive gesture, the bad boy more vulnerable even than when he had fallen apart. Eva gripped his hand tightly. "I told you you'd have as many hugs as you want, whenever you need them. I haven't changed my mind."

"Do you want to ask me if I did it? Is that the important thing?" Daniel kissed her hand. "That's what they always asked."

Eva couldn't pretend that she wasn't curious, but she didn't feel as if she could ask. "They never found her, did they? I wondered... Maybe she slipped, and I could never understand why they were so certain she hadn't. That someone had..." *Pushed.*

"We were dirt poor, Mum and me, and I'm not going to dress this up, because I was a little bastard. I shoplifted and stole whatever I wanted, I was always fighting, skipping school. I just didn't care." He closed his eyes for a second. "I was nowhere near an angel. There was this one woman and I made her life miserable because she was the weirdo, crazy hair, wild eyes, all that. She lived in a massive house on the edge of town, huge place, and I'd go over there with my mates and smash her windows, just to mess with her. She'd come screaming out the house shouting about how *you bairns are gunna knock me badly*. We'd cuss right back at her. If it was my kid, I'd go mad."

He smiled, perhaps at his own recollection of the Middlesbrough accent, but the smile faded too quickly and he went on.

"My friends were as bad as me, but there was one boy at school and he was as different as you could be. *Ollie.* He wanted to hang out with us, nine years old and smoking, swaggering about thinking we were really something." Daniel broke the bun in half and put it on the arm of the sofa. "And he always had plenty of cash, so he was the best kind of friend. His sister was Emily—"

His voice cracked and he bit down hard on his lip, breathing deeply.

Emily Shaw.

Eva stroked his shoulders. He really had been the sort of tearaway that came to her outreach workshops.

Although none of them had — "It's okay. We've got as much time as you need. You don't need to rush."

"Emily was *her*. The girl they said — I didn't, Eva, I said I did because —" He took another deep breath. "Typical little sister, always hanging around, trying to be part of the gang."

Eva nodded. Her own younger sister had been the same, following Eva and her friends wherever they went. Until that summer, when the bike rides had stopped and they'd had to play in the back garden, always under a parent's watchful eye. "Why did you say you did it?"

"Because I wanted to go to the seaside, and they don't let you out if they don't think you're sorry." He gave a defeated shrug.

"Did you have a nice day out?" Eva asked. What a thing to ask. Was it worth confessing to a crime he hadn't committed? And when he'd seen the sea again, had he thought of Emily Shaw?

"I was going to throw myself off the cliff like they said I had her," he whispered, his eyes filling with fresh tears. "But when I got there... When I got there I thought of Mum and that one holiday we had in Brighton and —"

Daniel threw his hand back against his eyes and let out a sob. Then he crumpled against her, a sound like a man in agony torn from his lips.

Eva held him, rocking him from side to side. What an awful thing for a child to contemplate. To find themselves in a situation so hellish and impossible that they would plan to destroy their young life. "And you didn't, you held on, you found the strength from somewhere to keep going. You were — you *are* — so brave."

"But if I'd not been so bad, nobody would've believed what Ollie said, but they wouldn't listen to me, some council house kid who was always in trouble." He sobbed out the words against her shoulder. "They wouldn't listen so I just stopped talking."

"Is that when you started to paint?"

Daniel nodded. "But I wanted to since we came to Brighton, me and Mum. That's why they didn't believe me about that day, because how would *I* want to paint?'

He lifted his head and blinked through bloodshot eyes. "When Mum took me to the gallery, I'd never seen anything like it. It was like magic, but I kept it to myself because I was Lee, and Lee wouldn't do something so stupid as paint pictures."

"But Daniel would?"

"Daniel did." He nodded. "Ollie's parents took us to the seaside for the weekend and because we were shits, we thought it'd be funny to give them a fright and go off to the cliffs. When we got there though, Emily trailing after us, I didn't want to just hang about and chuck rocks or whatever. All I wanted to do was explore, picture how those amazing scenes would look if I painted them, so I left Ollie and Emily to it. It was dark when I found my way back to the car and...and the police were there and Ollie was saying —"

"It's okay, you don't have to say it." Eva held his hand again. He hadn't done it. She believed him.

"But I didn't, and he had this whole story and he was crying and her parents were screaming but I *didn't*! I kept on saying that I hadn't been there, that I never did anything, and they wouldn't listen so I stopped saying it." He clenched his free hand into a fist. "And he told the police and the court and the judge and they said that I'd done it too, and I said nothing. I bit my tongue and I made it bleed and I said *nothing.*"

"It's odd to think that Oliver Shaw is out there somewhere, isn't it?" Eva took his fist in both her hands and tried to ease it open. "I hope one day he apologises. I hope he finally tells the truth. Kids make stuff up, they elaborate, and they don't go back on it because they're scared they'll get in trouble. Even if it ends up with someone else. Did he see her slip, and was so shocked that he..."

Or did Ollie push her? The irritating little sister who had tagged along all the time.

"I think he did it, but they were so close... A couple of weeks before, Ollie found Emily face down in their garden pond and dragged her out, so— It was in the local papers and everything, little hero Oliver." He pinched his fingers to his eyes, wiping away the tears. "And they put me away for it and Mum— You know what happened to Mum."

Eva nodded. "She loved you, you know that? It must have been awful for her, to feel as if she couldn't help you."

"The first time I won the Turner, I stuck a bundle of cash in an envelope with anonymous instructions for a stonemason back home and gave her a headstone, because she didn't have one. I just wanted her to be remembered." He shook his head. "I knew they'd go to the press, so I added a few extra thousand and asked them to keep it to themselves. I didn't realise until then how money can change things."

"Have you visited her resting place?" Eva knew the story was bleak, but the very idea that his mother had lain in an unmarked plot for years, after the newspapers had coined it in from pull-out spreads shrieking about *The Middlesbrough Monster's Mum*, was grotesque and cruel.

"A few times." He nodded. "It's very peaceful up there. I'm not supposed to, really, I don't know how it'd go down with my probation, but I've behaved for nearly twenty years, so they don't seem to think I need too much monitoring these days."

"I'm glad it's peaceful." Eva hoped like hell that no one had graffitied the headstone. His mother didn't deserve to be hounded in death after the way she had been treated in life. "I'm sorry, by the way, for joking about you being the *bad boy*, and I'm incredibly sorry for what I said the other day, when I called you a *monster*. I can't imagine how much that must've hurt."

"A *bad boy* I don't mind, because I'll admit to that. Not a monster though, I was never that." Daniel blinked and a fresh tear rolled over his cheek. "They let me out when I turned eighteen and the press went nuts, you must remember that, so I got this anonymity order. New name, new history, new everything. And Lee Carswell disappeared into Daniel Scott, once and for all. But he comes out in every single painting."

"What did Lee think of my critique?" Eva caught his tear with her fingertip. "I hope you didn't think I was being rude, Lee."

"I thought you had a point." He managed a smile and sniffed back another tear. "Daniel Scott got stuck, he just needed somebody to tell him."

"And it's taken a bunch of kids like Lee to point you in the right direction." Eva returned his smile. She couldn't undo the past, but she could help to brighten his future. "Do you know, Mr Carswell-Scott, I've had an idea?"

"Share it?" He squeezed her hand. "I love you so much."

"You know you want to jazz your house up?" Eva snuggled comfortably against him. "Why not get the outreach kids to paint murals on those lovely big blank walls?"

"I'll have to tell my probation officer, believe it or not," Daniel admitted. "But she won't say no. Shall we make it a party? Get the parents round too?"

"Yes! And if you like, I could get my mum to come over and help with the catering." Eva laughed. "She *loves* a party. And I want her to meet you."

"I didn't have a dad, not even on my birth certificate. Don't suppose there's a dad Catesby too, is there?"

"There is." Eva wondered what he'd make of her parents, the hippy and the banker. "Recently retired from his banking job, just started watercolour lessons. He might even join in with the murals!"

"I hope they'll approve of me." He sniffed and glanced down at himself. "I'll look a bit smarter when I meet them."

"They won't care, trust me." Eva kissed him. "They'll only want to know that we're happy."

"I didn't want to lie to you, but I'm not supposed to tell anybody," Daniel admitted. "You're the only one who knows outside of the people who *have* to."

"You didn't lie, not really. Daniel Scott is your official name, after all. And don't worry, I won't say a word."

"Do you think Mum would be proud?" His voice was small.

"She really, really would be, I'm sure of it." Eva combed back his hair. "And it's absolutely not your fault that she isn't here to see how far you've come."

For a long moment he studied her face, then he gave another tiny smile, like a ray of sun peeping through a storm cloud.

"I think she'd like your paintings a lot more than mine, though."

Eva laughed. "Do you know, I got a message from my agent saying someone wants dancing saucepans for a cookery book now. I seem to have found my niche!"

"I should sneak one in somewhere." He offered her half of the bun that he had split earlier. "A little Daniel Scott saucepan in Wayfarers hidden in the middle of a crowd."

"You should!" Eva laughed again, then fell silent as she bit into the bun. After a pause, she asked, "So what happens next? We go on our date, we get the kids up to yours for murals and partying…? Nothing changes, Daniel. That's what I mean."

"We go on our date," he whispered, as though he could hardly believe it. "And somehow I love you even more than before."

"I love you too, Mr Carswell-Scott."

Chapter Fourteen

Eva sat down at the table opposite Lyndsey.

"I'm so sorry I'm late, Lynds, I had to pop home first before I came out." Eva gestured to her hastily applied makeup. "How are you?"

"Not quite as glowing as you," Lyndsey replied meaningfully. "How is Sunglasses?"

"He's *extremely* well. Gorgeous and lovely." Eva squeezed Lyndsey's hand. "And you and Miles?"

"It's like we've known each other all our lives." Her friend beamed. "I adore the old sausage."

"Wonderful." Eva smiled. "And your ballet date was a success, was it?"

"Is it too early to say? Oh, Eva, I think he's *the one*!"

Eva almost squealed with excitement. "Really? Oh, that's so adorable! And to think, he was there all along, your good friend Miles. Wow, it's funny how these things happen, isn't it?"

Lyndsey's obvious glee at her romance was enough for Eva to push aside once and for all the misgivings she'd had about Lyndsey going out with her ex. If Lyndsey and Miles were happy, then that was all that mattered.

"All that time, there he was!" She clapped her hands together. "Now tell me about Mr Sunglasses! Is it still lovely?"

"Yes. He lets me work in his studio, and I stay over, and…it's like I've half-moved in with him already!" Eva had only gone home to change, pack some clothes in a bag and pick up her laptop. Some might think it was a bit too soon, but it was right. "And you'll never guess. Remember I said he wasn't the dating type? We are *actually* going on a date!"

"And a double one with us!" Lyndsey clapped again. "When?"

"Oh, Lynds, I can't…" Eva picked up the menu, even though she already knew what she wanted to order. "I don't think Mr Sunglasses has gone on a date in his whole life. I can't spring a double date including my ex on him!"

"It'll happen one day! Where is he taking you?"

"Maybe—hopefully before your wedding!" Eva laughed. "He wants me to decide, but I'm really stuck. I know the sort of place that I'd like to go to, but he's used to all those glitzy, sophisticated occasions, so I'm not sure. I'm more tagine in a Moroccan-themed café— he might want crisp white tablecloths and silver service."

"What about lovely pastels and cake stands?" *Pure Lyndsey, in other words.* "Choux buns?"

Eva tried to imagine Daniel sat there in his sunglasses and black suit. The picture in her head made her chuckle. "Hmm…not too sure. It needs to be a dinner date, really. An evening occasion. Can you think of anywhere?"

"Oodles of places really. It's all down to what sort of lovely nosh floats the boat." She took a sip of tea. "Black tie?"

Boat.

"Seafood," Eva said. "There's loads of speciality seafood restaurants in Brighton. I can just see him cracking his way through a lobster." And he'd make it look damn seductive, too.

"A chippy tea!" Lyndsey clapped and hooted with laughter.

"Mushy peas in a polystyrene pot in the rain! Not quite what I was thinking of." Eva widened her eyes and licked her lips. Maybe one day, for nostalgia's sake, but it didn't seem quite right for their first date. "A bit of glamour, that's what we need."

"What's the place—" She frowned and tapped her finger on the table. "Really chic, seafood. Oscar's? Maybe that?"

"Oh, yes, that'd be perfect!" Eva grinned as she took her phone out of her bag. "Thanks, Lyndsey, you're a lifesaver. I'd better ring now and book. You don't mind? I won't be a second."

"You won't get in without a ton of notice, but Miles knows the manager so I can do it for you? When do you want it for?"

"Even if I book it for the mighty Daniel Scott?" Eva had gone off calling him *bad boy* and *enfant terrible.* And neither was she going to dwell on the fact that during her relationship with Miles, he hadn't once taken her to Oscar's. "Well, if you could see if he'd squeeze us in, that'd be amazing. Table for two, tomorrow. It really is short notice, isn't it! Seven o'clock?"

Lyndsey lifted her bag onto the table and took out her mobile, flipping open its pink cover. "I'll ask Miles to give his chum a buzz. Consider it done!"

Her nails tapped over the screen before she put the phone down on the table between them, the cover open. Lyndsey and Miles beamed at Eva in close-up from the screen, a selfie on a sunny British beach. They looked like a couple, in a way that she and Miles never had. They fit together in that special way, just like she did with Daniel.

"So, if you're virtually moved in already, when is the official moving-in happening? Oh my God, Eva, should I buy a lovely new hat?"

"We're artists, darling," Eva deadpanned. "We don't do anything officially. Besides, I'd have to decide what to do with my little house. Rent it out, maybe, for holidays? Artists' retreats, perhaps, or..." She saw the mugshot of Lee Carswell again. "Subsidised holidays for kids who need a hand."

"I bet your neighbours would *love* living next to a crack den!" Lyndsey widened her eyes. "Or a knocking shop!"

"Lyndsey!" Eva rolled her eyes. Her friend would never understand, and she could never, ever know, of course, why Daniel was driven to help the children whose start in life had been like his. "Shall we order lunch?"

"I'm having an eclair today, to celebrate —" The phone buzzed and she peered at it. "Table confirmed!"

Eva clapped. "Oh, thank you, Lynds! And I think I might join you in an eclair..."

Chapter Fifteen

Eva hovered in the restaurant's bar, her eye on the door. Daniel should arrive at any moment. The taxi for his mystery tour had been booked to collect him from his house fifteen minutes earlier. Their first date. Slightly the wrong way round, but what a place to have it. And at short notice, thanks to the intercession of her best friend and her ex.

Her heart started racing as soon as she saw the car pull up, its orange *hire* light extinguished. As Eva watched, Daniel emerged from the rear seat. He was clad in black, sunglasses over his eyes, and he approached the restaurant with the same arrogant swagger that had carried him over the gallery floor to her on that first night. The maître d' hurried to open the polished glass door and a few words were exchanged before Daniel was shown with much polite ceremony to where Eva waited.

"Ms Catesby," the maître d' said to Daniel, as though there might be some doubt. "Enjoy your evening, sir, madam."

As he strode away, Daniel dropped the sunglasses down his nose just a touch and whispered, "Did you book company for the evening, Ms Catesby?"

Eva put her drink down on the bar as she went to encircle her arm around his waist. "Company?" She had no idea what he meant, and kissed him on the lips as a hello.

"They've got us down as a four." Daniel shrugged after they had exchanged a long kiss. "I let them know we're just a two. A happy, in love, two,"

"We have Lyndsey to thank, she helped get the booking. This is a very exclusive place, Mr Scott!" Eva would have kissed him again, but knew that snogging in the restaurant bar might be frowned on. "I wonder... Maybe we've been booked in as a four as a bigger table is more private? We won't be squashed up like sardines with other diners."

"Shall we have a drink before we go over, or are you ready to eat?" He slipped his arm around her.

"You could top up my wine for me." Eva held up her glass to him, grinning. "White, of course, to go with fish. Although I suppose you'll choose red?"

"Always." Daniel gestured to the barman and asked, "Another white, please, and whatever the best red you have is."

Then he kissed Eva's cheek and whispered, "The hotel's booked, so consider this a holiday."

"I packed my bag." Eva indicated her handbag, which could fit a toothbrush at most. She slid a menu across the bar towards them. "So what do you think of this as a venue for our first date? Do you like it?"

"I think it's perfect for two artists like us. Beats the pictures and a burger by a long way." He thanked the barman with a smile as the drinks appeared before them. "And tonight we have another magnificent bath, a bed with views over the sea, and the receptionist seemed to think I'd be interested in the fact that our shower is big enough for two."

"I'm rather interested by that too, Mr Scott. Do tell me more!" Eva chuckled saucily. "What do you fancy? The specials are up on that board, by the way."

"I don't even need to look. I'm thinking lobster." He raised his glass. "To art!"

"To art!" Eva clinked her glass against his. "And lobster."

"And another night without sleep, for the very best of reasons," Daniel added in a heated whisper.

A shot of desire burst through Eva and she brought her mouth to his again, but broke away from his tantalising lips. "I'm so tempted to go to the hotel now, but we really must have our date. Shall we order?"

Yet Daniel's attention was on the door, his face darkened by a frown. Then he asked, "Isn't that—"

"Surprise!" Lyndsey waved from the doorway as she glanced back at Miles as he strode along in her wake. She ignored the maître d' and headed for Eva. "Hello, lovely!"

"Erm… Yes, this is a surprise." Eva air-kissed Lyndsey, but struggled to smile.

A table for four? Oh, she hasn't…

She has.

"When I told Miles that you were eating here tonight, all we could think about was the sea bass!" She turned her dazzling smile on Daniel, receiving a faint quirk of the lips in reply. "But they couldn't fit us in unless we squeezed up with you and we didn't think you'd mind. Miles, come and meet the famous Daniel Scott!"

Miles, in his red and white striped shirt, which was supposed to be casual but worn by him looked like it should be under a suit, came forward and held out his hand to shake Daniel's. There was a nervous look on his face, and Eva wasn't sure if it was because he was meeting a celebrity or because he was meeting his ex's new man.

"Hi there, Daniel Scott. Miles Sutherland. Great to meet you. And… Eva, hope you're well." He glanced at Lyndsey, and an awkward smile came to his lips as he turned back to Daniel. "Heard a lot about you and your exhibition!"

"Pleased to meet you." Daniel shook his hand. "Can I get anyone a drink?"

"G and T!" Lyndsey beamed. "Miles, lovely?"

Miles had been staring at the specials board. Distracted, he nodded to Daniel. "I'll have the same, thanks."

The barman swung into action, not needing any further instruction this time.

Her first date with Daniel and she would have to endure Miles being awkward.

Fantastic.

Eva brushed her lips over Daniel's ear and whispered, "Sorry."

"I hear you've been keeping well, Miles." Eva rearranged her wrap. She was showing far too much cleavage to be at dinner with her ex and his girlfriend. "It's very sweet that you and Lyndsey are a couple now. You make a lovely pair."

Miles nodded, and looked to Lyndsey as if he were an actor who'd forgotten his lines.

"He's starstruck," Lyndsey explained, blinking at her own reflection in the sunglasses. "He's not used to famous gents."

"What do you do, Miles?" Daniel asked, perhaps taking pity on him. "You're not in the arts, right?"

Miles breathed out, like a punctured balloon. "No...no, I'm a surveyor. I go about with my binoculars, looking at the state of people's chimneys before they put an offer in on a house. Not quite as exciting as your line of work, but..." Miles laughed. Quite at what, Eva wasn't sure. "Hear you've bought a nice place?"

"My next project," Daniel said with a nod, squeezing Eva's waist. *Their* project.

"It's a gorgeous house," Eva told the gatecrashers.

"A little more spacious than your old place, eh?" Miles laughed. "But structurally sound, I'll give it that, Eva. Nice conversion job on those mews houses. By the way, Daniel, you'll want to keep an eye on those flat roofs on your property. Keep the gutters in good nick, too, as the last thing you want is a leak—1930s houses are a sod for that."

How excruciating. When Eva had first gone out with Miles, he had been fun. But one day he had changed, just as suddenly as if someone had flicked a switch.

"I'll keep one eye on that," Daniel deadpanned. "We're focusing on the interior right now, though. Making it a place for *us*."

"We're going to paint murals on the walls. It'll be amazing. The kids from outreach are going to join in," Eva told them.

Miles pressed his lips into a thin smile and laughed, a reedy sound that went straight through Eva like nails down a chalkboard. "You trust them in your house, Daniel? You're a braver man than I!"

"Richer too," Lyndsey laughed, nudging her boyfriend. "So when they steal the TV, Daniel can buy ten more anyway!"

Miles went on laughing, the reedy sound evolving into a snort.

That broken nose he got playing rugby at university isn't getting any better, even after the last surgery.

Lyndsey grimaced and said, "I've told you, that needs breaking and rebuilding. You need a full Michael Jackson. I'm not having you snorting and sniffing down the aisle when the time comes!"

Eva pasted on a smile. "It's good to give these kids a chance. Daniel's really got behind outreach, haven't you?"

Miles' laugh spluttered to a stop, his glance fixed on Daniel. "Hope they don't run off with your sunglasses! What d'you do then?"

Daniel lifted his sunglasses up into his hair and looked at Miles, unanswering. As Daniel parted his lips, the barman put down two glasses in front of the newly arrived couple. Lyndsey picked one up and exclaimed, "Big happy cheers, everyone!"

"Cheers!" Eva chimed in. She linked her hand with Daniel's where his rested on her waist.

"Your good health!" Miles nodded and held his glass up to Eva and Daniel. His glance stayed on Daniel again, as if he was surprised that under those sunglasses the man had eyes.

"How lucky are we, Eva?" Lyndsey took a sip. "Out with two boys!"

Unfortunately. Eva smiled politely. "Are you two ready to order? I'm absolutely famished!"

"Starters and mains and pudding." Her friend laughed. "A lovely big salad then my lovely sea bass. Miles wants soup and sea bass, don't you, darls?"

"Oh yes. The soup here is excellent." Miles put his arm around Lyndsey's shoulders. "They make their own bread, would you believe? Goes so well with the food. Really is good."

"Let's get our lovely nosh ordered and sit down, then," Lyndsey decided, resting her head on Eva's shoulder for a moment. It seemed to break whatever was brewing between Miles and Daniel, and he lowered the sunglasses over his eyes again. Now, though, Eva didn't wonder what he was trying to hide, because she recognised a change in her lover, a playfulness that they would never notice. He was playing at being the affected artist, playing at being a star, and when they were alone they would laugh at this despite the unexpected companions on their date.

Their orders taken, the two couples were led through the restaurant to a table that looked out over the prom. Eva laughed, pointing to a boat far out at the darkening sea. "Look, there's our dinner, it's on its way now!"

"Pinchy lobsters!" Lyndsey made claws of her hands and pinched at Miles, who batted her away with a smile. "Snap, snap!"

He leaned sideways in his chair, one arm over its back, apparently relaxed. "That leaves you and me, Daniel, as the only grown-ups!"

"Not me," Daniel replied. "I paint pictures for a living—that's not a proper grown-up job, thank God."

Miles turned rather pink and stared outside. As if he'd seen something outside to prompt him, he said to Daniel, "Been to see your show. Very interesting work, I must say. I'm not a particularly arty type—I'd say everything I know about art I've learnt from these two lovely ladies. But bloody good work. Modern stuff leaves me cold, but yours is very interesting."

Daniel relaxed just a little at her side. He leaned forward and picked up his glass.

"Coming from someone who doesn't care about modern art, I'm really pleased that my work touched you," he said. "We can only send it into the world. Once it's there, it's up to you."

Miles' cheeks turned a shade deeper. "It's not that I don't care about it—I struggle to get my head round most modern art. But yours, I understand... I think."

Quite an accolade from the man who had dismissed Eva's career as *scrawling*. She smiled at him, still wondering why he had changed. What had it been—the sudden advance of middle age?

"Too dark for me, not enough unicorns." Lyndsey laughed. "What do you see when you look at Mr Scott—*Daniel's* work, darling?"

Miles cleared his throat and fidgeted on his chair as if he wished he'd never brought it up. "Colours. I see colours. And the way the colours move." He tapped the side of his nose as if imparting a great secret. "Got to be visual in my job, you see. But in a very practical sort of way. So I probably look at paintings differently from how you all would. Anyway, I like them."

"Thank you." Daniel pushed his sunglasses up into his hair. "For seeing the colours."

Miles looked at Daniel, a little startled now that Daniel had lifted his sunglasses again. As Eva watched him, she knew that even if Miles had felt anything on seeing Daniel's paintings, he would never have admitted to it.

"Ah, look, here comes my soup!" Miles glanced away from Daniel at last.

Eva stroked the top of Daniel's thigh. This really wasn't how she had envisaged their first date. He caught her hand and squeezed it, only releasing her when their own food was set down before them. She could feel that he was relaxed though, caught that same mischievous smile as he dropped the sunglasses back into place.

Perhaps it wouldn't be a washout after all.

Their conversation wended its way to easier subjects. The different wines served in the restaurant, the bread and the fish. They chatted about favourite places to eat in Brighton, which could have been awkward when Miles mentioned a restaurant that he and Eva had gone to often while they were a couple, but she realised they had both moved on enough for it not to be difficult in the least. Miles brought up the topic of cars, while Eva showed Lyndsey her new handbag. They were, strangely, behaving not far off the way that couples on a double date would do.

"Handbag." Lyndsey said the word thoughtfully, her brow furrowing. She tapped her fork on her plate, then her eyes grew saucer-wide. "Oh. My. God."

Laughing, Eva set her handbag back down on the floor by her chair. What mini-drama was Lyndsey about to relate? "What's up? Have you just been cast as Lady Bracknell?"

"I was cleaning out my bag" — she began miming with her hands, taking invisible items from an invisible bag and putting them down on the table — "at work, whilst Rupe was bending my ear and— I had your keys, Eva, and I said, *oh heck, look at all the bits and bobs I'm toting around, I've even got Eva's keys!"*

Eva felt Daniel tense beside her, lifting his sunglasses. At the same moment Lyndsey looked at Eva.

"And I tipped the whole bag up and the man from *The Times* came and I had to whizz off and sort him out with his pass. You've still got mine, Mr Scott. When I came back, I don't remember seeing your keys again, Eva."

"Oh, Lyndsey…" Eva grasped both her hands over the table, forgetting about the dirty plates and glasses that stood between them. "Oh, God no… It *was* him then?"

"Just as well we got the locks changed." Miles stared at their joined hands. "Rupert, eh? Creepy bugger, if you don't mind me saying so. I want you to be careful around him, Lyndsey."

"He has a thing for Eva, not for me." She blinked her blue eyes. "I'm so sorry, I completely forgot about it until just now. I'm so glad you've got Mr Scott now, he'd bop Ru on the nose if he tried it again!"

Eva shivered. She let go of Lyndsey's hands and brought her wrap more tightly around her. "He made my bed. He tucked the duvet under the mattress. He smoothed the covers."

"It's all right," Daniel assured her, sliding his arm around her shoulders. "We'll sort it out with him."

Eva gazed into his dark eyes. His expression was unreadable. "How?"

"I'll get a restraining order on him if I have to." He held her gaze and she thought there was a flicker of something before he said, "I'm not going to hurt him, don't worry."

"I didn't think you would." Or did she? The little sod who broke windows, he hadn't pushed Emily Shaw off the cliff, but what would he do to Rupert? No, she couldn't think like that about him. He had changed. "I hate to say it but…oh God, I'm going to have to pull out of the auction. I'm so sorry, but I can't… The thought of him makes my skin crawl. And a restraining order — I can't go back to the gallery, can I?"

"We can sort out the auction," Daniel told her, but there was the promised exhibition of the children's work too, not to mention the memories of Lee Carswell and his mum wandering wide-eyed through the gallery thirty years ago. "That's not about him."

"I'm sorry, I don't want to mess everything up." Eva hated Rupert all the more now, for making her feel guilty. That was just the way a creep like him operated. "Maybe it's better if I hold my head up high."

"That's the spirit!" Miles grinned. "That's just what I always liked about you, Eva. You never let anyone walk all over you, and this Rupert chap shouldn't be an exception."

"And so like him to break into a house like a weird beard and tidy it up," Lyndsey observed, reaching to take Eva's hand. "I'll talk to him at work, don't fret."

Eva stared outside. She saw a figure pass along the prom and her heart was in her throat. Surely it wasn't — no, it wasn't Rupert. Everything was all right.

"I suppose I'll have to tell the police that he had access to my keys." Eva shivered again. "I can't not say anything."

"And they'll come to talk to him and he'll make my life miserable if he doesn't find a reason to sack me there and then!" Lyndsey's mouth turned down at the corners, tears filling her eyes. "We've changed the locks, why does it have to be a big fuss?"

"Come on, there, there... It's okay, Lyndsey." Miles brought her into his arms, gently kissing her face and stroking her hair. He looked up from his girlfriend to Eva and Daniel. "The police are very busy, Eva. All you need to do is ask Daniel here to have a word, and Rupert won't be bothering you ever again. Isn't that right? I know what I'd say to a man who'd been creeping about uninvited in Lyndsey's house!"

"It's for the police to deal with," Daniel told him, earning a strangled sob from Lyndsey. "Let's not turn vigilante over it."

"No, just get fired over it!" Lyndsey pushed her plate away. "I'm not hungry now, I don't want anything!"

"Now, now, come on Lynds, that's my girl..." Miles cooed over her, demonstrating that he was just the sort of man that a drama queen like Lyndsey needed. "You won't get fired. None of this is your fault."

Eva stared in surprise at that remark, picturing her keys on the desk as they fell out of Lyndsey's handbag in front of Rupert, but she didn't say anything. Besides, she was still surprised that despite what he had gone through, Daniel was happy for the police to deal with Rupert.

"Promise you won't tell them, Eva, please?" Lyndsey dabbed her napkin at her eyes and sniffled. "For me? For my job? We're best friends, aren't we?"

"Of course we're best friends!" Eva didn't comment on anything to do with the police. What a dreadful situation to be caught in, but she didn't know what else to do.

"So you won't tell them," Lyndsey pressed. "The locks are changed, you've got Daniel now and Rupert isn't exactly Jack the Ripper. Please, Eva? Do this one tiny thing for me?"

"Yes, I know, we've changed the locks, everything's great." But Eva would still tell the police. What if Rupert went after someone else, and what—what the hell would have happened if he'd let himself into her home when she had been in there by herself?

"Please," she whispered. "Why're you being so selfish?"

"That's not fair—" Daniel began, but he was silenced when Lyndsey's entire face crumpled with misery and she pressed it to Miles' shoulder, sobbing.

Eva could hear the chatter from nearby tables quieten, and cutlery stilled on plates. *Art world bad boy makes local arts administrator cry.* Was that what the newspaper would say?

"I wonder if perhaps it might be time to"—Miles looked up at Daniel and Eva, miming his two fingers walking over the tablecloth— "call it a night?"

"I haven't had my pudding," Lyndsey whispered sorrowfully. "If I'm losing my job tomorrow, I want my pudding."

"Do you want to know what the police will do?" Daniel asked, his voice hard. "Nothing. They'll do nothing because Rupert went to the right school, plays golf at the right club and has the right handshake. At worst, they'll laugh it off as *high spirits*, but more likely they'll promise to make a note of it then go back to the crossword. Have your pudding and for Christ's sake, stop roaring."

Miles' mouth dropped open. "Now look here, you might be a big-shot artist, but I won't have my...my girlfriend talked to like that."

Eva threw her napkin down onto her plate. Was the evening going to end with her boyfriend and her ex battling their way up and down the seafront? "Can we all just finish our dinner, please, before the fisticuffs erupt? This was supposed to be a date, not a—not whatever this has turned into."

"I want that raspberry cheesecake." Lyndsey pointed across the restaurant to another diner's plate, her equilibrium restored as quickly as a child coming out of a tantrum. "Mr Scott's a much-needed voice of sense, isn't he? Fisticuffs, as if either of these boys is the violent sort!"

Eva folded up her napkin. "I'm going to pass on dessert. Daniel and I—" She glanced at him. "I'm rather tired, actually."

"Let's go to the shake shop and get fat," Lyndsey urged Miles, pinching his cheek. "Still BFFs, Eva? Mum's coming down soon, she'll be heartbroken if we're scrapping over keys!"

"Of course we're still friends!" Eva left her seat to give Lyndsey a hug. Her strong floral perfume reminded Eva of a lazy summer's day, and she smiled. *How exhausting it must be to be Lyndsey.* "Everything's okay. You couldn't have known what would happen."

"I'll get dinner, since you scored the reservation." Daniel held out his hand to Miles, who received a jab from Lyndsey's elbow. "Nice to meet you, Miles."

Miles shook. "And you too, Daniel. Jolly decent of you, by the way, getting the bill. If you're sure. My treat next time?"

"A fair deal," Daniel agreed, gesturing for the bill. Somehow, by the time they were back on the street and Lyndsey and Miles had departed in search of their sugar fix, the crisis was averted. There were hugs and more handshakes and everyone parted in what seemed like good spirits.

"We're not far from The Mallard, are we? Shall we walk? It's a warm evening." Eva slipped her arm through Daniel's and sighed. "That really did *not* go how I'd planned."

"The lobster was amazing though," he observed. "And I'm sure the hotel can do something tasty for pudding for Salome and her escort."

Eva chuckled filthily. "Something creamy that I can lick from your nipples, I hope!"

"The receptionist can probably get anything you could wish for." Daniel slid his sunglasses up into his hair. "And tomorrow, because tonight isn't for serious, I need to know how you ended up with such a crazy best friend."

"Entertaining, isn't she?" Eva snorted. At least he was asking her about Lyndsey, rather than Miles. Discussing an ex on a saucy stay over didn't seem like a good idea. "She's a sweetheart, really. Tends towards the dramatic, but... Don't worry, all shall be revealed."

"Slowly, I hope, once we get to the hotel." He darted a kiss to Eva's cheek. "That dress is a work of art."

"*Slowly?* You tempter." Eva slid her hand down his back and rested it on his toned bottom. She let her wrap fall in a less demure fashion. After all, she was Salome, heading to a hotel room with her escort.

"What exactly did you tell the taxi people?" Daniel's voice was tinged with humour. "He was giving me a very funny look in the mirror."

She swung her handbag back and forth, a skip in her step and a giggle in her voice. "I pretended that I run an *agency* called Brighton Belles, and told them to please collect Mr Scott for an appointment with one of my clients. It's not my fault if they assumed I run an escort agency!"

"Do you know what he said when he dropped me off?" They paused on the hotel's steps and Daniel slipped his arms around her. *"Wish I had your job, mate!"*

"Oh, that's brilliant!" Eva tipped back her head and laughed. "You weren't too embarrassed, were you? Possibly as embarrassed as *I* was when you sent the taxi for me?"

"I gave him your number and told him to ring for an interview."

"You sod!" Eva pretended to swipe at him, then kissed him slowly on the lips. "Your client awaits, Mr Scott…"

"The room's booked under your name, Salome Catesby," Daniel informed her. "And I aim to send my client home *very* happy."

"I should think so too." Her arm linked with Daniel's, Eva strutted through the door of the hotel up to the reception desk. "Salome Catesby," she said in a breathy whisper.

"Ms Catesby, you're in the beautiful room four." It was a different receptionist this time, but no less polished and smiling. She too turned away from the computer to the large diary and she too had that same smooth demeanour in the face of her visitors. "The champagne is on ice. Can I get you anything else?"

"A dessert. Maybe a rather tart raspberry mousse?" Eva glanced at Daniel as she licked her lips. "And cream. Lots of whipped cream."

"Of course. I'll show you to the room." She took the key from a drawer and raised one appreciative eyebrow when Daniel reached out and plucked it from her fingers.

"No need," he told her. "I know the way."

They headed along the plush corridor to the hush of the bedrooms. Although not much of a hush, as the distinct sound of a spank came through the door of room two, followed by a groan. Eva chuckled, even as she found the sounds of other couples at play arousing. There was no doubt that Daniel felt it too, as he caught her by the waist and kissed her fiercely, pushing her back to the wall. His erection pressed to her through their clothes, the heat in his lips coursing through her blood in turn.

What sounded like another spank landed on the guest in room two, and this time they moaned. It echoed the need in Eva's veins, and she gasped into their kiss, fumbling with Daniel's belt. Were they allowed to do this in the semi-public space of the corridor? They surely wouldn't be the first. "Oh, I want you…"

"Here?" He gasped, massaging her bottom.

"Yes…" Eva sighed. "*Can* we?"

"So long as we make it fast," he purred. "And hard."

Eva slid her hand into his back pocket and found the foil packets that he kept there in readiness. She drew one out, tore the packet open with her teeth and nudged down his zip to put it on him. No underwear, of course, and that delicious erection of his was easily freed. Eva raised one leg, crossing behind Daniel's waist, and the silky length of her satin skirt rose up to reveal herself to him. He lifted her easily, the sounds of a stranger's pleasure echoing their own as their bodies joined.

"Brighton Belles?" Daniel whispered, arching his eyebrow.

"What else?" Secure in Daniel's arms, Eva lifted her other leg and crossed them around him. Thrusting against him, she whispered, "Salome Catesby, proprietor and procurer."

"I hope I'm your star attraction?" He dipped his head, nuzzling Eva's throat.

"Oh God, yes!" Eva's words escaped her on a sigh. "You're the man they all clamour for, but I keep you all to myself."

"I'll never want anyone but you." He gasped, thrusting harder. "I love you."

"I love you too!" Eva sighed her lover's name. She threw one arm up above her head, almost knocking a picture off the wall behind her as the occupant of room two moaned again. Daniel was silent apart from his gasps then, devoted to bringing them both to the peak of their pleasure. As the unseen man groaned behind the wall, it seemed like this was a secret they would all share, each caught in their desire.

Eva's pleasure rushed at her and through her, and she grabbed Daniel, holding him tight, her climax leaving her sighing and breathless. His head dropped to her shoulder as he caught his breath, soft groans still in his throat.

"To our room?" Eva stroked the nape of his bowed neck as she brought her feet back down to the floor. She heard the sound of him tidying his clothes, the scrape of the belt buckle and zipper before he scooped her up into his arms.

"Before the cheesecake gets there," Daniel told her with a wink.

Off they went along the corridor, the cries of whoever was in room two diminishing behind them. When they reached their room, Daniel turned the key in the door and threw it open with a flourish before carrying her over the threshold as though this was their wedding night. A thrill of anticipation went through Eva as the door closed behind them. The room was just as plush as the one they had shared before, the huge bed inviting. And tonight, they would stay here together, not make their separate ways home.

Chapter Sixteen

Eva lay across the bed, a sheet draped over her in an accidentally artistic way. She blew across the surface of her tea. "Despite all that pleading from Lyndsey yesterday evening, I'll have to, won't I?"

"Have to?" Daniel took a bite of his breakfast croissant and offered it to her. "What do you mean?"

Eva sat the antique cup back in its saucer. "Go to the police. Seeing as I reported it to them, someone being in my house. If Rupert had access to my keys, then I really should tell them, shouldn't I?"

"You do understand why I can't deal with it like our friend Miles thinks I should, don't you?" He kissed her shoulder. "It's not because I don't care."

Eva caressed his cheek. "Because you have a record? Miles is talking a load of nonsense. He wouldn't say boo to a goose, let alone *have words* with someone like Rupert. I bet he's scared of him." Eva started to laugh. "I bet he's scared of Lyndsey too!"

"It's not the record, but I'm on probation *forever*. I go to his office, we speak calmly, nobody loses their temper, we say goodbye." He leaned into her touch, closing his eyes a little. "But if Rupert decides to tell the police that I hit him or threatened him or anything like that, I could go back to prison. They don't play about with an order like mine, they come down hard."

Eva blinked, trying to stop herself from crying. Not because he wouldn't — couldn't — protect her, but because his life had been so straitened by something he hadn't even done. "It's not fair, is it? For you. That someone like Rupert can carry on like he does, his word counting for more than anyone else's. And I bet if he went to court for trespass, he'd have some expensive barrister saying it was *my fault* for the tepid snog we had. I was clearly asking for some creepy sod to come into my house and move my shit about."

"You don't really believe this would go to court?" Daniel gave a dry laugh. "Someone might have had a key and might have let themselves into your house and made your bed. He wouldn't even *need* a barrister — it'd never make court, you must know that."

"If he keeps doing it, though, it would have to." Eva sighed. "But he's not going to get the chance. I'm not going to let him. You might think it's only a little thing, but I was so scared."

"I don't think it's a little thing, but without some proof they won't do anything." He blinked, his expression darkening. "Do you really think I don't understand how frightened you were? I spent the first ten years waiting for someone to realise who I really was — I *know* what it's like to be terrified of who's in the shadows."

Eva kissed his cheek. "Ten years? That's a long time to always be looking over your shoulder."

"Even now, all these years later, I still wonder sometimes when someone looks at me a little too long." Daniel took a deep breath. "I don't not care about what happened in your house, but we both know the coppers aren't going to do much."

"I know. And nothing's really happened since. Maybe he's given up?" But did men like Rupert ever give up? Eva told herself that he *would*, otherwise she'd fret over it and it would do no one any good. She held Daniel's hand. "If it makes any difference, I had no idea who you were, or used to be, until I thought of Mr Carswell, and...well, you know."

"And I only used that name to book our room here. It was a stupid risk, but you know why I did it." His head moved to rest against Eva's shoulder. "One happy night."

"The first of many." Eva turned her face to brush her lips against him. "I love *you*, whatever your name is."

"Not Salome, that's for sure!"

Eva put her tea aside and danced her fingertips across his chest. "Do you want me to tickle you, Mr Scott, because I will!"

"What I *want*," he told her casually, "is for you to move in with me."

Eva sat up in surprise, and her face split with a grin. "Daniel! I don't know what to say! I mean...I *do*, but— You're sure, aren't you?"

"I know you've got your own place and it's a big thing to ask you to leave it," Daniel replied. "But I'd like us to live together *somewhere* whenever you're ready to say yes."

"I've half-moved in already. Bit by bit." Eva kissed him, then whispered, "We can make the house *ours*, can't we?"

"Our home." He smiled, touching his forehead to hers.

Chapter Seventeen

Eva parked outside the gallery. She'd packed her car with as many of her belongings as would fit. It was the first trip to load up and move into Daniel's. And as such, new beginnings and all that, she needed to have a word with Rupert.

She smiled at the receptionist as she went into the gallery. "Is Rupert in? I need to have a word."

"He's out at lunch at the mom—"

"Eva!" The doors swished open to admit Rupert, his pinstripe jacket thrown over one shoulder. "To what do I owe the pleasure?"

Eva nodded politely. Her skin was covered in goosebumps, but she was fairly sure it wasn't down to the air conditioning. "Rupert. I just popped by to have a word. If you have time?"

"Step into the office." His tone was cooler than the conditioned air and he turned his back on her to stride across the lobby towards the stairs without waiting.

Eva gave the receptionist a small wave and followed Rupert up the stairs. She saw a flash of colour from the corner of her eye, and knowing Daniel's artwork was here made her feel as if he was too. He had endured so much, and she only had to confront a creep.

"I've had Lyndsey in here this morning." Rupert opened the office door and threw his jacket onto a mahogany coat stand just inside the room. "Chattering on with all sorts of rubbish about keys and your house."

"That's what I want to talk about." Eva loitered in the open doorway, not confident enough to close the door behind her. She wasn't thrilled at the thought of being shut in with him. "I know what you did, Rupert."

"I've never heard such rubbish in my life. Making your bed, wasn't it? Carrying bloody vases around?" He laughed, but the sound was cold. "Is it that boyfriend of yours? Been sharing his marching powder?"

Eva shook her head. "It was you. You did it." Her controlled voice began to rise in pitch. "You had the opportunity to take my keys, because whoever it was had keys to get in, and— It was *you*, I know it was!"

"I applaud you, Eva, I really do." Rupert puffed out his chest and folded his arms. "Why bother with the guy who owns the gallery when you can fuck the artist and get to the top?"

"*What*?" Rage flared inside Eva and she slammed the door behind her. Was it just Rupert who thought that, or everyone in Brighton? "You really think I— That the only reason I didn't want to go out with you is because I thought *ooh, goodie, I've snared a famous artist?* No, actually, it's because I *don't like you*. Do you understand? How dare you! And I don't care if Daniel is famous or not—and it has *nothing* to do with you anyway!"

"It will when I'm hosting your boyfriend's auction and your chavs are displaying their work proudly in my gallery!" he shouted, his face reddening. "I know a few journos who'd like to hear about his coke habit, maybe I'll have an anonymous word in an ear or two? Do they still do doorstepping these days?"

"Oh, a threat? To go to the press?" Eva's throat tightened and she saw Lee Carswell again, a frightened little boy standing in front of the camera in a police station. The media might never know who Daniel had once been, but they loved to destroy a golden boy, and Daniel Scott would be savaged. "And that would be wise, would it, with your gallery stuffed full of Daniel's work?"

"Would it be wise to drum up scandal and column inches about a man whose work is in my gallery, this bringing in even more proles?" He tapped his finger against his chin. "You really are pretty but stupid, Eva, I didn't quite realise until now."

"Proles? Wow... Do you have any respect for *anyone*?" Eva shook with anger, ice creeping into her voice. "You don't, do you? Not a shred. You disgust me."

"Trot on, I've got calls to make." Rupert's hand closed over her elbow. "And when the journalists are rooting through his bins, be sure to tell Daniel you sent them!"

Eva froze as he grabbed her arm, her flesh prickling as if an army of insects were walking over her. "You dare, Rupert—I will rip your phones out myself! This is your revenge, is it? Because I wouldn't go out with you, you'll try to destroy a decent man? Well, I hope the press enjoy rooting through his bins and finding nothing but empty tubes of paint and my old lipsticks!"

"Like the used condom the pair of you left in my office?" He jabbed his finger into her face. "There're tarts like you all over the scene, darling. Wait until he gets a sniff of the art groupies and you'll be out like the slut he thinks you are! When it happens, come back to Uncle Rupert and maybe, *maybe*, I'll let you hang a little drawing on my toilet wall."

He pushed her back against the door and kissed her, his mouth tasting of cigars and whiskey. Eva tried to battle her shock at his outrage towards her, tried to push him off, tried to scream against his damp lips. She knew then what she had noticed during that unimpressive kiss on their failed date. This was power for Rupert, not love, or affection, or even lust. He wanted to control and possess.

Out of nowhere, there was a knock at the door. Rupert started back, releasing her elbow and wiping his hand across his mouth as the knock sounded again. There was a trace of Eva's dark coral lipstick on his face.

Eva shoved him away. "You bastard! You obnoxious shit!"

"What the fuck is this?" Daniel threw the door open, Lyndsey following in his wake. For a moment they were silent, then he stalked into the office, his black eyes blazing with fury as he pointed at Rupert. "You piece of shit!"

Eva grabbed Daniel by the arm. All she could think of was his warning—that Rupert might decide that Daniel had attacked him, and Daniel would be back behind bars. "Time to leave…come on…"

"Come on, bad boy!" Rupert beckoned Daniel forward and his arm tensed, his muscles tightening beneath her hand. "Didn't you know this is what tarts do? I had her over the desk a couple of days ago, didn't she tell you?"

"You filthy pig!" Lyndsey's voice was a brittle whisper and she shrank back into the doorway. "You dirty, filthy, lying pig."

Eva shook her head and tried to drag Daniel into the corridor after Lyndsey. She heaved for breath as she spoke. "How dare you, you revolting, repulsive man?"

"Daniel, please." Lyndsey joined in as Daniel pulled his arm free and started into the office, the air fizzing with fury. He was going to hit Rupert, Eva realised. He would hit Rupert and Rupert would report him and —

"This isn't finished," Daniel told him in a voice as cold as ice, his tone somehow too calm despite his fury. Even Rupert was stilled, his ruddy face paling. "This isn't finished at all, but you are. You're fucking *done!*"

"We need to leave, Daniel. Now."

"I'm going home," Lyndsey decided. "Can I have a lift, Eva? I don't want — "

She stifled a sob against her hand and Daniel turned, telling them both, "Let's get out of here." He looked at Eva then, and she wondered when their gazes met if he had seen that tiny smidgeon of doubt, the one she had dismissed immediately.

They headed along the corridor, Eva primed for the sound of Rupert in pursuit. But she heard nothing. Not even the sound of him making his threatened telephone calls.

"I just wanted to draw a line under it," Eva said, her voice quiet as they went through the foyer. "It was stupid of me."

"Not your fault," Daniel told her, taking a deep breath of fresh air as the doors opened for them. "I mean it, though, I'll finish the fucker."

There was such venom in his words, and it surprised her to hear it echoed in Lyndsey when she added, "That's the worst thing, I feel sick thinking that he did that."

Eva drew her best friend and her lover into an embrace. "Let's just...just calm down a bit, shall we? He's a horrible man, Lyndsey—" Daniel would help, wouldn't he? He could find Lyndsey a new job with all those contacts of his. "But we need to go. Erm... I can squeeze you into my car, Lynds, if you still want that lift? Do you want to come back to ours and help me unload?"

"Could you drop me at Miles' office instead? Is that all right?"

"Yes, of course, anywhere you like." Eva kissed Lyndsey's cheek, then Daniel's. "I'll see you at home, darling?"

"I've got something on tonight that I can't cancel, but I don't want you in your own," Daniel told them, his voice still clipped with contained anger. "Lyndsey, how'd you fancy coming over and keeping Eva company for a few hours? I'll even buy you a takeaway."

"Shall we have Thai, Lyndsey?" Eva tried to smile. They'd make the best of it—they had to. Lyndsey nodded, weeping, and blinked fresh tears away, but there was something in Daniel's face that she couldn't read and this mysterious *something* he was suddenly doing... What was it?

"If you want to report this to the police," Daniel told Eva, "I'm one hundred percent with you. And,

Lyndsey, I know a dozen galleries that'll jump to take you on, don't worry."

"Thank you, darling." Eva stroked his jaw, which seemed tight with contained rage. "I *will* go to the police. Lynds, let's head off. I'll see you later, Daniel."

Eva unlocked the car and opened the passenger door for Lyndsey. "You'll just need to hold this box on your knee, if that's okay."

"I'll see you later, Daniel." Lyndsey smiled as Daniel brushed his lips against Eva's cheek.

"I'll follow in my car," he told them. "I want to stay close."

Eva checked in her rear-view mirror as she drove Lyndsey to Miles' office. All the way there, Daniel's blue sports car with its white stripe on the bonnet followed behind like a guardian angel.

Chapter Eighteen

Eva put her pair of pottery candlesticks on the wide blank ledge above the fireplace in Daniel's lounge. They looked rather small there, so she crossed the room and put them on the windowsill. A little bit better, perhaps. It was nice to do normal things like this, to try to calm herself down from what had happened earlier. She'd rung the police, and they'd been kind and said they'd make a note on the file, but Eva knew there wasn't much they could do. Unless Rupert committed an even bigger outrage, and Eva really hoped he wouldn't.

She had given up asking Daniel what he was up to that evening. Despite the combined efforts of her cajoling, kissing and tickling, he wouldn't yield up his secret. Maybe it was something to do with his previous life, something that would have to remain a secret.

"Do they look okay on the windowsill? Or are they too diddy?"

"They look great. I like that my house is suddenly full of candlesticks." Daniel fastened the remaining buttons on his clean black shirt. "And thank you for trusting me enough to not demand an explanation about tonight. Tickling got you nowhere either, but you'll find out soon enough."

"All I'm saying is, it better not be a lads' night out with Miles!" Eva laughed at the idea of it, an entire evening of Miles staring at the lenses of Daniel's sunglasses while warning him about the dangers of a 1930s flat roof.

"You found me out." He slipped his arms around her. "And I'm not going to challenge Rupert to a duel either, I'll leave that to the coppers. Just have a good time and I'll be back before midnight."

Eva nodded sagely. "Or your car turns into a pumpkin." She heard someone on the driveway and told herself not to panic. "That'll be Lynds!"

"Takeaway money's on the hall table. I promised it'd be my treat." He kissed her nose. "Don't wake the neighbours."

"Don't worry, darling, we can do that when you get back later." Eva laughed as she headed to the front door.

"I'll bring dessert. Just for us." Daniel's keys jangled as he twirled them on his fingertip. The bright smile that he bestowed on Eva disappeared into the much-photographed artistic scowl as the door opened to admit Lyndsey, her arms filled with bright pink flowers.

"Lynds! Are you practicing for your wedding, or are those a gift?" Eva gave her a hug.

"They're for you. Miles and I wanted to do something to show you how much we love you." She held out the flowers. "I know I can be an old silly, but you had such a horrid day."

"You'll ruin my reputation if you put them in a window." Daniel kissed Eva's cheek. "Have a good night."

Eva laughed again. "Bye, darling! See you later!" She turned to Lyndsey. "These are gorgeous. Let's put them in the vase that got moved about. Make something happy of it."

"Put them in the middle of a prominent window," Lyndsey told her as told Daniel closed the front door. "What a gorgeous house, not bad for a boy from care!"

Eva showed Lyndsey into the kitchen and carefully laid the flowers down on the marble worktop. "He's done really well for someone who had a hell of a lot against him." *If only Lyndsey knew.*

"How does a person just end up in a home, though?" Lyndsey perched on a stool and rested her elbows on the counter surface. "Does he not have any parents? I imagine you know all there is to know about the mysterious Mr Scott!"

"Let's just say he had a very difficult childhood. He could've been one of the outreach kids." Eva tried to think of Kieran and Sam, Jayden and Wai, rather than Lee Carswell. "And now he has an enormous kitchen with its own wine fridge. Would you like to choose?"

Eva knew that sounded flippant, but she was doing her best to skate over the ice.

"Anything rosé for me." She drummed her fingers against the marble. "The police haven't rung me yet to ask me what happened, but I imagine they'll get to it. What a rotter Rupe was!"

Eva produced a Spanish rosado from the fridge and took two glasses from the cupboard. "I don't think there's much they can do, Lynds. I rang them earlier, and they didn't exactly fob me off, but I get the impression that they'll only act if he does something far worse. I doubt he will, I hope he won't. But I don't think they'll be phoning you or Daniel."

"I suppose you can't put a man away for a life for a snog, even if it *was* a horrible sleazy one!" She pouted. "Is that where Daniel's gone off to tonight? To box his rotten old ears?"

Eva winced as she poured the wine. "It was foul. And when I saw my lipstick on his face afterwards, it somehow made it worse. Do you know what I mean? Like him making my bed…as if there's intimacy where there isn't." She pushed the wine across the worktop to Lyndsey. "Daniel's busy tonight. Something important, apparently."

"A mystery something?"

"Would appear so…" Eva grinned. "I joked and said he was going on the razzle with Miles! Can you imagine what that would be like?"

"Poor old Miles, he's not the most artistic boy, but he *is* trying." Lyndsey laughed. "I'm educating him!"

"I was impressed that he'd actually been to look at Daniel's paintings. More than can be said about most of the people who turned up for the private view!"

"We've now unofficially sold them all. People like the darkness, it would seem."

Nodding, Eva pushed away the image of that wronged little boy again. "That's one of Daniel's talents, I think, expressing something very dark which is inside us all."

"Even unicorns," Lyndsey told her with a wink.

Eva patted Lyndsey's hand. In her gentlest voice, she asked, "Are you okay after what happened earlier?

You seemed really upset." There had been something in the way Lyndsey had reacted that worried Eva. *Had* Rupert made a pass at her, despite what she'd said the other day?

"It made me think—" Her lips wavered again, just the hint of a wobble. "It reminded me of something that happened once, I won't depress you with it!"

"Oh, Lynds…" Eva put aside her glass to hug her friend. "If you'd feel better for a chat about it, you can tell me. That's what friends are for."

"You've never asked me where my dad is, in all the years we've known each other." And Eva hadn't, because Lyndsey had never mentioned anyone but her dotty mum. It wasn't the sort of thing someone could ask either, especially not with Lyndsey's penchant for drama. "I haven't seen him since I was six."

"I'd always assumed your mum and dad had split up." Eva now thought she knew the reason why. A child of six, his own daughter? Rupert's vile kiss came back to her, and she wiped the back of her hand across her mouth. "Gosh, Lynds, I'm so sorry."

"Well, that's why I won't ever go back to work with Rupert." She shrugged, her lip firm once more. "Someone should teach him a lesson though, something he won't forget. People like that should suffer the way I did, *we* do. Prison wouldn't do it, they'd come out and throw money around and do it to someone else. It needs to be a real lesson, something they have to live with, like a disease that eats away at them. A rotten, horrible disease."

Eva knew Lyndsey wasn't exaggerating. To have gone through whatever she had as a child, at the hands of a parent who should've protected her, had to have left a scar. One she had dressed up behind smiles and pretty frocks and manicures, but the shadow was still there.

Was that why she hadn't liked Daniel's art, because the darkness in his work too closely resembled her own? A child unprotected and afraid.

"I rather think Daniel will use his contacts to teach him a lesson. Rupert can't go on doing that. Creepy, horrible man. He'll get his comeuppance, you'll see."

"He'll sell the gallery to someone else and make a fortune." Lyndsey clutched the wine glass and raised it to her lips. "Or he'll swagger about just like he does now and nothing will change, you wait and see."

"He's just lost himself an excellent administrator, hasn't he, and incurred the wrath of Daniel Scott. If he keeps on the way he does, he's eventually going to get himself into a whole world of trouble." *I hope.*

"It's funny, isn't it, how Daniel started out as the victim and now, if he wanted, he could deal out the punishment?" She blinked her blue eyes, the tears dried now. Then she took a sip from her glass and smiled. "Let's talk about something happier."

Eva opened the drawer where Daniel kept his takeaway menu stash and fanned them across the worktop. "Let's talk about...dinner!"

"A far happier subject." Lyndsey laughed, before downing the remainder of her wine in one spirited gulp.

Chapter Nineteen

The next morning, Eva was up and dressed, ready for another run down to her house to collect more of her belongings. She was halfway to the bottom of the stairs with a large, empty suitcase when she heard the sudden burst of a loud engine speeding up the driveway. She dropped the suitcase where it was and hurried into the hallway.

"Is someone stealing the car?" Daniel called playfully from upstairs. "What's the noise outside?"

Through the glass panels of the door, Eva saw Lyndsey's car hurtling over the gravel.

"It's Lyndsey!" Eva shouted in reply as she unbolted the door to open it. "Maybe she left her lip gloss last night!"

Lyndsey flung open her car door and stumbled from the interior in her hurry.

"Eva!" she called urgently. "Have you heard?"

Eva stepped aside to let Lyndsey enter the house. Her remark about lip gloss couldn't have been more unfortunate, as Lyndsey's usually careful makeup was a mess of tears and streaks. After what Lyndsey had confided in her last night, Eva wondered if this could be something serious. Had her father come back? "Heard what, Lynds? Are you okay?"

"Rupert—" She looked over Eva's shoulder to the front door where Daniel stood, dressed in a robe of midnight-blue silk. "Someone killed him!"

"Killed—? What the hell happened?" Eva slid her arm around Lyndsey's shoulder and guided her towards the lounge. She met Daniel's gaze. It wasn't him, she knew it. He had never been nor ever would be capable of taking a life. But what if someone thought he was?

"I don't know but Joyce went in last night—" She took a deep, shuddering breath. "To clean after... We had a charity group in and Miles gave the keynote, so Joyce went in to clean after the guests went home and she found him in his office!"

"His *office*? I thought you were going to say he'd been killed at home, or in a car accident. But his office?" Everything from yesterday flashed before Eva's eyes. The office, the very room she'd been in with the man, and only hours later, someone had killed him there.

"All bloody!" Lyndsey crumpled down onto the sofa, sobbing. "Oh God! I got there to clear my things and there are police everywhere and Joyce says he was murdered!"

"Murdered?" Daniel took a few steps over the threshold. "He can't have been."

"Could it have been an accident, Lynds?" *Please, God, let it be an accident.* "Had he been drinking at the charity do and tripped or something? Fell over and knocked his head?"

Lyndsey shook her head very slowly, her eyes wide as she peered over Eva's shoulder at Daniel. "That's not what she said."

"What did she say?" Daniel asked in a whisper.

Eva caught his glance. He was thinking the same thing as her, surely he was. That if someone knew his history, the finger of suspicion would swing Daniel's way.

"Lyndsey, come on…" Eva tried to coax her. "What did Joyce see?"

"He'd been beaten to death," she whispered behind her hand, as though sharing a playground secret. "She says the hat stand was smashed up and there was blood everywhere."

Eva recoiled, as if she could smell the metallic tang of Rupert's shed blood. "Was he robbed?" Because that would make sense of the brutality, somehow.

Lyndsey shrugged, her gaze still on Daniel. Then she murmured, "Who could've— Poor Joyce!"

She had no pity for Rupert, then, but Eva wasn't surprised. Why did Lyndsey keep looking at Daniel, though? He wouldn't have, no matter how angry he had been yesterday.

"Makes you wonder— if someone did it in a rage, was it some other woman he'd assaulted? But more than a…" *Kiss.* Eva couldn't say it. The memory of his kiss came back to her, and before her was the bloodied, smashed face of a dead man.

"I'll get you a drink," Daniel murmured. "You too, Eva?"

"Yes…" Nausea washed through her. Rupert wouldn't torment her ever again, nor anyone else. But to be killed in his own office, beaten to death? Was that justice, or savagery? "They say hot, sweet tea is good for a shock, don't they?"

She heard Daniel's bare feet padding away, and Lyndsey's sobbing getting louder.

"God!" she exclaimed, clutching Eva's hand. "Can you imagine?"

"I'd rather not!" Eva swallowed. "I couldn't stand him, but...I'm not sure anyone deserves to die like that."

"You probably want to talk to Daniel?" she whispered. "Don't you?"

"Why, what would I need to talk to him about?" Eva shook her head, trying to push away her mounting disquiet. Surely Lyndsey, her best friend, couldn't think that Eva was living under the same roof as a killer? "They had that big thing yesterday—" Eva's voice rose, her throat tight. "Daniel was furious with Rupert, but surely you don't think he'd beat a man to death over it? Finish him in the art world, yes, but—Good God, Lyndsey, Daniel's not a killer!"

"Men get heated, anything can happen, and he was so angry!"

"Lyndsey, you surely don't think that every man wandering around out there could fly into a murderous rage and savage someone to death—like that?" Eva clicked her fingers. "The human race wouldn't last very long if that was true!"

Lyndsey sniffed deeply and whispered, "I won't tell the police, don't worry."

"There's nothing to tell!" Eva realised she had clenched her hands. She straightened out her fingers and had to look away from Lyndsey. Maybe going through what she had as a child at the hands of the one man in the world a girl should trust had soured her perception of the entire gender. And it wasn't Eva's place to be angry with her for that.

"How late did he get back? Where was he?" She sniffed again. "Do you not even wonder?"

"Wonder what?" Daniel asked from the doorway, a steaming mug in each hand.

Eva watched the steam curl up from the cups and dissolve in the air as she tried to find a calm response. "Thanks for the drinks, darling!"

"What were you asking, Lyndsey?" He padded into the room, greeted by silence from their guest. As the silence deepened, he put down the mugs and waited.

Eva snapped round to look at Lyndsey. "I'm not going to say it, Lyndsey, because you shouldn't even *think* that about the man I love."

"I didn't think anything," she protested. "But you reported Rupert and Daniel was furious and — you *did* go out, Daniel!"

"Out," he repeated. "Not murdering people!"

Eva took his hand. "Lyndsey, please, you're upset. Take a moment and just *think*. You're seeing guilt where there isn't any."

"I don't think you did anything," Lyndsey protested quickly. "But the police might ask, that's all. After the report yesterday."

"And if they do, I'll tell them where I was," Daniel promised.

Yesterday, Eva had tickled Daniel on that very sofa, both laughing as she tried to make him tell her where he was off to. And he wouldn't say. Wherever he had been, Eva hoped the police would believe him.

"Don't worry," Daniel told them both, kissing Eva's hair. "The half dozen people I was with can tell them too."

"So there you go." Half a dozen people. Had he been on a stag night? A fairly sedate one for him to arrive home sober before midnight. The tension drained out of Eva and she sagged back against the sofa.

From Lyndsey's bag, her phone trilled into life, and she whispered, "I can't answer that, I can't speak to anyone!"

Eva patted Lyndsey's arm. "You really should. What if it's Miles, or your mum?"

Lyndsey fished out the mobile and peered at it. She said to Eva, "It's Mum."

"Talk to her, Lynds. You'll feel better for it. You've had a terrible shock." Eva began to drink her tea. They'd *all* had a shock.

"Can I—" She gestured to the hallway and Daniel nodded, as though he would do anything else. Lyndsey rose to her feet and left the room, tapping at the screen as she went.

Eva glanced over her shoulder. Her candlesticks still weren't in the right place, even now. It bothered her more than it should. *A man has been killed, and I'm fretting over candlesticks.* She pulled Daniel into her embrace. Only then did she realise she was shivering.

"I didn't go anywhere near him," Daniel whispered, clinging to her. "That's not where I went last night, I swear it."

"I know you didn't, you wouldn't have." Eva held more tightly to Daniel and the shivers ebbed away. "I'm sorry for Lyndsey accusing you, but please don't be angry with her. She has little reason to trust men."

"She didn't accuse me, she thought what anybody would've." Daniel sighed. "I'm going to ring my probation officer and let her know what's going on. Believe me, there's no way I could've been doing anything last night other than what was in my diary. It's meant to be a nice thing, but— It'll be all right."

A nice thing. Eva brightened at his words. Something nice in a world where a man had been killed in his own office. "I know it will be all right, darling."

"And the Lyndseys of this world…" His lips were softly reassuring against her hair. "There'll always be Lyndseys."

"She—" Eva looked towards the door into the hallway. She could hear Lyndsey on the phone, but not make out what she was saying. "I'll tell you later. What do we do, though? Just go on with the day?"

"What else can we do?"

Eva nodded. "I was going to fetch some more things from my house, but would you mind coming with me? If you're not busy, I mean."

"We'll spend the day together. I don't want you on your own."

Eva saw her house again, the bed made by an invisible hand. Now the hand of a dead man. "I know it sounds ridiculous, but I'm scared. As if I'll go in there and meet…" She glanced at Daniel before looking away. "As if I'll meet Rupert's ghost."

"You're not alone anymore."

"Mum's coming down on the next train." Lyndsey stood in the doorway, holding her phone. "Can I wait here until she arrives? I feel all at sixes and sevens, I keep thinking—I should care."

"Of course you can wait here, it's fine." Eva forced herself to think of something else. Not of Rupert, not of the flash through the window or the silent intrusion into her home. "Do you want anything to eat? Me and Daniel attempted my mum's rock bun recipe if you're feeling brave!"

"Are they sweet?" She dabbed her eyes with a tissue. "I need something sweet before I pass out. I've always struggled with shocks!"

Eva went over to her friend and slipped her arm around her. "There's chocolate in the fridge as well. You're bound to be shocked, you saw him every day, and now…"

"I'll go and throw some clothes on," Daniel decided. "And make that call."

"Anything as long as it's black." Eva winced after saying it. Were they supposed to dress for mourning? She smiled gently at her friend. "Come on, Lynds, let's raid the kitchen."

Yet even as they did, she couldn't help but think of Daniel trying to explain this to his probation officer, one of a handful of people who knew who he truly was. Someone had killed Rupert, and the only thing she knew was that it couldn't have been Daniel.

Chapter Twenty

Eva had hoped that shifting boxes and suitcases and spider plants and goodness knows what else all day would have worn her out enough to sleep. But as she and Daniel lay in bed together that night, his arm around her, she was far from being able to sleep. Her body was on alert, awaiting some unnamed, faceless threat. What would it be, a car pulling up outside? But not Lyndsey this time, no—a car with a blue light and a siren.

It was almost midnight when she heard Daniel's phone beep with an incoming message. She jumped despite herself and he kissed her hair before picking up the mobile and swiping the screen.

"Daniel, who is it?" Eva wasn't about to crane her neck to see, but she couldn't shake her trepidation. What if it was bad news? The worst kind of news. That Daniel was going to be taken away.

"I didn't want to spoil the surprise but—" A low light filled the room when Daniel reached out and flicked on the lamp. It spilled across the bare walls that would one day boast the children's art, the vast white expanse above the bed where the mermaids would soon swim beneath the pier. "You haven't asked where I went last night. Nobody ever trusted me like that before."

"Of course I do. I couldn't love you if I didn't." Eva held his hand.

"I had two appointments last night." Daniel looked down at their linked hands. "The first was with Kieran and his mum at their place. I wanted to talk to her about some opportunities for boys like him, funds to help him develop that talent of his. I didn't tell you because, well, I wanted to ask him to work with me and organise the other kids on a bit of a project for you. A thank you bash, and a mural right across the foyer in your honour."

Eva started to laugh, with relief and with love. "Daniel! That's the loveliest thing! Oh…I don't know what to say."

"And Kieran was completely up for the idea of being the boss. His mum started crying, she was so happy." He laughed gently. "But I wasn't there all night. I had a second call to make."

"Go on, Mr Mystery…"

"I missed you at the Tate." Daniel reminded her of that first conversation. "And I need to put that right. There was no way that sketch of the kids was being auctioned in Rupert's place after what he did to you so… I pulled some strings."

And he fell frustratingly silent.

Eva gasped. "You didn't… The Tate? Is the auction going to happen at the Tate? Daniel! I'll have no choice but to tickle you again!"

"I had to agree to giving them a few exclusives, but the outreach artwork will be displayed right there in the turbine hall alongside some new Daniel Scott pieces." He snuggled her tight in his embrace. "And that's where our auction's going to be. The kids and their folks are my guests of honour—let's give them a night they'll remember forever?"

"I can't quite believe— You're the best of men. Really, you are. That's the most wonderful thing anyone's ever done for those kids, you do realise that?" Eva couldn't reach his lips from where she was lying, so she pressed her lips to his chest instead, over his heart.

"And I don't want it to end there, I want to see them on the right path. I spent *hours* with these gallery suits last night sorting this." A watertight alibi indeed, just as he had said. "It could be the start of something bigger, couldn't it? Something to help kids who don't have to be able to paint really. The only qualification is wanting to be there and create something. It doesn't have to be perfect, it just has to be *yours*."

"If we could get more space, more kids, more paint and paper and God knows what else— It would be amazing, Daniel." Eva grinned. "There's kids every-where who could do with outreach. Other groups that need help to keep running, or people who want to start one up and just need a nudge."

"And you've got to keep on working at those sketches, dancing saucepans or not." As he settled back into the pillows, Daniel drew her down with him. "Keep painting, keep drawing. We can make something really special together."

"We most definitely can!" Eva curled her legs around his, cocooning herself against him.

"When we went to that hotel, I wanted to give Lee Carswell one happy memory," he told her. "You know you saved my life, don't you?"

Eva shook her head. "I had no idea," she whispered.

"You put me on the right track, but it's my responsibility to keep myself there, I know that." Daniel pressed his lips to her hair. "It wasn't just as an artist that I was stagnating. I was so full of anger and bitterness, so incapable of being loved. But I wasn't, and you showed me that."

Eva propped herself up on her elbow and smiled at him. "You deserve as much love as anyone else, darling. *More*, I think, to make up for —" She brushed away a tear. All those years and a whole identity that Daniel had lost. "And you give it back, to me, to the kids… You have a very big heart, and I want you to always be happy."

"I've been in the dark so long." He studied her face for a few seconds then gave a bright smile. "Must be the sunglasses. I love you, everything about you."

Eva laughed and swatted at him playfully, but as soon as her fingertips met his lips, she drew nearer to him and kissed him. The day had been so filled with emotion and anxiety, with Lyndsey's tears and the fear that some unspoken somebody might come for Daniel at any moment, but now, with only the sound of the ocean and the stars glittering through the floor-to-ceiling windows, all of the anxiety was shoved aside. The world might be going mad but here things made sense.

Chapter Twenty-One

The following day, Eva and Daniel went for a drive. As the blue sports car travelled through the dazzling sunlight, it was difficult to think that not far away, the earthly remains of Rupert Hawley lay in a morgue while the police hunted for his killer.

Lyndsey had suggested they meet up for a walk, and Eva had been so concerned about her friend that she had agreed. She couldn't bear to think what nightmares from the past had been stirred in Lyndsey, but fresh air and sunshine might distract them for a while at least.

"I can't imagine what she went through as a child," Eva confided. "And it's all swirling about inside again, poor girl."

"Lyndsey's mum." Daniel frowned. "Is she like Lyndsey? What I mean is, she's so emotional and I just wondered, if her mum's the same, could that make it worse? I suppose she's got Miles though, and he's anything but emotional."

Eva snorted with laughter. "Are you saying my ex is a bit boring, Daniel? Well…let's say he's a very steady sort of bloke, and that if anyone can keep Lyndsey rooted, it's him."

"When I was inside, I met all sorts of people. You can imagine." And she could, but she didn't want to. "I've only met him once, so tell me if I'm wrong, I feel like there's nothing there. He's walking around, he's talking and breathing, but...he gives me the strangest feeling."

"He can be very charming, or he used to be, at least." Eva shrugged. "But he changed. And that was that. You're right about Lynds' mum, though. I think *dotty* might be the polite way to describe her! Dotes on Lynds like she's still a little girl, but I suppose you can see why, after what happened in their family."

"Maybe my time at HM's pleasure made me cynical, but do you wonder if there's even the slightest possibility—" He glanced at her then said, "Forget it, let's try and have a good day."

The car park was almost empty when they arrived, except for a rather bored man in an ice cream van reading a newspaper.

"I'm glad it's not too busy. I came for a walk out here once and nearly got knocked out by a stunt kite." Eva grinned at Daniel as she tried to tidy her hair. "The joys of living by the sea..."

But Daniel's attention was elsewhere as he climbed from the car and looked out over the horizon. The land seemed to fall away into emptiness, as though the world itself ended at the cliff edge, where nothing waited other than a sheer drop down to the sea below.

Oh.

Eva tucked her hair behind her ears but the breeze caught it and blew it loose. The long strands whipped against her face as she reached for Daniel's hand.

"Darling, if you'd rather not…we can go back home again if you prefer. I'll send Lynds a text. I'll say I didn't feel up to it after all."

"It's going to make life by the sea tricky if I can't look at a cliff." He kissed her cheek, but she heard trepidation in his voice. "Kick coke, walk on a cliff, fall in love. A successful year!"

Eva laughed. She screwed up her eyes against the sun and peered along the path. There, on the headland, were three figures silhouetted against the bright, sparkling sea. "That's them, I think. Shall we?"

"Let's go." He nodded. "Meet the parent!"

Eva waved as they made their way over the tufty grass that clung to the sparse soil and chalky earth. The figures returned her greeting. Miles was clad in another of his striped shirts, a jumper knotted carefully around his shoulders. Lyndsey's mother was wearing a cerise-pink skirt suit with a flouncy blouse that billowed in the wind, and her shoulder-length grey hair blew about her face. Her entire outfit looked crumpled, as if she had slept in it—which was, Eva had learnt over the years, par for the course. She looked even more crumpled stood next to Lyndsey in another of her immaculate ensembles.

"Afternoon!" Eva greeted.

"Hello!" Lyndsey seemed so much happier today. Her cheeks were flushed, her hair perfectly groomed and her smile in place. Her mother didn't look quite so delighted, Eva noticed. She seemed to have aged decades in the few months since their last meeting. "Mum, this is Daniel. I've told you *all* about him, haven't I?"

"Yes." Mrs Davis kept her hands in her pockets and bestowed only a curt nod. "The artist, aren't you?"

"That's what I tell everybody." Daniel smiled and took off his sunglasses. "Pleased to meet you. Good to see you again, Miles, Lyndsey."

Once again, Miles stared at Daniel as if he had just heard a loud and surprising bang. Did it really startle him so much that Eva should have found a new partner?

"And you, too." Miles extended his hand to Daniel. "Glorious day, perfect for blowing out the old cobwebs!"

The men shook hands and Lyndsey, standing dangerously close to the cliff edge, snapped a photo of them with her phone.

"For posterity." She smiled. "Two friends beside the sea."

Her heart hammering, Eva looped her arm through Lyndsey's, bringing her away from the edge. "Right, then...off we go."

They strolled along the cliff path, but the farther they went, the more the atmosphere thickened. Perhaps Mrs Davis found the presence of the art world's celebrity enigma a little troubling, because she kept glancing back at where he and Miles walked in awkward silence, and it seemed as though only Lyndsey had anything to say, chatting merrily about this and that but never, ever mentioning Rupert.

Lyndsey was clearly aware of it too, and her efforts to draw her mother and boyfriend into the conversation grew more clipped until Eva had a feeling that trouble might be on its way. She heard the slight huff in her friend's voice, saw the tightness in her jaw and the flash of childish annoyance in her eyes when she asked, "Miles, shall we share our news?"

Miles glanced at Mrs Davis before nodding to Lyndsey. "Yes, I think we should."

Mrs Davis stopped and slipped off one dust-covered court shoe to rub her toes. "Never mind me," she muttered.

"News?" Eva did her best to sound upbeat. "Oh, go on, spill!"

"What happened yesterday has shown us that life can be horribly short." Lyndsey reached out and seized her boyfriend's hand. "We can't get along without each other and we wouldn't want to. Miles and I are engaged!"

Eva clapped her hands together. "That's so lovely! Oh, congratulations, you make such a lovely —"

Mrs Davis interrupted with a huff. "I don't want to hear about it. Lyndsey, you've knocked me badly!"

"Don't you dare."

Lyndsey sounded utterly furious, but even she was silenced when Daniel addressed Mrs Davis and said, "I knew you were familiar from somewhere."

His voice dropped to a menacing whisper and he asked Miles, "What the fuck's going on?"

Defiant, Miles raised his chin and stared at Daniel. "Lyndsey and I are getting married. There's no need for bad language, even from an *enfant terrible* like you."

"Miles!" Mrs Davis snapped. "That's enough!"

Eva moved too slowly to catch Daniel's hand. He seized Miles' chin in a violent grip and stared at him, his black eyes blazing with an emotion that she couldn't quite read. Then he whispered, "Ollie?"

The wind blew with more fury along the clifftop, rattling the salt-stiffened grass.

'Ollie?'

"What?" Eva's stomach lurched. This wasn't right. Miles was Miles, he wasn't Oliver Shaw, he wasn't the boy whose lies had condemned Lee Carswell. "Daniel, come away... Let's go back to the car. Let's go home."

"You put me away! You killed your sister and you put me away for it!" Daniel shouted, his words searing with fury, and still Miles stood there, silent and unmoving as Daniel yelled. "We were mates! How the hell do you push your own sister off a fucking cliff and —"

"He didn't." Lyndsey held out her hand to her mother. "Did he, Mum?"

"You'll hold your tongue if you've got any sense, my girl." Mrs Davis' hands were still in her pockets, bunched now into fists. "But you haven't. All I did for you, and you plan to seal your existence in an act of abomination with *him*."

Miles broke away from Daniel's stare and glared at Mrs Davis. "Shut up, you mad old witch! We love each other!"

"Why can't you be normal?" Lyndsey thundered at her mother. "Why do you have to talk like there's something wrong with you? All you did for me? All I did for *you*!"

"*Normal*?" Mrs Davis' deep laugh shook her body as if the very ground she stood on was about to crack apart. "Says the girl who wants to marry her own brother!"

"Shut up!" Miles swung his fist in rage and frustration. "Shut *up*, you mad bitch! And as for you, Mr Artist, I don't know what the fuck you're on about. I never pushed anyone off a cliff! Why? Did *you*?"

Eva couldn't move. The wind blew with more violence by the second, whistling and shrieking around them. Images came to her. Emily Shaw in her school photograph, Lee Carswell's mugshot.

But she had never seen Oliver Shaw.

Until now.

In fact, as his fist connected with Daniel's jaw and sent him sprawling across the grass, she saw him all too clearly. Oliver and Emily had been here all along, the abused girl living her life with the crazy lady who had once lived in the big house, the woman Daniel had *knocked badly* with his loutish mischief. The woman who had masterminded all of this.

Because surely a child couldn't —

Suddenly Lyndsey's words made all too much sense, her calls for Rupert to be punished beyond anything the law could do, to be gnawed away from within over the years. Was that what they had done to the father who'd abused her? Spirited away his victim and left him to live out the years not knowing what had become of her? Punished not by the police, but by the torment that she had been taken from him by the actions of a boy who had been innocent all along.

Lee Carswell hadn't been locked away for a crime he didn't commit.

He had been locked away for a crime that never even happened.

"Get up, Lee!" Miles taunted. "Didn't you learn to fight in Borstal? You fucking idiot scum, come on then!"

"Ollie, don't act the fool," Lyndsey told him, cringing as though he'd told an off-colour joke. As Daniel pushed himself onto his hands and knees and spat out a thick wad of blood, Lyndsey's hand lashed out like a whipcrack and caught Eva's wrist, pulling her close. In her other fist she held a small, bright-bladed penknife, which she pressed against Eva's throat. "I was so scared when Ru went for you. Miles gave me this just in case. I think this counts as *just in case*, don't you?"

"Lyndsey!" Eva could barely speak, scared that her slightest movement could bring the blade into her skin. "No. Emily, that's who you are, isn't it?"

"Emily's dead," Lyndsey told her with that same bright humour in her voice. "She died the first time her daddy climbed into her bed and told her, *This is our secret.* Well, Miles and me had an even bigger secret, didn't we? All these years, the biggest secret of all and the best mum a girl could want."

Daniel stumbled to his feet, his gaze still fixed on Mrs Davis. Then he asked, "So this was your idea? You took her and ran and the whole world thought—"

"Of course it wasn't *her* idea, does she *look* like she's capable of coming up with an idea like that?" Lyndsey laughed. "I was eight years old, but thanks to daddy, I was a *very* grown-up girl. It was *my* idea, Lee. I wrote it all down in my jotter and showed it to Ollie and one day, when Mum—Mrs Davis to you—was all upset and crying about the little girl she had lost, we showed the jotter to her too."

She pressed the blade closer to Eva's skin, the edge just biting into her flesh. "That crazy woman in the big house who you and your little friends used to torment was grieving for her *own* child, Lee. She'd had a baby and she lost it, and you were smashing her windows and writing dirty words on her wall, and is it any wonder that she hated you? You were a nasty, horrid little chav and, in all honesty, I think we did you a favour."

"He was a child," Eva murmured. "The world did him wrong. Just as it did you!"

"No one wept for little Lee Carswell." Mrs Davis' tone was cold and detached. "But little Emily Shaw, what a beautiful child! Hair like wisps of gold, and *I* loved her, properly, as a mother should. Not that pathetic bitch who did nothing in the face of that unnatural monster she'd married, no. I gave you a home. And how do you repay me? You're twisted, Emily, you always were!"

"*I'm* twisted?" She scoffed. "It was Ollie who caved Rupert's skull in, not me! I only said someone should teach him a lesson, Mum!"

Miles puffed his chest out with pride, then grabbed Daniel by the front of his shirt. "Hear that, do you? I killed a man for the woman I love. And you? What did you do? Shouted and carried on a bit, a fucking yob just like you always were!"

Daniel was silent, staring into Miles' eyes. Then he spoke, the anger in his voice still there, though Eva could sense the effort he was making to keep it in check.

"Let Eva go, Lyndsey. She's your best friend." He looked straight through Miles, as though he wasn't even there. "She's never done anything but be kind to you."

"You don't understand, Lee." Lyndsey smiled. "I *love* Eva, really, she's a sister to me, but when she picked *you*, that was sort of it. You're still a horrid little council house rat and I think she could do so" — she jabbed the blade again — "much" — another jab — "better."

Still held by Miles, his rugby player physique never more bulky than it seemed now, Daniel seized the moment that Lyndsey had given him and slammed his fist hard into Miles' belly. He crumpled and Daniel turned, clearly intent on reaching Lyndsey and Eva.

"Stop it!" Eva cried. "Lyndsey, *please*."

"You always were a tart, Eva!" Miles spat through heaving breaths. "Going with *him?* With a Borstal brat?"

Miles lunged for Daniel's legs, toppling him over. The two men grappled with each other, heading for the edge of the cliff. Eva couldn't move, could only scream, and Lyndsey hadn't let her go.

Mrs Davis did nothing but stare at them all with empty eyes.

"What's going on?" a voice asked and there, innocuous amid all this violence and truth, was a party of three middle-aged women clad in sensible hiking boots and Gore-tex. In their hands they held walking poles and on their heads, despite the warmth, were woolly hats. They were prepared for anything, it seemed, but not this. "Is that— Call the police, she's holding a knife!"

But Lyndsey wasn't looking at the women, nor was she really looking at Eva anymore, and as Daniel and Miles tumbled towards the edge of the cliff she let out a howl of panic because she saw, as clearly as Eva did, that their momentum would carry them over.

The man she loved and his paintings and the warmth of his embrace and the passion in his every kiss and— Eva was about to lose him.

And there was nothing she could do.

Miles grunted like a beast, and did he really not see it? Could he not see the edge of the cliff?

At the last, their limbs somehow came undone and she saw Daniel's arms flailing even as his momentum took him sliding down the crumbling bank. One caught onto the jagged face of the rocks, the other locking around Miles' wrist. She heard earth fall, rocks scatter and Miles, his arm still held by Daniel, disappeared over the edge. With a cry of pained exertion Daniel forced his heels into the ground and was caught there like Prometheus on the rock, his back pressed flat to the steep incline, one arm wrapped for dear life around a sharp outcrop, the other hand keeping Miles from his death.

Alone he would have been safe, but with the weight of the other man dragging at him, it was only a matter of time before both fell. Certainly before the emergency services the hikers were summoning would arrive.

A thin wail rose from Miles, the cry of a terrified child. The cry of Oliver Shaw as he condemned his friend to prison. And now the cry of a man who was about to die.

"You're coming too!" Miles' shout echoed against the cliff face, as if his voice was far away. "You'll die with me, Carswell!"

Eva slowly closed her hand over Lyndsey's wrist and with a quick movement pulled her arm away. Her head pulsed with blood at the sight of the drop that fell hundreds of feet below, of the chasm of air noisy with the crashing waves and the shriek of gulls.

Helpless, unable to go any nearer to the cliff edge, she held out her hand, but it was too far for Daniel to reach. "Daniel, don't go...don't!"

And she already knew that he wouldn't let go of Miles because he wasn't the sort of man who could do that. He wasn't the sort of man who would let anybody fall.

Lyndsey screamed her brother's name as she dashed towards the edge, scattering a loose fall of rocks as she went. Yet she wasn't intent on violence now, but on saving the man she loved from the fate that the world thought had befallen *her*. Her momentum carried her over the coarse grass and stone, the soles of her ballet flats scraping for purchase that they couldn't find. It was like watching someone trying to keep their balance on a carpet of marbles and, in a shower of tumbling rocks, Lyndsey Davis—Emily Shaw—plummeted down onto the merciless rocks below.

Even the waves fell silent for the space of a heartbeat. Then a dreadful sob came from Miles as he cried out, "Emily!" He sobbed again, the most desolate wail of sorrow Eva had ever heard. "I can't live without her...let me go with her, Lee! For God's sake, man! Let me go!"

"We were mates back then, whatever you did," Daniel gasped, his knuckles white against the rock. "I'm not letting you fall."

"Then you'll die with us too!" Miles yelled. "Do you want that?"

Eva crawled towards the edge. She couldn't get close enough to reach, but she could see Miles dangling below, his lips drawn back and his teeth bared as he bit Daniel's hand. The bite tore a cry of pain from Daniel's lips but still he held on, even as blood began to seep from between Miles' teeth. A hand closed over Eva's shoulder and she turned to see the face of a police officer, whose eyes were wide at the sight he was witnessing.

And when Eva looked back she could see her lover's fingers slipping from the rock, smearing blood from the sheer effort it was taking to hang on. Perhaps it was the sense of that hand on her shoulder that did it, perhaps just sheer desperation, but she lunged forward, straining every muscle to catch Daniel's fingers in the second that he let go of the outcrop. Another hand joined hers and someone, somewhere, caught her by the ankles just in time to stop them all following Miles as he fell, his body thudding onto the rocks at Lyndsey's side.

Eva squeezed her eyes tight shut. She couldn't look, couldn't bear to see the two still figures on the rocks below. But he was safe, wasn't he? The man she loved. "Daniel… Daniel…"

She was being hauled away from the edge by strong arms, but there was a hand still in her grip, fingers sticky with blood, but those same fingers were clutching her with all their might.

"I'm here," Eva heard him whisper. "Just."

At last, Eva opened her eyes. Daniel was as white as the chalk cliffs, his clothes dirtied and his hair stiff with sweat. But he was alive.

Eva held him, clinging tightly to him as she wept. "Is it over now?"

She could hear the women telling the tale of all they had witnessed, of Lyndsey and the knife, of her fall, of Daniel's heroic efforts to save his friend and next to them, there was Mrs Davis, impassive, serene, looking out to sea.

Then she turned and calmly walked over to the police car, waiting there to tell her story.

Chapter Twenty-Two

Two years later

Private views didn't usually offer orange squash and lollies to visitors, but this wasn't an ordinary exhibition. The artist beamed in front of his paintings as the cameras flashed, and his mother nudged him to fasten his trailing laces. No arrogant bad boy posturing for Kieran at his debut solo show.

With baby Joanne on her hip, Eva wandered through the gallery, and the children from her outreach workshops waved and loudly greeted her. She grinned at Brighton's art crowd, who struggled to maintain their poised *hauteur* as they ate sherbet. How disappointed they must have been when they found out the only available drink with fizz was pop.

Not that Daniel seemed bothered. He wore black, of course, but this time his shirt was a deep blue and his sunglasses were not over his eyes, but pushed up into his hair. He stood beside Keiran as the flashes popped, both smiling as broadly as the other.

Daniel Carswell's protégé, the first to emerge from the charitable foundation established using that *undisclosed amount of compensation* that the press had reported on so breathlessly. They had catalogued every new twist and turn in the same excitable tone, and some said that it had helped the *bad boy* to his fourth Turner. He, of course, had made no comment.

Joanne waved at her dad as if seeing him surrounded by photographers was the most normal thing in the world. Which, to her, it was. Leaving Kieran to his public, he bounded across the gallery, past Eva's celebrating outreach kids, to his wife and daughter.

"They want some photos of the lady behind the outreach," Daniel whispered, offering his finger to Joanne. "Whenever you're ready. I'll mind the muse!"

Joanne grabbed his finger and smiled broadly as she tugged it. Eva hefted her over to Daniel and pressed her lips to the top of her baby's head. As she watched father and daughter together, Eva wished that Daniel's mother had been able to see both her son's success and the family they had created. But her memory lived on in the baby who had been named after her.

Eva took her place beside Kieran and his mother, and the flashes pinged again. They didn't make her jump with fright anymore. No one was waiting in the darkness outside now.

On the sidelines, Daniel and Joanne watched, doing their best to distract her with their waves and silly faces. Eva doubted anyone would've suspected that Daniel hid such a playful interior, yet the passion still flowed when they found themselves alone.

After what had happened, after death and revelations, Eva and Daniel had clung ever closer to each other. They had survived through the nightmares together, through the inquest and the investigation, and the curiosity of the public and the press. The boy who had been erased had been exonerated, and Daniel had reclaimed his name. And despite all of it, despite the wasted years and the drugs and the fear of discovery, he held no grudge. How could he, when all of that had led him here, to his own little family?

Once the camera flashes had finished, Eva rejoined her husband and her baby. Joanne was no longer interested in either parent and instead gazed at the paintings around them, her young eyes attracted by the bursts of colour.

"She's contemplating her own future masterpieces!" Eva laughed. Daniel slipped his arm around her and held her close. He pressed his lips to her cheek and bestowed a soft kiss.

"I love the pair of you," he whispered. "My mermaids."

Want to see more from these authors? Here's a taster for you to enjoy!

The Ghost Garden
Catherine Curzon & Eleanor Harkstead

Excerpt

1925

The gap between each floorboard seemed to call to Cecily. *Drop the ring*. But she gripped it even tighter.

She'd cleaned off the dirt after finding the ring in the rose garden. No one ever went behind the ancient brick walls, and Cecily had only braved its thorns and twisted branches to rescue a cricket ball. The pupil who had accidentally knocked it in there had cried, frightened of a telling-off, and Cecily hadn't had to go far into the overgrown garden to retrieve the ball.

And there had been the ring, half-hidden in the ground as if it had risen up through the drought-parched earth just for her.

Cecily glanced over her shoulder, along the length of the corridor, but Hugh, her husband, was nowhere to be seen. *Busy in his study*, Cecily supposed as she knocked on the Culpecks' door.

The late summer sun was dying, throwing a blood-red tide over the floorboards of the masters' quarters and she knocked again, keen to be in the cozy confines of the Culpecks' rooms. Somewhere, someone was tuning a piano and she could hear the occasional sound of leather on willow from the playing fields outside, where school life went on as it ever did, as it ever had since she could remember. She was part of the fabric here, as constant as the buildings themselves.

"Close the curtains," Harriet instructed from inside the rooms. "Our circle is now complete." The bolt slid back with a metallic thud and the door opened to reveal Harriet Culpeck, her yellow summer dress a flame in the gloom. She smiled and said, "I was worried you'd thought better of it!"

"No, not at all!" Cecily stepped inside. Harriet's curious glance fell on Cecily's knitting bag. "Just in case the spirits are quiet, I have a pullover I'm knitting for Hugh, you see."

"Graham has a meeting with the headmaster," Harriet explained as her husband appeared on the threshold of the sitting room, struggling to find the sleeve of his dark gray suit. He greeted Cecily with a warm smile, as different from Hugh as any man could be. "It'll just be you and I."

The headmaster. Never 'Hugh', never 'Mr. James', always that stern-faced, rheumatoid-eyed headmaster, even to the people who have known him all these years.

"Good evening." Cecily nodded. "I hope your meeting goes well."

His look was one of sympathy, the same look the world had given Cecily all her thirty years, when the world looked at her at all. Then Graham fastened his jacket over his rounded belly and said, "And your circle of two."

"We shall see — perhaps it will be more by the end of the evening. There might be quite the party going on by the time you get back!" But Cecily still clung to her knitting bag. Until the bolt was drawn on the door, she couldn't trust Hugh not to arrive unannounced. He would be extremely displeased to know that Harriet was holding a séance in the masters' quarters. And even more so if he knew that Cecily was taking part.

"We shall be one hour," Graham told them, holding up his index finger. Cecily nodded an acknowledgment as the clocktower chimed its mournful six bells. When the clock chimed again, *the headmaster* would stalk along the narrow, dark corridor that led to his study, his black cape billowing at his back. He would descend the wide staircase into the oak-paneled hall and make his way over the courtyard, through the archway and around the path — never over the grass — toward the rooms she shared with him.

And she *must* be at home to meet him.

Harriet presented her cheek for a kiss, then Graham was gone. She slid the bolt back into place and asked Cecily, "You have the ring?"

Cecily put her knitting bag down behind the sofa, then held out her palm to Harriet. The gold ring, with its inlaid pattern of white and dark red stones, shone in the dim light.

"I managed to get the dirt out of the inscription this afternoon — it says *'My love, my secret'*. And then a letter C. I suppose an antiques dealer would know how old it was, but they couldn't tell us who this C is, could they?"

Cecily glanced expectantly toward the séance table. Or dining table. She had never been to *a circle* before but whatever Cecily had been expecting, it hadn't been a cheery crochet square in the colors of the rainbow, nor a bowl of russet apples beneath the pink lampshade, its tassels blowing a little in the breeze that fluttered the closed curtains. Two stubby candles already burned, settled into green saucers, and a steaming teapot sat next to the bowl, alongside two cups and a milk bottle.

A milk bottle on the table. She couldn't even imagine what Hugh would have to say to *that*.

"Would you like a tea before we start?" Harriet held out her hand. "Can I see the inscription? How romantic, a ring in a rose garden!"

Cecily nudged the ring into Harriet's palm. "Yes, it is romantic, isn't it?"

Romance was lacking so entirely from Cecily's life that she wondered if it was just something made up for songs, books and films, a lie to cling to. Harriet squinted at the inscription and gave a sigh of appreciation before she handed it back.

"I'll pour and we can start!"

Cecily held the ring tight once more. It had become her little piece of treasure, something she wrapped in a handkerchief and kept under her pillow. Hugh knew nothing of it. If he did, he would send it to the auctioneers in Tiverton. But it was hers—the one little piece of romance that had fallen to her.

She pulled out a chair at the dining table and sat down, her chin in her hand. "I wonder if the C stands for Caroline?"

"Once we've reached your brother, God rest him, we can ask!" Harriet took her seat and poured out two cups of tea. Then she clasped her hands in front of her breasts and told Cecily, "We'll start with a prayer."

Cecily placed the ring down in the center of the table and pressed her hands together. Sitting around the table, she and Harriet looked as if they were about to say grace before dinner, rather than contact the dead. Together they recited the Lord's Prayer as the candle flames fluttered and the curtains moved gently. Then

Harriet reached her hands across the table and offered them to Cecily.

"We mustn't break the circle until we've said goodbye," Harriet told her. "Ready?"

Cecily took her hands. She would grip on for dear life, because what would she do if Sandy got trapped in limbo, or wherever it was spirits went if the circle broke too soon? "I'm ready."

Harriet tossed her head to throw her graying copper curls from her eyes, then closed her eyelids. She took a deep breath, then another, and asked in a clear voice, like the dorm matrons ordering the boys into line, "We wish to speak with Lieutenant Pincombe. Sandy. Are you there, or is anybody with us who can call Sandy forward?"

Cecily stifled a sob. She'd promised herself not to cry, but the thought of her poor brother lying cold in the cemetery outside Ypres for a decade was too much to bear. Though she hadn't cried when news had reached them that Sandy had been killed. Her father hadn't allowed it.

"Sandy, it's me, it's Cecily. Please talk to us."

The mantelpiece clock ticked on, counting out the empty seconds. The sound of the piano had stopped and, into the silence, Harriet called, "Can anybody come forward? Sandy or perhaps the lady who lost her ring in the rose garden? We'd love to know who gave you such a pretty trinket. Who was C? Were you one of the Whitmores of Whitmore Hall?"

One of the candles guttered, the flame sputtering and dying as though someone had passed a breath across it. Then it flared again, the wick spitting back into life.

"Is there a Whitmore with us?"

Thump.

Cecily jolted and almost let go of Harriet's hands. Cautious, she asked, "Is that a footstep, Hattie? What is it?"

Harriet's fingers tightened and she gripped onto Cecily as her eyes sprang wide open and her mouth grew slack. As Cecily watched, her friend began to work her jaw as though chewing tough leather, then she asked, "What ring?"

Yet it wasn't Harriet's voice at all, but a rasping, low, male voice. A voice that sounded as though it hadn't been used in a very long time. It sounded like alcohol and tobacco and a stern loathing that Cecily had heard from her father, just as she heard it from her husband and now from this unnamed, uninvited visitor.

"Answer me, my girl." Harriet stared at her, unblinking. "Whose whore are you?"

"I'm not anybody's..." Cecily swallowed, her throat dry with alarm. Her voice had become tiny again. "Not anybody's whore. I'm not."

"Don't take it!" Harriet's voice was a scream of terror, a woman's scream, high and shrill. Her hands were so tight on Cecily's now that her knuckles were white as bleached bone. "No!"

"Take what? The ring?" Cecily implored Harriet, or whoever was speaking through her. This wasn't what Cecily had hoped for when she'd agreed to sit in Harriet's circle.

"Keep it safe," the woman's voice implored. "Keep it from him."

"I will, I promise." Though Cecily had no idea who *him* was supposed to be. "Is it yours? Are you C?"

"Shh." Harriet looked over her shoulder, as though listening for someone. Cecily found herself listening too, her heart pounding at the approach of whoever the woman was so afraid of. The clock ticked again and

Harriet leaned forward across the table to whisper. "Isabella."

Cecily recognized the name. She closed her eyes, trying to recall where she had heard it in relation to Whitmore Hall. Of course, the memorial inscription on the floor of the chapel.

Isabella Whitmore, whose earthly remains lye interr'd elsewhere, under her husband's connstant gaze untill the Daye of Judgement.

Isabella, the woman whose own husband had tried her and found her guilty of murder.

A chill rushed through Cecily. Whyever had she agreed to this? Her brother had not spoken, and instead Harriet had managed to dredge up a dark, dark episode from the old days of Whitmore Hall. Long before her grandfather had bought it and turned it into a school.

"Find me," Isabella's voice implored. "And let us rest as one."

The candle flames flared again then went out, plunging the room not into the gloomy sunlight that the curtains should allow, but an inky blackness, darker than any night she had ever seen. Cecily willed herself not to move, not to cry out as the hoarse rasp of the man's voice sounded again and told her, "I am always watching."

Cecily shivered. It sounded just like Hugh. Could it really be that Harriet had made contact with the dead, or had she managed to read what lay hidden in the depths of Cecily's mind?

"You leave her be, you bully!" Cecily said under her breath. Yet she could be entirely alone in the room if not for Harriet's grip on her hands. The clock was silent, the birdsong too, and here they sat in this sudden, unexpected tomb, watched by whoever possessed that ancient, cobwebbed voice.

"Sorry to interrupt, but the door was open," a new voice said in an accent that she didn't recognize. For a second Cecily readied herself for a new horror but instead a match sparked into life and the candles were illuminated. As though someone had flicked a switch, the clock resumed, the piano sounded and outside the window with the billowing curtains, a bird was singing.

Cecily blinked against the light and saw a man in the doorway. She had no recollection of ever having seen him before. He was rather short, an imp of a man, with an uncombed thatch of tousled dark hair and bright blue eyes. He was grinning—beaming in fact.

And he was handsome.

Still holding on to Harriet's hands, Cecily gave him a polite nod to mask her mounting surprise. "Good evening. And you must be…?"

"Rafael de Chastelaine. *Raf.* They tell me you're having a problem keeping your Latin masters?" As he replied, Harriet sucked in a gasp of air as though she had just been revived after drowning. She released Cecily's hands, just as she had told Cecily *not* to do. As she did, Raf took a step into the room and pressed his hand to his crumpled shirt, holding it over his heart as he told the unseen visitors, "Thank you, spirits, for joining us, go safely on your way. Lord grant peace to us and those who speak here."

He recited it as though it had been learned by rote, his accent lending the words a strange flamboyance, a world away from the hideous rasp of the spirit. Then he dropped his hand and Cecily realized that the new arrival wore no tie.

Hugh won't like that at all.

"I am so, so sorry!" Harriet settled her wide gaze on Cecily. "Did we get anyone, Cecily? Did your brother come through?"

Cecily stared at her open-mouthed. "Did you not… You couldn't hear what you were channeling?" Maybe it was better to pretend. She could tell her that Sandy had said hello, and that he was playing cricket in Paradise with the shade of W.G. Grace. But no, she couldn't lie to Harriet—she had few enough friends as it was. "A gentleman and a lady came through. He sounded angry. And she said her name is Isabella."

Cecily took the ring from the table and held it safely in the hollow of her palm once more. She offered the new arrival a smile. "Sorry."

"Did your bro—" Only then did Harriet seem to notice the crumpled Latin teacher in the doorway. She rose rather shakily to her feet and said, "Did my husband let you in?"

"The door was wide open!" Raf repeated, still beaming. He gave a very polite nod of greeting. "I'm a day early but there wasn't a reply from Dr. James' rooms so I thought I'd give his deputy a try instead!"

The bolt was fastened, Cecily remembered, a chill running through her again.

"Graham— Mr. Culpeck, the deputy headmaster, is with Dr. James." Harriet rose to her feet and quickly swept the curtains open, flooding the sitting room with welcome light. There was a giggle in her voice, an obvious note of excitement at this new arrival who seemed so untypical of the men of Whitmore Hall. "This is Mrs. James. Cecily—Mrs. Headmaster!"

Cecily rose from the table and, with a confidence she didn't feel, approached the new arrival. "How do you do, Mr. de Chastelaine? Have you traveled far? We are rather tucked away in our corner of Exmoor—I trust you did not have too many difficulties finding your way here."

"All the way from the Yorkshire coast," he admitted, though he didn't sound like any Yorkshireman Cecily had heard before. "By way of Romania, in case you were wondering if this is a typical Yorkshire accent!"

"Romania?" *No White Russian emigré, then.* "My goodness, I don't believe I've had the pleasure of meeting someone from your country before. You are very welcome here in Devon, Mr. de Chastelaine."

"I've been wandering around the grounds," he admitted in a conspiratorial whisper, as though it was quite the shocking confession. "It's a beautiful place."

"Mrs. James was born here." Harriet beamed. "Tea, Mr. de Chastelaine?"

He to/pok a battered silver pocket watch from the pocket of the rather rumpled tweed jacket he wore and opened the case with a flick of his thumbnail. "I wouldn't want to hold you ladies up."

Cecily glanced at her watch. "We have twenty minutes."

"Mrs. James is a marvel in the gardens." Harriet smiled and Cecily couldn't help but return it, because she knew her friend well enough to recognize the embarrassment in her bluster. She had been caught in her séance by this newcomer, and she felt rather silly about it. "Cecily, dearest, why don't you show Mr. de Chastelaine the grounds before he meets the headmaster?"

Cecily's heart blanched at the very thought of it, the idea that she would stroll alone at dusk with a man, any man. She had been punished for far less over the years.

"I can show you from the window, if you'd like. There's something rather special for you to see, actually."

Maybe Mr. de Chastelaine would be interested in what Cecily had spotted, even if her husband had not been. Yet Harriet wasn't about to let the matter drop so easily and suggested, "Oh, you can't see anything at twilight! Take Mr. de Chastelaine to see the gardens, Cecily." Then she patted Cecily's arm. "They never end their meetings early. Nobody need know."

Something in Harriet's voice implied, *I won't tell.* But someone else might if they saw Cecily and the substitute teacher through the school's many windows.

"If you should like to see the grounds quickly, then I have no objection in showing you, sir." "Really, call me Raf," he told her. "And I'd love to see the grounds with you. Don't tell, ladies, but gardening's what I do these days. Gardening and enough Latin to help a mate in need!"

Nerves. That's what Hugh had said was wrong with Mr. Brennan when he went off in his father's car, whiter than anyone Cecily had ever seen in her life. *It's always nerves.* Mr. Brennan had nerves, she had nerves. Nerves were for weak people, Hugh always said.

Where on earth did the bookish Latin teacher meet this man, though? They hardly seemed to be from the same planet, let alone be mates.

"This way please, Mr. de...Raf." Cecily gestured toward the door. Over her shoulder, she said, "Thank you, Harriet. That was certainly...interesting. Oh, I nearly forgot my knitting bag!"

Cecily's emergency excuse sat behind the sofa, and she hurried to pick it up, the ring still clutched in her other hand.

"Never break the circle," Raf told Harriet with a very mischievous wink indeed. Not the sort of wink that one saw in a school intended to turn out middling cabinet ministers and respectable bastions of the civil service.

In reply, Harriet giggled and held her hand to her lips like the girl she had once been. Her giggles grew a little sillier when Raf added, "You never know who might be knocking about."

Home of Erotic Romance

Sign up for our newsletter and find out about all our romance book releases, eBook sales and promotions, sneak peeks and FREE romance books!

About the Authors

Catherine Curzon

Catherine Curzon is a royal historian who writes on all matters of 18th century. Her work has been featured on many platforms and Catherine has also spoken at various venues including the Royal Pavilion, Brighton, and Dr Johnson's House.

Catherine holds a Master's degree in Film and when not dodging the furies of the guillotine, writes fiction set deep in the underbelly of Georgian London. She lives in Yorkshire atop a ludicrously steep hill.

Eleanor Harkstead

Eleanor Harkstead often dashes about in nineteenth-century costume, in bonnet or cravat as the mood takes her. She can occasionally be found wandering old graveyards, and is especially fond of the ones in Edinburgh. Eleanor is very fond of chocolate, wine, tweed waistcoats and nice pens. She has a large collection of vintage hats, and once played guitar in a band. Originally from the south-east, Eleanor now lives somewhere in the Midlands with a large ginger cat who resembles a Viking.

Sign up to receive their newsletter at
https://curzonharkstead.co.uk/newsletter/

Catherine and Eleanor love to hear from readers. You can find their contact information, website and author biographies at https://www.totallybound.com.

www.ingramcontent.com/pod-product-compliance
Lightning Source LLC
Chambersburg PA
CBHW050557260626
47157CB00002B/598